The Souring Seas

Alan Kemister

The Road to Environmental Armageddon

Book One

The Souring Seas

Alan Kemister

In 2022, oceanography students in Halifax, Nova Scotia's Dalhousie University are studying ocean acidification. When they add carbon dioxide to their aquaria, the acidity increases, and they observe explosive growth of marine plankton. Tony Atherton discovers removal of the extra planktonic biomass to the sediments will reverse global warming. He imagines a natural remedy for increasing carbon emissions. His enthusiasm withers when he realizes other aspects of climate change will destroy global ecological balances before his 'cure' kicks in.

Beth Manville, an actress with an interest in environmental issues, steals Tony's heart. She joins his fight to convince people to treat ocean acidification seriously. Her enthusiasm waxes as his wanes.

Then he discovers the importance of acidification and excessive plankton growth in other climate change endgames. It's playtime, and he's rejoined the battle.

Prelude

Spring, 2049

My name is Tony Atherton. The story of my life as a scientist, professor of oceanography for twenty-three years at the University of British Columbia, and climate change crusader began thirty years ago. That's when I arrived in Halifax to begin work on my Master's degree in engineering. My timing was poor. The coronavirus pandemic of 2020 hit us five months after I arrived. The university closed its doors, delaying the completion of my degree. My research project was withdrawn, forcing me to fall back on my second choice. After the reset, I designed and built an automated system for adding chemicals to an enormous aquarium in Dalhousie University's oceanography building.

Jacinta Lopez was the first to use my system. In May 2022, she learned that plankton grew more rapidly when she added carbonic acid to the aquarium. Her simple observation inspired my twenty-seven-year career as an oceanographer.

Jacinta's discovery also brought Beth Manville into my life. She became my one true love, the mother of our children, and a dedicated environmentalist. She reinvigorated my interest when it flagged and led our fight to convince everyone we must take climate change seriously.

Our efforts, and those of thousands of other activists, came to naught in 2049. Our blighted planet spiralled into chaos. Millions died. North American survivors struggled to endure without the technical infrastructure we'd become so reliant on.

Carl Linnaeus, the father of the modern system of nomenclature for organisms, gave our species the name Homo sapiens. This Latin term means wise or discerning man. Some would call him 'thinking man'.

Our thinking ability served us well for millennia. We made great discoveries and recorded countless cultural achievements. Longevity and the quality of life improved. Humans thought they were making progress.

In recent centuries, our expanding industrial capacity overwhelmed the natural environment. We became technological marauders, bending nature to our will.

Humans became obsessed with making anything they could. We seldom considered our need for it or our ability to build and use it without destroying our environment. 'Do it and ignore the consequences' became consumer man's mantra. That, I would contend, led to civilization's demise and consumer man's struggles to cope after the collapse.

In the spring of 2049, electronic communication came to a crashing halt. No internet, no cell phones, no communications satellite signals, nothing. A few days later, we smelled smoke. It was too early for forest fires, and the smoke drifted north from the United States, not south and west from the British Columbia hinterland.

Then American refugees arrived at the border. Thousands of cars with people telling stories of massive explosions and fires wherever they looked.

Our daughter Hannah and her baby were home with me in Vancouver when the chaos erupted. Our son Michael, his wife, Vanessa, and family were at their home nestled in the Coast Mountains one hundred and fifty kilometres to the north. Beth was in Ottawa, attempting to resurrect a political career that collapsed some months earlier.

No mysterious blasts occurred in Vancouver, but we couldn't escape their effects. Fires emanating from nearby Seattle were spreading north and approaching the international border. They'd also jumped through the San Juan Islands toward Victoria and southern Vancouver Island.

My thoughts were fragmented. I worried about the relentless fires. Tremendous efforts were being made to slow their progress, but no one appeared confident anything could halt their spread. I worried about the university and our attempts to establish early warning networks. Those well-meaning efforts seemed pointless, a pathetic response to the disaster we'd encountered. I worried about the complete absence of the electronic communication we'd become so dependent on. Did that suggest the problems were global? More than anything else, I worried about Beth. She was alone and far from home in a hazardous environment. The lack of communication channels meant we couldn't discover her fate.

Two things sapped everyone's will. The first was the absence of communication with Calgary, Edmonton, or anywhere farther east. Had massive electromagnetic pulses destroyed our communication systems? Or was it a consequence of the global integration of everything web-based? The second was our feeling of hopelessness in the face of relentless fires. People's thoughts were on escape and finding refuge.

I was in a better position than most. I'd worked for several years on a series of stations monitoring environmental conditions along BC's outer coast. Bill Robertson, an indigenous man and an ex-student, returned home to Haida Gwaii to manage a station. He was a survivalist and ham radio enthusiast. At his suggestion, I set up a shortwave radio transmitter in our Vancouver home. I was now one of the few people with radio communication capability.

I also had the inside track on a potential haven. Michael and his family were living near Pemberton in the Lillooet River valley. Could the narrow valleys in that glaciated and snow-covered area of BC's Coast Mountains escape the ravages of the relentless fires?

Less than a week after the disaster struck, Hannah and I decided she and little Alice would be safer with her brother. We could hit the road before the expected exodus, and I could return to Vancouver if it was still safe. With the batteries topped up and our electric SUV crammed with basic foodstuffs, we departed at dawn on Friday, May twenty-eighth.

The road wasn't too congested. We made the one-hundred-and-fifty-kilometre trip in four hours. After recharging the car's batteries, I returned. The most notable feature of the return trip was the increased traffic struggling to the north. Back in Vancouver, I learned fires to the east of Vancouver had crossed the Fraser River and were spreading westward. That meant they threatened Vancouver and the Sea to Sky Highway to Pemberton. Vancouverites would soon be trapped between the fires and the Salish Sea. Many fled, some by boat, others on the few open roads.

I immediately changed my plans. As the batteries charged, I reloaded our SUV with more food, more clothes, my ham radio, and data from my university office. Zeke Barlow, Alice's father, appeared. Soot from days fighting the fires advancing from Seattle covered his face and clothes.

"Time for you to get Hannah and Alice outta here. We can't stop the fires. Vancouver will burn. You should head north."

"They're already at her brother's place in Pemberton Meadows. Last-minute packing. I leave once the batteries are full. Will you join me?"

"I can't leave, but you should go. Tell her I'll get there, somehow, someday. I'm not abandoning them. It just can't be today. Go now before it's too late."

I tried to convince him to join me, but he was adamant. A few minutes later the charge light turned green, and I joined the slow-moving exodus. Along the way, I thought about Zeke and how he didn't live with Hannah and Alice but always appeared when they needed him. He was doing it again, and I was sure he'd fulfill his promise.

My thoughts turned to Beth. Our relationship also started rocky, but we overcame our difficulties. We had a loving and sometimes exciting life together, fighting the opponents of climate change. I feared I'd never see her again, but at least I'd be with our children and grandchildren.

As my SUV crawled north in the erratically moving convoy of refugees, I relived our first years together. Years when Beth and I led the charge to convince humanity we must fight climate change. I was investigating a major problem in climate change research. Together, we were spreading the word on the need for progressive action. This is our story.

I crafted it in 2045 as a third person narrative. It would be my contribution to a multi-authored history of our fight to beat climate change into submission. I could only hope that someday, someone would read it and benefit.

Part One

An Intriguing Experiment

Chapter One

Monday, May 2, 2022

Tony Atherton's mobile chirped as he stepped from the shower. He ran naked and dripping to where his phone was charging on rickety shelves beneath his studio apartment's largest window.

A young blonde with long hair and the posture of a runway model stared from a window in the next building. Her shimmering blue gown suggested she'd just returned from an all-night party. He hesitated, transfixed by her smiling eyes only five metres away.

"Jesus fucking Christ," he exclaimed. Several heartbeats later, he grabbed his phone and slithered to the floor.

He tapped the incoming call button. "Heyo."

"Good morning, Anthony. Jacinta Lopez Martinez speaking."

"Morning, Jacinta."

"I hope I have interrupted nothing important."

Tony glanced at his bedside clock: 8:05. He was hiding from his neighbour when he should have been enjoying a relaxing end-of-term break. Hilarious perhaps, but unimportant, and nothing he'd discuss with Jacinta.

He took a deep breath and imagined laboratory disasters that could produce the early morning call. He focused on his system for controlling chemical concentrations in Dalhousie University's largest aquarium. Jacinta was using it to measure changes in phytoplankton as she slowly increased the acidity. It must be the problem. "Something's wrong with the aquarium, eh?"

"The matter is the pH control system has failed, and I need your help."

Tony metaphorically patted himself on the back for correctly assessing the situation. "Can't Herr Professor solve it?"

"Professor Krueger is at a conference. Only Rosalind and I are here to manage the aquarium, and we are uncertain. I would not have called if it was not important."

Rosalind Parker, Rosie to everyone but Jacinta, was an undergraduate working for the summer in their research lab. Neither would solve mechanical problems without help.

Tony struggled to concentrate on the call rather than the blonde he imagined laughing at his expense. "Explain what happened, and, you know, I may suggest something."

"There appear to be two problems. First, all pH sensors failed. Many algae have grown over the weekend, and they are inhibiting the sensors. Second, all the carbonic acid has discharged into the aquarium."

"Experiment's ruined. Why not abandon it and start again?"

"We should not stop until we understand the rapid algal growth."

A picture of slimy goo overwhelming the experimental setup he designed and built displaced images of his blond neighbour. Dissecting the computer records and determining the exact conditions when the system failed were the obvious next steps. But something else was equally important. "Give me forty-five minutes."

Tony refused to creep like a cowardly dog in his apartment. He stood, hoping a bevy of female roommates with cellphone cameras hadn't joined his neighbour.

Her window was empty. Vaguely disappointed, he rushed through his morning routine before dashing to the university.

A brisk fifteen-minute walk through chilly South End Halifax streets took Tony to the university campus. In the Life Sciences Building, he diverted into the oceanography department's aquarium annex. The humid concrete cavern housed the ten-metre-diameter aquarium where Jacinta was studying the effect of a more acidic ocean on phytoplankton. The plastic-lined pool was two metres deep, and a rotating arm with two giant paddles provided mixing. A thick scum and the smell of decomposing vegetation assaulted his senses. The huge tank's constant mechanical stirring caused Jacinta's algal mass to roil like the witch's cauldron in *Macbeth* but didn't disperse it.

He strode from the aquarium to the laboratory he shared with Dr. K's other students.

Jacinta emerged from her office with the grace of a flamenco dancer. The PhD student looked the part with her abundant curly dark-brown hair, brown eyes, olive complexion, and delicate facial features. Add castanets and a colourful flowing skirt, and she'd be ready for the stage.

"Hello, Anthony. I apologize for taking you away from vacation," Jacinta said in her charmingly accented English as she swept up to him. "Rosalind thinks you will not have breakfasted, so we have coffee and muffins." She paused with head cocked. "Have you regarded the pool?"

Tony scanned the room, searching for the promised treats. "Strolled by as I came in. Sickly yellow colour of a cheap curry."

"I also observed the unusual colour. Rosalind has taken samples to the nutrient laboratory and asked Senorita Stewart to hasten the analyses. She promised us results by Thursday."

"Average pH is now 7.26, so up a few hundredths," Rosie said as she skipped into the lab. The robust country girl towered over Jacinta. She always wore cowboy boots, jeans, and plaid shirts. Her appearance and attitude were as rosy as her name implied. She paused, smiling mischievously. "Cynthia's after your bod. She'd analyze the nuts faster if you asked."

"Rosalind, you should not say such things, and calling the nutrient samples nuts is undignified." Jacinta turned toward Tony. "We need the nutrient results, so, Anthony..."

He stood straighter. The bubbly cowgirl's mildly sexual banter boosted his ego. Something he needed after his neighbour appeared unimpressed by his early morning performance. "I'll talk to Cynthia. If they're so important, you should, you know, collect extras."

"The intensity interests me," Jacinta said as she watched Rosie gather bottles for the additional samples. "The textbooks say we cannot generate a bloom without a pulse of nutrients, but I cannot imagine a reason for high concentrations. How do we explain such growth?"

"No idea, but I know something." Tony paused while biting his bottom lip. He imagined slimy sea scum gumming up the electronic sensors that measured chemical conditions in their aquarium. "We need electrodes that don't fail."

Something had ruined several months' effort, disrupting Jacinta's plan to wrap up her laboratory work. She was treating it with equanimity. Her reaction when the coronavirus pandemic disrupted everything for over a year was similar. When he'd questioned her about the shutdown, she smiled and said, "God challenges us to do our best. We must accept these setbacks and try harder to complete the tasks He sets for us."

He found her reliance on guidance provided by her Catholic faith annoying but accepted Jacinta's need for divine motivation. Tony's generosity, however, didn't extend to fundamentalist Christians who claimed global warming reflected God's will. They, and millions of others, wouldn't accept the reality of climate change. Individuals, corporations, and governments who recognized the problems but refused to alter their behaviour were no better. Add academics who studied climate change but left action to others. The resulting progress-defying inertia stifled interest in humanity's greatest environmental challenge. It was driving him crazy.

Fortunately, Jacinta had her mind on the immediate problem and didn't elaborate on her religious motivation. "That gives us two reasons to continue the experiment. Can we keep the pH stable between 7.2 and 7.3?"

"I can recharge the acid tanks and set it to whatever value you choose."

"Will the fouling not recur?"

He nodded, convinced the fouling problem wouldn't fade away. "We can clean the electrodes every few hours while I devise a solution."

Jacinta turned after taking two steps toward her office. "I must identify the organisms responsible for the bloom. Rosalind and I shall collect water samples for biomass and species identification. Then she can help with the electrodes. If she takes over electrode maintenance, you can resume your vacation."

After the promised coffee and muffins in the graduate students' common room, Tony instructed Rosie on electrode maintenance. He left her to determine how long they'd function between cleanings. In the lab, he cleared a section of bench and focused on the fouling question.

Rapid water flow, he hypothesized, should inhibit adhesion to the electrodes. The simplest solution, force water past the membranes with motorized impellers. That should keep the membranes clean.

As Tony sketched impeller housings, he imagined plankton growing in shallow coastal waters during the Cretaceous and Jurassic periods. Had a more acidic ocean generated massive plankton blooms? Had it generated the biomass that produced the world's oil and gas deposits in those prehistoric eras?

Did Jacinta's results suggest human-induced climate change was pushing the world into another period of exceptional primary productivity? Would it generate massive accumulations of organic carbon in new oil and gas deposits? Would it slash atmospheric carbon dioxide concentrations and reduce global temperatures? Could it lead to a new ice age?

Too many tough questions, but one thing was clear. Jacinta's experiment foreshadowed results that would impact their understanding of ocean acidification. She'd estimated a tenfold increase in growth rate, and several characteristics of the bloom made no sense. Would low pH become a critical factor in the global ecological response to climate change? Could it disrupt the way industrial societies functioned?

Chapter Two

After four days designing, building, and testing new electrode housings, Tony had a working aquarium. It wouldn't be robust until he installed components produced by a machine shop's computer-operated tools, but it should function.

That afternoon, he approached the busy coffee shop near his apartment with a spring in his step. Inside Cuppa Java, he bought a medium house blend and scanned the glass-topped cast-iron tables and matching metal chairs.

The blond bombshell from Monday morning gazed into space from a window table. She was wearing a white sundress splashed with red and yellow flowers. An odd choice for a chilly spring day, but sexy as hell.

He wandered over. "Heyo, neighbour, is this seat taken?"

A frown creased her brow as a black cloud hid the late afternoon sun. "Feel free."

"You may not recognize me, but we're neighbours, eh?"

"Sorry," she said. "Was I, like, staring? You looked familiar, but I couldn't place you."

Tony glanced around with one hand on the chair back before placing his mug on the table. "Anthony Atherton at your service, but everyone calls me Tony."

He made an exaggerated bow with a majestic sweep of his right arm. He imagined holding a big medieval hat instead of his Boston Red Sox ball cap, but one couldn't have everything.

She scowled. "Elizabeth Manville. Friends call me Beth."

He pulled back his chair and brushed away imaginary crumbs. "You know, I've often seen you here." That was stretching the truth—he could only remember seeing her a few times. "Perhaps now we're acquainted, we can become coffee shop friends."

"My work leads to too much coffee drinking, but, yeah, coffee shop friends. I could handle it."

He watched as Beth fiddled with her mug. Her frown suggested his exuberance was annoying, but he wouldn't let that deter him.

"Whatcha do, eh?" he asked.

"My boyfriend and I are actors. That means drinking coffee while waiting for endless auditions. If I get a job, I'm like drinking more while I wait for my few minutes before the camera."

Tony leaned forward, mug halfway to his lips. "Exciting! A film or television actress. Should I, you know, recognize you?"

"Doubt it. Bit parts in a few movies and TV shows. Mostly commercials. If you recognize me, it'll be an insipid soap commercial or something similar. Or a stupid smiling face staring from a magazine ad. Nothing romantic or exciting." She tipped her mug until the remaining coffee reached the rim. "What about you?"

"Student at Dalhousie starting on a PhD in oceanography. I'm studying the effects of global warming."

She smiled as the sun returned from behind the dark cloud. "Sounds fun. Tell me."

"You sure?" he said, his confidence evaporating. "I'll, you know, bore you."

"No way! I'm real interested in science and the environment. I should have gone to university and studied biology. This will be some good."

His eyes widened. Her reaction was too good to believe. "Stop me when I get boring."

"Get going already." Her smile broadened as she thumped her mug on its coaster.

He took a deep breath before launching into his standard explanation of the relationship between fossil fuel use, carbon dioxide accumulation in the atmosphere, and global warming.

He'd barely begun when Beth held up her hand while shaking her head. "The previous federal government's attitude was real negative. The latest Ontario government and the previous US administration didn't treat it as an important problem. And Trudeau talks progressive but subsidizes heavy oil production. They're, like, squashing people's interest."

"Totally agree. Our government's attitude is inconsistent—green-friendly high-profile pronouncements but little concrete action."

Beth tapped her index finger on the table. "Someone should challenge them. Learn why they're taking us down this road to ecological crises."

"Wow, you *are* interested in environmental affairs."

Her smile reappeared. "Whenever my career bogs down. But what about you? Where do you stand?"

Tony hesitated, surprised by the depth of her interest in environmental politics and the way her scepticism of government policies paralleled his. He took a deep breath and plunged into his description of the potential problems without committing to any political approaches. He focused on his interest, the effects of carbon dioxide emissions and increasing acidity on the marine environment. Tony described the pH control system he developed for the large aquarium as his master's project and Monday morning's puzzling problem.

When he digressed into an explanation of how carbon dioxide alters the ocean's pH, she interrupted him.

"I know about that. Crazy unit chemists use to measure acid concentrations. The higher the acid concentration, the lower the pH."

Tony nodded and resumed his narrative. After several minutes of sometimes incoherent explanation interrupted by numerous questions, she drained her coffee and put down her empty mug. "Sorry to stop you, but it's, like, time to go."

She leaned over and gave him a quick peck on the cheek. "I wasn't bored. Next time, we can have another oceanography lesson. And incidentally, I liked your performance Monday morning. But your cursing was too much."

Beth strutted away, but before she disappeared, her shoulders slumped.

She's messing with my friggin' mind and hiding something I must discover.

Monday morning, Professor Krueger stormed into the laboratory, brandishing Jacinta's summary of their efforts. Their research director was a large, exuberant man, and storming around was his normal behaviour.

He stopped before the whiteboard on the wall between two student offices. A fume hood and glass-fronted cupboards with bottles and equipment lined the remaining interior walls. Two laboratory benches dominated the floor space, and windows lining the exterior wall provided natural light.

He picked up a marker and addressed his team. "Good morning. I compliment you on a job well done. Your results are intriguing, but we have much to accomplish before shouting Eureka."

"Good morning, sir," Jacinta replied. "I trust your German trip went well."

Dr. K nodded. "An interesting meeting, and you've produced a fascinating new observation. It's your discovery, Jacinta. What do you propose?"

"We must identify the mysterious pennate diatom that dominated the bloom."

"That's important, and I can help verify your identification." Dr. K took three paces and stared through a window. He strode back to the whiteboard. "Isolating it and determining how it responds to pH change will follow. For that, we'll need smaller aquaria."

Tony smiled from his perch on a laboratory bench. When Dr. K found something interesting, he jumped in. If Jacinta wanted to control her experiment, she must stand up to him. But she was too respectful.

Dr. Krueger charged on. "This is a job for you, Tony. If you begin today, I'll pay you retroactively from the first." Tony nodded, and Dr. K continued. "We'll need aquaria with pH control like we have for the large pool."

"Presumably, you're imagining static aquaria." Tony sketched a series of three-dimensional boxes bristling with electrodes on the whiteboard. "We'll need pH meters and electrodes, and separate acid control systems for each aquarium."

"Buy them. We shouldn't dismantle the pool system." Dr. K replied, before turning toward Jacinta. "You should repeat the latest experiment."

"What about the nutrient question?" she asked. "We do not understand where the bloom found the nutrients it needed."

Tony considered techniques to control fluctuating acid concentrations as Dr. K and Jacinta droned on about biology. A tricky engineering problem was better than nebulous biological considerations. He reconnected when Rosie joined the conversation.

"Last week, Jacinta sent me to the library to investigate other low pH environments. I learned many oceanside lakes have freshwater sitting above saltwater washed in from the sea. Lakes like that around here?"

"Porters Lake may be one," Tony suggested.

Dr. Krueger waved the marker like a conductor with a baton. "Surveys of saline lakes are a good idea, Rosie. If a lake has runoff from acid rain, we may see low pH and ocean salinity. Put Porters Lake on our agenda, but first, we must get the aquaria working."

On his way out, Dr. K beckoned to Tony. He strode to his book-cluttered office and closed the door behind Tony before saying anything.

"We must consider how last week's observations lead to other investigations. But first, we should firm up your duties for the summer."

Tony frowned. They'd discussed those plans during April while he corrected errors in his master's thesis. "I'm to manage the aquarium system and pursue short-term research you outlined. In September, I'll register for my PhD."

"Correct, and the aquarium management job becomes more complex. The experiments I planned no longer interest me."

"Sir, you want me to focus on engineering problems?"

Dr. K sighed. "Rather like your master's project, but, yes, that should be our immediate priority." He paused, staring out the window. "Jacinta will concentrate on her biological observations. You should monitor her efforts and consider how you could build a thesis project on that foundation."

"Other climate change research may be more interesting."

"I'm not suggesting you abandon your training and become a biologist."

"Then, you know, what are you suggesting?" Tony asked. If Dr. K was trying to push his thinking in a certain direction, he wasn't making his intentions clear.

"Keep an open mind. Jacinta's endeavours should inform a project that suits your interests."

"So that's my task, eh? Establish protocols for controlling pH in smaller aquaria?"

"With Rosie's help. Then you can watch over the experiments she conducts for Jacinta."

Tony borrowed pH meters and electrodes that wouldn't be needed until September from a chemistry department teaching lab and idle computers from the Chemistry Student Resource Centre. When he reached the aquarium annex with his new equipment, he discovered Rosie was a step ahead of him. She had six large sea-water-filled aquaria on a reinforced bench along one wall. He installed the electrodes and other plumbing and transferred his control program to the six computers. By evening, they were experimenting with pH control in fifty-litre tanks.

Their first experiments without plankton in the tanks were confusing. All six drifted to lower pH. That confounded the conventional understanding that natural processes would generate an upward drift. He added a second control loop that introduced sodium carbonate and reprogrammed the computers.

Experiments with plankton from the large aquarium also failed. Two grew rapidly, an observation that intrigued Jacinta, three grew at rates similar to those in the large aquarium, but in one, the plankton died. An experiment where Rosie added nutrients also gave confusing results. Nutrient concentrations had little impact on growth rates.

Dr. K made frequent visits as they struggled to control pH in their new aquaria. He waxed poetic about their work and its potentially earth-shattering implications for climate change. He repeated his comment about being on the cusp of a significant breakthrough and never expressed frustration with their lack of progress. By month's end, his happy-go-lucky approach had worn thin.

The ongoing climate change discussion in the graduate students' coffee room was equally frustrating. A twit named Steve Matthews droned on about the Gaia Hypothesis. He claimed the biological system could look after itself without intervention by climate change scientists. Add politicians and climate change deniers on the Christian right who insisted God would look after everything, and you had a recipe for Earth-destroying inertia.

If Jacinta's observations were so important, shouldn't they identify the problems, jumpstart the research, and announce the results to the world?

Chapter Three

Wednesday, June 1, 2022

Beth sat at her favourite window table in Cuppa Java, willing Tony to appear. She should have been celebrating her recent success, her first role as a guest star in a drama series since they cancelled the children's show she starred in three years earlier. But try as she might, she couldn't look back on the six years since she graduated from high school with a sense of satisfaction.

The years when she had an ongoing role in *Kiddie's Corner* had been exciting. She was busy every day with acting and other activities related to the show and partied most nights with her best friend Bernadette. She'd acquired her first lover, fashion photographer Justin Kilburn, and when Justin followed his photographic muse to sunnier climes, she became enthralled with the brooding actor Jeremy Foxcraft.

Her life should have been a young woman's romantic dream come true, but by the time she met Tony, that life felt hollow. The tedium of endlessly chasing fewer and fewer promising opportunities, and festering questions about the pedestal Jeremy placed himself on, had worn her down. She realized abandoning her passionate interests in biology and environmental degradation after high school had been a huge mistake.

Tony strode into Cuppa Java, bought his usual mug of medium roast, and sauntered up to Beth's table. "Hey, Beth, a while, eh? Hoped I'd see you sooner."

She stretched to kiss her tall, sandy-haired companion's cheek. *He really is more handsome and better company than either Justin or Jeremy.* "Been hoping you'd show."

He grinned as they both sat. "You always greet casual acquaintances with kisses?"

"Something actors do. You'll, like, get used to it."

"Hey, you know, bring 'em on. How's it going, anyway?"

"Real busy. Snagged a part where my name lights up the opening credits."

"Will I recognize the show?"

She shook her head, trying to imagine Tony downloading the show onto his computer. "*Smugglers Cove* adventure series for teens. Guest star in their first season's final episode. Could lead to an ongoing role in their second season."

"Sounds great, eh? When will you know?"

"They'll start filming again in the fall, so I'll know by August or September. Until then, I'll be waiting and worrying." She placed her hand on his. "You can distract me with your adventures in an acidic ocean."

Tony glanced at the serving counter before gesturing at her mug. "Your cup's empty. Refill before I start?" She smiled as she passed it over. Somehow, his trivial offer seemed more meaningful than a temporary improvement in her career.

"Last time, I said we're studying the impact ocean acidification could have on phytoplankton," Tony said after he returned. "You need some marine biology to understand our results. That'll be your next oceanography lesson."

She sat upright with her shoulders back and breasts pushed forward. *Flirting with this guy is, like, so much fun.* "I'm listening."

He stumbled through a very broad-brush description of terrestrial and oceanic food webs. He sighed before summing up. "Masses of phytoplankton underpin an enormous food pyramid that supports all higher marine life. If human activity destroys that base, the whole structure comes tumbling down."

She frowned as she wagged a finger. "Your biology professors would say that's a gross oversimplification."

"I'm an engineer, eh? And you're doing a lousy job of looking stern."

"Yeah, right," she said, laughing. "You don't hack it as a girl-crazy engineering student who's only interested in parties. I'm, like sure you understand the details."

He shrugged. "We're, you know, looking at the effect of changing pH on the types and amounts of phytoplankton."

"And you're finding?"

"When the pH drops to 7.7, we get a persistent month-long bloom of a mystery organism we can't identify."

She leaned forward, placing her hand on his. She had to ensure she understood this. "Hang on. Seawater has a pH of eight, so it's slightly basic. If added carbon dioxide pushes it down to 7.7, that's a change of zero-point-three units. You've, like, doubled the amount of acid, but it's still basic, right?"

"Close. The current pH is 8.15, so at 7.7, we're closer to three times as much acid."

She rolled her shoulders, confident now she'd remembered those old school lessons correctly and could return to her teasing. "I'm real glad I can remember this stuff."

He glanced away. "We must identify the organism and determine its source. Also, how it can be so tolerant of lower pH, because, you know, it's still growing at 7.3."

"Neat, like a detective story. What's next?"

"Tomorrow, Rosie Parker and I are heading for Porters Lake. It's an environment where acidic water from acid river runoff mixes with saline water that floods in from the sea. We may find unusual plankton tolerant of both low pH and salt, maybe even our mystery organism."

When she prepared to leave a few minutes later, she prolonged the now obligatory kiss. Her flagrant flirting was unfair, but every minute they spent talking about his research exposed another of the lies she'd been hiding from. He was becoming a lifeline she couldn't abandon as she struggled to redefine her existence.

*****

The following morning at nine, Tony backed the oceanography department's Boston Whaler onto the Porters Lake Provincial Park boat ramp. He and Rosie jumped out and transferred their gear from truck to boat. Then he untied it and passed her the painter.

"Tell me when she floats off the rollers," he said before gingerly backing the trailer into the lake.

Rosie tugged on her rope. "Now! It's running away."

"Pull it to the shore and hang tough. I'll, you know, park the van, and we'll be off."

A rusty pickup roared up after Tony backed their rig off the access road. The brown pickup screeched to a halt, blocking their van. A burly man hopped out. "You from the D-F-O?" he demanded, using the local vernacular for the federal Department of Fisheries and Oceans.

Tony pointed to their van's black and yellow Dalhousie University logo. "Dal. Sampling for an oceanography department project. Doesn't involve the feds."

"Well, they should investigate our fish kill. Wouldn't surprise me if those buggers sloughed the job off on someone else."

"Sorry, not us. Your fish kill a problem related to this spring's high runoff?"

"How the hell should I know! Dead fish and more lake weed than usual. We called the bloody experts, but they haven't shown their chicken-shit faces."

"Problem here or the inner lake?" Tony asked.

"Inner part mostly, but they'd launch their bloody boat here."

Tony shrugged before nodding toward Rosie and their boat. "I must get back to our boat. Long day ahead, and we're, you know, not sampling the inner lake."

The man glowered, with his feet apart and his hands on his hips, as Tony stepped around him and strode toward the whaler.

"What's happening?" Rosie asked.

Tony hopped aboard and clambered to the stern. "Later. Keep the stern pointing out while I start the motor. Then jump aboard, and we'll get going."

"So, what's with Mr. Grumpy?" Rosie asked as Tony swung the whaler toward inner Porters Lake.

Tony explained as they slowed in the narrow passage joining the inner and outer lakes.

"Is the high runoff important, changing environmental conditions in favour of the diatom that bloomed in Jacinta's experiment?" she asked.

Tony stopped where the lake widened to five hundred metres, and Rosie dropped their anchor. "Possible, and if it is, this sampling trip may tell the tale. Here's the plan. One station where it should be freshwater, so not supportive of marine plankton. Then downstream, sampling more frequently as we encounter water that's fresh on top but saltier underneath."

"Okay, and I see you have the department's inshore CTD for temperature, salinity, and fluorescence, and a water sampler for nutrients, chlorophyll, and species identification—"

"Oxygen too, because we may encounter anoxia."

Rosie nodded, then pointed at a torpedo-shaped device. "What's that?"

"Bathythermograph, it gives us changes in temperature with depth."

"But the CTD does that."

"Not until we download the data in the lab. The BT gives us an immediate answer. We can, you know, use it to choose the water sample depths."

"And you want to sample the boundary between salt and fresh water—the boundary between warm and cold."

"Correct. A surface sample, one below the boundary, and one at depth. Shall we start?"

"What's first. Your BT? You must show me."

Tony described the procedure as Rosie lifted the BT from its cradle.

"Wow, it's heavy," she said.

"Solid brass. Heavy, so it drops straight down."

She held the torpedo dangling over the side from the lanyard attached to a tie point between its tail fins. "How fast?"

"Hand over hand, don't hurry. And count the knots. It's only twenty metres."

"Here goes." She lowered the probe from one knot to the next, mouthing the numbers until she reached eighteen. "What now?"

"Haul it back onboard."

Rosie looked up after setting the BT in its cradle. Tony handed her a small device. "Unclip the microscope slide and place it in this reader. What do you see?"

She squinted into a microscope-like eyepiece. "A trace of temperature versus depth. It's seven degrees at the surface, stays constant for two metres, then between two and five it drops to three, and almost constant to the bottom.

"Gold?" she added after checking the slide.

He nodded. "I get them plated at the university's electron microscope facility. In the BT, a stylus scratches a trace in the gold."

"Neat, but such an old-fashioned museum piece."

"It tells us what we need when we need it."

"I get it. Water samples at one metre, four or five metres, and what, ten metres. We use your torpedo to decide on sampling depths, but later the CTD gives us the actual data."

"Exactly. Start collecting the water samples. I'll give you a hand after I deploy the CTD. When we're done, it's on to the next station."

Six hours later, they'd collected samples from ten stations and were approaching the Provincial Park. A pickup truck with its motor running blocked access to the boat ramp.

"Not Mr. Grumpy's truck," Rosie said.

A different truck driver, taller, leaner, and less aggressive, sauntered to the foreshore and helped Rosie pull the whaler onto the sand. He waited until Tony joined them at the bow. "Fair weather. Hope your sampling was successful?"

Tony hesitated, unsure how to interpret this new, friendlier approach. "Foggy morning, but the afternoon was good."

"And your sampling?"

"Won't know until we process the samples."

The stranger sighed. "I represent Porters Lake Environmental Stewardship, and we'd appreciate access to any data you collect. Here's my card. If you'd give it to whoever's in charge and ask him to contact me..." He looked back at his vehicle. "I'll move my truck and let you get on with it. Unless you'd like a hand?"

Tony inspected his card. "We're good. Don't see how our data will help in a fish kill fight, but I'll see Professor Krueger gets your card."

"Why didn't you mention the hydrogen sulphide at the first station?" Rosie asked as they headed to Halifax.

"Because we shouldn't comment on what's normal or abnormal from one measurement."

"Earlier, you said hydrogen sulphide could have killed the fish."

"But we can't say it did."

"I don't understand. You want to stay out of this environmental issue, but you're ready to fight about climate change."

"Because we're developing a solid knowledge base for anything we say about climate. If we commented on the fish kill, we'd be guessing."

Chapter Four

Wednesday, June 8, 2022

Six days after Tony and Rosie ventured to Porters Lake, Steve Matthews raised a ruckus in the graduate student's coffee room. The gaunt New Englander saw himself as their leading intellectual. He was younger than most but disparaged everyone's views. He never shied away from expressing his ideas.

Steve smirked from his seat at the central table as Tony poured his coffee and dropped a loonie into the collection tin. He slid into the only empty chair.

The venom in Steve's voice pierced the air. "An engineer should realize the obvious. Your concern for plankton blooms and carbon dioxide accumulation has a simple solution."

Tony's heart raced as he struggled to contain his anger. *What's with the annoying little runt? It's been months since he accused me of poaching a coed he was lusting over. That can't be his problem.* "You referring to blooms generated by large additions of ferrous sulphate to nutrient-depleted surface waters?"

"Those, and efforts at carbon capture. The global warming problem was never the slightest bit interesting." Steve snorted before waving his hand dismissively. "Simple, practical solutions. You'll be heading to the drawing boards to develop projects that investigate something that's actually unknown."

Another student joined the fray. "The iron fertilization experiments solved nothing. No proof they remove anything on extended timescales."

"Polluters buying carbon offsets by funding those fertilizations is a joke." Tony's brows furrowed as he tried to get a line on Steve's purpose. "What about side effects like toxic algal blooms and the development of anaerobic zones?"

"Really, Mr. Matthews," Jacinta interjected. She seldom entered these heated discussions. When she did, she always commanded everyone's attention without raising her voice. "We are doing as you suggest, investigating principles of ecology in the low pH environment we could encounter in relatively few years."

"You may be, but Mr. Engineer is talking about politics, not fundamental oceanographic processes."

Tony stood, towering over his pint-sized adversary. "Screw it, Steve, what's your point?"

"Not to intimidate anyone, that's for sure," he replied, his all-knowing smirk more prominent than ever.

Tony sat after realizing his mistake. He'd let Steve's barb burrow under his skin. He'd learned not to overreact when outsiders expressed disdainful disregard for his climate change research. An attack from an insider, however, surprised him. Didn't everyone in the department agree they must address climate change?

He took a deep breath. "Okay, no intimidation. What's your point?"

"Oceanographers, marine biologists, and natural philosophers should expand our understanding of the environment. The answers to the climate change questions are obvious. Stop wasting time on them."

Tony gulped his coffee. *His bloody no-it-all smile is so annoying.* "Crap. We only recently learned lowering pH to a critical threshold produces a bloom like the one Jacinta observed. That was, you know, unknown and still unexplained. Claiming we shouldn't work on it is nuts."

"But that doesn't interest you, does it, Mr. Engineer?"

"That's Jacinta's question. I'm considering carbon removal on regional or global scales and how the removal links to Jacinta's biological observations."

"They're engineering, not scientific considerations," Steve replied.

"So, that's your concern, eh? You suggesting I shouldn't be in the oceanography department?"

Steve shook his head. "Offering friendly advice to a fellow oceanography student. Your proposal will be rejected because it doesn't investigate a fundamental oceanographic problem."

"No way," said the geochemist who'd entered the fray earlier. "The answers to Tony's questions aren't known. They're not trivial questions, and the solutions will be important for society. Why wouldn't they form the basis for a solid thesis topic?"

Steve picked up his mug and theatrically savoured his coffee. "Look at the governing principles for thesis topics. A fundamental oceanographic question is a requirement, not an option."

Tony shook his head as he wandered back to his lab. Steve's statement about thesis topics was illogical and even self-defeating. Shouldn't the university brain trust feel an obligation to tackle climate change without worrying about academic purity?

The following day, Tim Wilkes, another of Dr. K's graduate students, dropped a computer printout on Tony's desk. Tim was of average height with brown hair and brown eyes, but there was nothing average about his intellect or his dedication to academic research. Super smart without the haughty arrogance Steve Matthews displayed.

Tony read the two-page report before glancing with eyebrows raised at Tim sitting on a nearby bench.

"What do you think?" Tim asked.

Tony checked the top of the first page. "Not sure. Where's it from?"

"An environmental organization with links to Cuba. The bloom in a shallow bay on Cuba's north coast resembles the one Jacinta generated in our pool aquarium."

"Know anything about this bay?"

Tim shook his head. "Unidentified bay, one of many inlets joined to the ocean with narrow passages."

"Like the Bras d'Or Lakes?" Tony asked, referring to Cape Breton Island's large brackish lake.

"Not as deep and more saline."

"Can we, you know, contact someone and get samples?"

"May be difficult. It's a tourist area. I doubt they'll be open about problems."

"Maria Consuelo?" Tony suggested. "You know, the student who arrived last year from Cuba but spends her time learning English. Should Jacinta talk to her?"

Tim nodded before wandering toward the lab's large whiteboard. "And there's a cooperative research agreement between Dalhousie and a Cuban university. Perhaps Dr. Krueger could set up something."

"Never heard of it," Tony replied as he followed Tim. He stopped and wrote Cuban bloom and a question mark on the board.

"Nothing active happening, but I suspect it got Maria here."

"I'll do some digging. We'd love a real-world example of a bloom triggered by low pH."

In the Muse, a week after his spat with Steve Matthews, Tony queried Tim on a niggling problem with his slowly developing research proposal. "Can Jacinta's blooms produce enough biomass to make a global-scale difference?"

Tim shrugged as he raised his beer. "Too soon to say." He listed several biological concerns someone must address, ending with the biologist's standard mantra regarding nutrient limitation of phytoplankton production.

Tony glared at his friend. *Why did biologists always raise dozens of complicating factors while ignoring the core observation?* "Jacinta's producing masses of biomass without high nutrient inputs."

"Don't get your knickers in a twist. To produce carbon, you must pump in nutrients. Where will they come from?"

Tony stared at his beer. Tim's Canadian accent always made the British expressions he learned from his parents sound odd. "Something to investigate, but it's a good question, eh?"

"Don't expect a simple answer."

"I want a complex problem that generates enough results for a good thesis."

Tim stopped with his glass halfway to his mouth. "Run it past the good doctor. But is it your best bet?"

"Suits my math and engineering background, and it isn't too biological."

"Are you ready to battle the right-wing fundamentalist deniers of climate change?"

"Or other deniers," Rosie said as she appeared from behind and placed her hand on Tony's shoulder. "I thought you guys were waiting for me?"

Tony filled a third glass from the pitcher they'd ordered. "My note said meet us when you're free."

She stared, one of those disdainful, blank, whatever stares. "What we talking about?"

"Tony stealing your results for his project," Tim suggested, smiling.

Her eyes widened as she focused on Tony's. "You're not, are you?"

"After you and Jacinta publish them, I'll, you know, calculate the impact your little buggies have on oceanic carbon dioxide uptake."

"But why does Tim suggest you'll battle climate change deniers and other insignificant opponents like our political leaders?"

Tony sighed as he thought about the problems. Answering the scientific questions was difficult. Convincing everyone to address the issue, well-nigh impossible. "Global-scale impacts could become controversial."

She turned to Tim. "I don't get it."

"If, as he's hypothesising, your enhanced productivity has large scale implications, he'll find himself embroiled in the climate-change controversy."

"But why?" Rosie asked. "It would be an investigation of natural changes, not some effort to force green behaviour on people."

"Scientists may separate the study of natural changes in carbon budgets from impacts on society, but the public will link them." Tim turned as an argument about recently increased carbon taxes on gasoline boiled over at a nearby table. One participant insisted climate change scientists were responsible for the unjustifiable increase. "See," he said.

Rosie stared at her beer, her brow furrowed. "What about Tony's project? Shouldn't increased primary production lead to increased carbon removal? Removing CO_2 people insist on pumping into the atmosphere should be helpful."

"Go back a step," Tim replied. "Increased anthropogenic emissions produce the low pH that spurs phytoplankton production. Will the carbon removal Tony's talking about be insufficient to compensate for the increased emissions, just right to balance them, or too much?"

"I get it," Rosie exclaimed. "It would be wiser to reduce emissions than take a chance with your question."

"Scientists think it's obvious," Tim said. "But reducing CO_2 emissions will cause major changes in some industries, and smaller, but not insignificant, ones for everyone else."

She raised her beer. "But we must do it, right?"

Tony hesitated, drawing circles in the moisture left on the table by the beer glasses. "Masses wish to contribute but can't decide where to start. Others worry about government regulations affecting their businesses or activities. A huge mess with large-scale uncertainty."

"Which means we must define things more clearly and limit the uncertainty," Tim added.

"On that point," Tony said, raising his glass, "I agree with Tim."

She shook her head before joining the toast. "That means you're leaving it to the politicians."

"No choice," Tony replied. "The political process or individual actions must, you know, take charge. No external authority will decide for everyone."

"You mean like God?" Rosie said.

"You still rely on people making the right decisions. Our job is to provide the best possible knowledge."

"And that's your plan?"

"That's what climate scientists do." Tony tilted the pitcher, judging its contents. "Eh, Tim? Another beer while she nurses hers?"

"Why aren't we doing more?" Rosie asked. "It's obvious Canada won't meet its Paris Accord targets, and the American's reconnect with the accord is problematical, to say the least."

Tony sat back with his refilled glass. "People won't address fuzzy problems that won't bite them for decades."

Tim nodded. "My wife's a psychology student, and she'd agree. We solved the problem of sulphur and nitrogen oxides in car exhausts and also the ozone hole. But people refuse to give up cigarettes, and the current global warming problem seems intractable."

Tony rubbed his upper lip with his left forefinger. Discussions of human reactions were always difficult. "We solved problems amenable to technological cures that weren't too difficult or expensive to implement."

"Or too disruptive of people's everyday activities," Rosie added.

Tony glanced from Rosie to Tim. "Should I, you know, add disruptive to my characteristics for intractable problems?"

Tim tied the threads together. "We'll need ministers or behavioural scientists to convince everyone to address those problems."

Or my new environmental activist friend Beth, Tony thought as he strolled home after a third beer. Tim had increased the complexity of his climate change question. Its solution would require an approach that was broader than one PhD project. His evolving project, however, should provide an important part of the story. But how could he, or anyone else, convince humanity to take the problem seriously?

Industrialists exploiting the environment weren't going away. They included oil drillers and others with dubious schemes that use iron to sequester carbon by enhancing phytoplankton growth. He could add climate change deniers and politicians hiding their heads in the sand. It produces progress-stifling inertia.

Ten days earlier, Steve Matthews harped about departmental requirements for thesis projects. The conceited twerp couldn't say anything without sticking in a barb, but his message made sense. A graduate student must focus on new scientific discoveries. *How can I do that while pushing those damned politicians in the right direction?* A project that showed how the ecological changes implied by Jacinta's results would alter global carbon cycling should fit the bill.

Great dream, but fighting the opponents of climate change action was like punching fog. Nameless and faceless adversaries they couldn't see or identify were out there. They must challenge them, but often as not, they couldn't even find them in the fog.

A poster from the previous fall's provincial election caught his attention. It was hanging by a few staples from a telephone pole. The parties were supposed to remove them after the election campaign, but this one escaped their attention. Tony pulled it down and scrunched it into a ball.

He strode along, juggling his projectile until he came to a bus stop where he tossed it into a waste bin. *Will an inspired political leader put aside political infighting and attention to short-term goals and tackle climate change before it's too late? How could he help make that happen?*

Chapter Five

Beth rushed into Cuppa Java. When she spied Tony slouched over an empty coffee cup, she stopped before joining the queue. "Don't go anywhere. I need a favour."

She returned with pastries and two steaming cups. One had a paper tag draped over the rim.

"Tea?" Tony asked.

"Herbal tea. You got something against tea?"

He shrugged. "Thought you were, you know, a coffee addict."

She took her tea and a sticky bun from the tray. "I've, like, gone off it. But getting back to my favour—"

"Sorry. What's the problem?"

"Going to the Laurentians next week on a photo shoot, and I'm like visiting my sister and her kids at their cottage in the Muskokas. My chance to schmooze with Ontario film people." She paused, placing her spare keys on the table. "I don't want to return to an apartment full of brown plants."

"Muskokas," he said as he stirred sugar into the coffee she brought him. "Ritzy, someone has money."

She rolled her eyes, imagining her sister's pompous ass of a husband. "He's a Bay Street banker. He either has money or pretends he does. I suspect the latter."

They discussed house-minding logistics before Beth placed her elbows on the table and leaned forward with her hands cupping her chin. "If that's under control, you can like tell me the latest on the acidic ocean problem."

"Last time, Rosie and I were, you know, planning to collect samples in Porters Lake."

"I remember."

"At first, I thought we were onto something—locals were upset about an unusual fish kill, and we found anoxic water in the inner lake. We thought it might be important, but when Jacinta analyzed her phytoplankton samples, she found none of her mystery diatoms. Interesting observation but it didn't help answer Jacinta's questions."

Beth laughed, imagining an easily impressed undergraduate fawning over her new friend. "Bet you and Rosie got a nice day on the water. Anything else?"

After summarizing Jacinta's latest explanation for her observations, Tony gulped the last of his coffee and grabbed her keys. "My turn to rush away. Have fun cavorting with the intelligentsia in the Muskokas. I'll see you in August, eh?"

Beth settled back to enjoy her second cup of tea and the sticky bun he hadn't taken. *He's such a teddy bear, and he'd be so easy to love. How can I manage it?*

*****

Tony strode into the bright sunshine of the year's hottest day. He was late for an appointment with Dr. Willard Wharton at the offices of a consulting company, where he focused on water quality modelling. The physical oceanography professor was on leave pursuing practical uses for his models.

Steve Matthews' criticisms of his project ideas had been bothering Tony. He needed another opinion and hoped Dr. Wharton would be the one to provide it.

"Steve's correct," Dr. Wharton said after thirty minutes' discussion. "You must focus on the physical or biological oceanographic principles of your problem. The justification can include its relevance to society, but you must delve into unknown science."

Tony hesitated with his brows furrowed as he struggled to balance Dr. Wharton's words with the interest he'd expressed in practical applications. "What should I do?"

"Consider the investigations you've described. Ask how biogeochemical models will help you understand your observations."

"How does applying existing models help?"

Dr. Wharton sighed. "Models that solve your problem won't exist. You must identify the important questions and develop experiments and models that address them."

Tony glanced at the rosewood furniture and large aquarium with tropical fish. The place looked like an upscale lawyer's office. Defending academic purity in surroundings trumpeting the value of research into practical problems seemed odd.

"What about convincing politicians to respond to climate change challenges? Or convincing the deniers they're wrong? Or developing engineering solutions to these problems?"

"You're showing your bent for engineering rather than academic science. Use those arguments to justify the study. They can't be the focus."

"Isn't that rather harsh when scientific arguments don't convince our leaders to address the crisis?"

"I'm overstating the case to help you understand my colleagues' perspectives. You must comprehend them."

Tony paused, puzzled by Dr. Wharton's deadpan expression. "But you don't restrict your investigations to these narrow academic channels."

"If you sign up for my modelling course, we can investigate these boundaries and how water circulation models may be useful to you."

They discussed water circulation models for several minutes. Then Dr. Wharton pulled a sheet from the papers on his desk. "Here's a website you should visit. It's hosted by environmental scientists with an interesting approach to climate change action. They describe a grassroots approach, encouraging individuals and companies to make small contributions."

"You're suggesting this is the mechanism to convince the government, but my project should be more academic. Keep those interests separate."

Dr. Wharton nodded. "Check them out and decide how you can contribute. Now I must bring this discussion to a close."

"Thank you, sir," Tony said as he reached his hand across the table. "It's been an enlightening discussion. I'll let you return to more productive work."

"Don't worry. I remain an academic at heart. Time spent helping inquisitive students is never wasted."

At home, Tony googled ClimateChange&U.com. The site developed by five American scientists promoting climate change action illustrated the complexity of Dr. Wharton's view. He defended academic purity and the isolation of academic research from real-world problems. At the same time, he supported academic scientists pushing for climate change action outside their ivory towers. *Why does he insist on that separation?*

ClimateChange&U targeted computer-savvy adults interested in saving their environment from the impacts of climate change. It had three main objectives. First, explain the science of climate change to an intelligent and receptive audience. Second, explain how citizens could reduce their carbon footprints by making small changes to their lifestyles. They showed how these contributions could produce community-wide improvements without disrupting individual's lives. Third, use the mass appeal of this grassroots effort to convince governments to join the party.

Tony sent messages to the website describing his own experiences. He also suggested a new thread on their forums about similarities and differences between Canadian and American perspectives.

He popped open a beer as frozen chili thawed in his microwave and considered scientists' contributions to the public campaigns for climate change. Many participated in marches, rallies, and the occasional sit-in. A smaller number became active in political parties. Some, usually more senior members, wrote essays and contributed articles to newspapers. A few wrote populist books.

He sat in his one comfortable chair, trying without success to imagine himself participating in protests or joining a traditional political party. A climate change scientist had entered provincial politics as leader of the British Columbia Green Party. That seemed like an anomaly and not something he wanted to do.

Getting more deeply involved in ClimateChange&U, however, was a possibility. It was a new social media approach to influencing public opinion, something that may have an impact. If the website organizers were encouraging, he could offer to host a companion site, ClimateChange&U.ca. It could launch a groundswell of popular interest in doing something about climate change in Canada.

Tony returned to his supper-making, encouraged by his latest thoughts and foolishly impatient to hear back from ClimateChange&U. He already had some ideas for a distinctly Canadian website.

Several days later, Dr. Krueger slapped a file folder on Tony's desk.

"What's this?" Tony asked before he opened it.

"Our agenda. You, Jacinta, and I will visit Cuba to do some sampling and discuss potential collaboration with colleagues from a polytechnic institute."

"Shouldn't you take a more senior person?"

Dr. K shook his head. "We'll be collaborating with members of a limnology and oceanography program. They're an engineering school, so you should fit in. Primarily, it's an opportunity to investigate the low pH bloom you sent me information about."

"Probably long gone."

"My contacts say it's been active for two months and shows no signs of abating. And Jacinta's lab studies suggest these blooms persist."

"Can't Jacinta handle it?"

Dr. K laughed. "Can you imagine Jacinta on a small, run-down boat with a communist crew?"

Tony remembered the one time he accompanied Jacinta on *CCGS Hudson*, the Bedford Institute's survey ship. "Hardly, and she'd probably be seasick."

"Seriously, your highly productive blooms could choke these inshore waters. This trip gives you an opportunity to spread the word and discuss its relevance with local scientists."

"But I don't speak Spanish."

"Under control. You remember Pedro Gomez?" Tony shook his head when Dr. K paused. "He was a Dal student who returned to a professorship at the Polytechnic. He'll coordinate the sampling with you, and I've arranged for Maria Consuelo's participation. She'll be in Cuba for a wedding and has agreed to help with communications."

"Is this part of the bilateral agreement Tim mentioned?"

Dr. K nodded. "My chance to kill two birds with one stone, as you would say."

Tony's promise to look after Beth's apartment popped into his head. "When will it happen? I'm, you know, committed until late July."

"It's in the folder. We leave on July thirty-first. That gives you time to sort out the sampling details with Jacinta and Pedro and ship anything we need. We'll have a week in Cuba. You'll be on a boat in a tropical paradise while Jacinta and I languish in endless meetings."

Chapter Six

Tony, Jacinta, and Dr. Krueger met Pedro Gomez at Havana's José Marti International Airport. He hired a taxi to transport Jacinta and Dr. K to a hotel near the university and waited with Tony for their gear.

"We have seven-hour drive to the boat tomorrow," Pedro said. "Tuesday and Wednesday, we are on the water. Then we return to Havana. Friday you can visit the university and meet my colleagues. It is all right?"

"Fine. I wondered how we'd arrange the sampling."

"That is my plan. We bring the last boxes to the boat tomorrow and set everything up. No hurricanes, so we should have good time."

"You had one a few weeks ago. Did it affect the bloom?"

"We worried also. The bloom dispersed but re-established." Pedro paused, pointing at a man approaching with a cart. "Here is your gear. Soon we shall leave."

Twenty minutes later, they had Tony's equipment stowed in an old truck made by an unfamiliar eastern European manufacturer. Tony tossed the sports bag with his gear into the space behind the seat, and they drove off.

"Tonight, we drive on the *Carretera Central* to the town where I live. I arranged a room for you in small inn. Tomorrow, we drive to the boat."

After thirty minutes travelling through farm fields and villages as twilight faded to darkness, Pedro parked beside a modest two-storey building. Tony's eyes swept around the room they entered. It was the reception area, dining room, and bar rolled into one. "Should be fine, but I suspect they don't speak English."

"A young lady who works here in the morning is neighbour. I will see you are okay tonight, and Agata will look after you in the morning. We will collect you at eight."

Monday morning, Agata ensured Tony was well-fed and ready when Pedro and a passenger arrived in the truck. Carlos, the passenger, belonged to the environmental group that publicized the bloom.

They began a tedious trip eastward along the *Autopista Nacional* with three adults crammed onto the bench seat of the decrepit old truck. The engine misfired under load, and wheel bearings groaned around every bend.

Along the way, Pedro described the history of bay-choking blooms fueled by a sugar refinery's waste discharge. Previously the blooms had been sporadic, short-lived, and always green. This year's more persistent bloom was yellow.

They arrived at a small village on a narrow inlet connecting a north coast bay with the Old Bahama Channel. A commercial pier for shipping products from the sugar refinery protected a small floating dock.

The university's survey boat, a ten-metre-long steel vessel that looked older than Pedro's truck, rested against the dock. An enclosed space behind the wheelhouse served as laboratory and sleeping accommodations for the boat's two-man crew. The open afterdeck had motorized davits for deploying sampling equipment and larger winches and cranes for fishing gear.

Several of Carlos' environmental activist colleagues collected him. Tony and Pedro spent three hours setting up their sampling gear in the sticky heat.

Jacinta and Maria arrived in a 1958 Ford Fairlane 500.

"Some vehicle," Tony exclaimed as the two-door hardtop's enormous doors swung open.

"It's my family's," Maria replied before patting the hood. "I miss her when I'm in Halifax. Toyotas may be practical, but this is what Cubans imagine when anyone mentions a car. How can we help?"

"We're almost finished," Pedro said. "Few last things."

"And I want to join you tomorrow," Maria replied.

"I am not so certain," Jacinta added. "This boat does not look safe, and I do not manage well on the water."

Tony shook his head. "Sampling inside the bay for the first few hours. You could go ashore before we collect the offshore samples."

Early Tuesday morning, they steamed into the bay. The boat's engine ran more smoothly than the truck's, but water sloshed in the bilge. The constant gurgling of pumps made Tony sympathize with Jacinta's nervousness.

With Maria's help, Tony measured temperature and salinity using Dalhousie's CTD, a device with electrodes that recorded the results as it descended. He also collected water samples for nutrients, pH, and oxygen. Pedro collected samples for chlorophyll, a plant pigment that gave them a measure of biomass, and species identification. He and Jacinta processed the biological samples within the boat's tiny laboratory, and Tony made the oxygen and pH measurements.

"Definitely below normal," Tony said after recording the pH of the second sample they collected at their first station. "And oxygen is low for such a shallow bay."

"That confirms our observations," Pedro replied. "I worried because we made the measurements the next day at the university."

"Ready for station two?" Tony asked as he watched Maria in animated conversation as the captain positioned the boat.

"What the hell?" he yelled as they lowered their temperature and salinity probe. He pointed at a large creature with a prominent dorsal fin but no vertical tail.

"*Delfin,*" the captain replied from the wheelhouse.

"Dolphin?" Tony asked Pedro. "Do you see dolphins in such shallow waters?"

"Many manatees in these bays," Pedro replied, "but we never see dolphins."

They occupied six stations over the next three hours before dropping Jacinta and Maria on the dock. The dolphin remained nearby. Was its continued presence animal curiosity or was it monitoring their progress? It tagged along when Tony and Pedro collected coastal water samples on their way to a second bay. It circled the boat while they sampled and cavorted around their bow as they steamed back to the dock. When Carlos arrived with the truck, it squealed a high-pitched dolphin squeal and hightailed it back to sea.

"Where do we stand?" Pedro asked after Tony chose a table in the hotel bar.

"Chlorophyll's high and oxygen's low. That's interesting, but not surprising."

Pedro banged his glass on the table. "Fine. Excess growth depletes oxygen when it decomposes. But what about pH? That's what we came for."

Tony punched a final entry into his laptop with a theatrical flourish. "Patience." He watched the screen for several seconds. "Average is 7.55 plus or minus 0.12, with no significant vertical or horizontal gradients. I haven't done the statistics for the second bay, but no measurements are less than 7.9."

"I find acid sources?" Carlos interjected, the first words he'd uttered in English. He'd obviously been following the conversation, so his English was better than Tony thought.

"You must have a pollution source."

"We study for months," Carlos replied. "Not sugar refinery."

"No," Pedro added. "They've been operating for years with no recent changes in protocols."

"Then what's the acid source?" Tony asked.

"Two possible," Carlos replied. "One small power plant. They build sulphur remover from smokestack."

"It would generate sulphuric acid from the sulphur dioxide in the flue gas, but generally, you know, it's trapped and sold."

Carlos tilted his head back and raised his eyes skyward. "Not known where acid goes. Other possibility is small businesses that rebuild car batteries and recycle metals."

"Acid from the batteries could be the problem," Tony suggested.

"Now we have proof of acid in bay, we find source," Carlos replied, summing up the situation as Jacinta and Maria strolled into the bar.

On their second morning, the dolphin, or another just like it, waited by the boat. They loaded the first day's samples into Styrofoam coolers in the trunk of Maria's car, and the women headed to Havana. Tony and Pedro reoccupied three stations in their first bay and began a longer alongshore trip to the west. Their destination was a larger, more industrialized bay where they completed their sampling by mid-afternoon.

The dolphin shadowed them until the approached their final docking place. It got Tony wondering if the dolphin had a better understanding of their activities than they appreciated. The ability of organisms to detect and avoid harmful environmental conditions was well known. Did the dolphin know their first bay was a toxic environment? Could it know they were there to study and hopefully improve conditions? It seemed inconceivable, but he was reminded of a woman he met at a Greenpeace meeting. She was convinced whales, and that could include dolphins, were aware of the harm humans caused with climate change and other pollution problems. They, she claimed, were quite capable of intervening to put things right.

Thursday and Friday, they conducted the various analyses. At an impromptu mini-symposium on Saturday, Tony presented the physical and chemical oceanographic results, and Jacinta and Pedro described the biology. The patrician director of the oceanography group synthesized everything. He would present his summary to Cuban authorities. The bay where they started sampling looked like a giant version of Jacinta's original experiment, but none of their results suggested anything more than a localized industrial pollution problem. No one mentioned the dolphin.

Sunday, during their return flight to Halifax, Jacinta placed her hand on the open pages of Tony's novel. "Friday, Rosalind left a message describing a problem with my experiment in the large pool."

Tony had paid scant attention to Jacinta's recent effort to repeat the observations that jumpstarted their current focus on plankton behaviour at low pH. He'd been too busy shipping gear to Havana and making preparations for their trip to pay closer attention.

His week in Cuba had been exhausting, and his weary mind struggled to digest the new information. "Going well, wasn't it?"

"Very well, better than I expected. Acidity reached 7.7 ten days ago. Since then, we observed rapid growth. We have a better record of the growth rate changes."

He closed his novel and stuffed it in the seatback. A successful repeat of May's disastrous experiment should be good news. "If the electrodes haven't failed, what happened Friday?"

"That is not clear. Rosalind claimed salps invaded."

"What the hell are salps?"

"Tunicates, small gelatinous chordates. They're efficient predators of phytoplankton."

He imagined tentacled lumps of jelly inundating his electrodes. "Gelatinous, like jellyfish? They'll, you know, gum up everything."

"Rosalind consulted Mr. Wilkes, and yesterday, they suspended addition of acid until we returned."

"Poor Rosie. Tough decision, but probably the right one."

Tony and Jacinta strode from the Halifax airport terminal near nightfall. Sergio, the Spanish Consulate's chauffeur, waited in a no-parking zone. He drove them to the lab, where they found Rosie sitting on the giant aquarium's observation platform.

"You okay?" Tony asked as he rushed up. Jacinta followed at a more dignified pace.

"Up all-night Friday keeping the stupid salps from gumming up the electrodes, and last night I couldn't sleep."

Tony wrapped his arms around her. "Worried about the experiment?"

"The bloom's toast," Rosie wailed. "The damned salps roamed the aquarium like little vacuum cleaners sucking up the phytoplankton. Now they're drunken sailors passed out on the bottom."

Tony stared into the water, impressed by Rosie's colourful description as she turned to Jacinta. "Tim says I'm knackered and should have gone home, but I wanted to be here when you arrived."

Jacinta led her to the hallway and pointed at her chauffeur, smoking a cigarette outside the aquarium annex. "Give us a summary, and then Sergio will take you home. Sleep in as late as you wish tomorrow."

Rosie launched into her tale as soon as she returned to the aquarium table. "Friday morning, the bloom looked wrong, anemic, like something had drained the colour. After I checked the pH, I saw the strange strings of goo." She paused for breath. A tear slid down her cheek. "When I couldn't reach you, I consulted Tim."

Jacinta displayed an unusually compassionate side to her normally imperious character as she drew the younger woman into an embrace. "Do not worry, *mi chula*, you did well."

"I stayed here Friday night cleaning the muck off the electrodes. Saturday morning, when Tim arrived, the colour was gone. He said salps resemble locusts, sweeping through an area and eating everything in sight. He suggested we turn off the pH control system, and I agreed. I was too tired to argue."

Jacinta reached for Rosie's lab notebook. "You should not worry. The experiment confirmed the results of our earlier one. And this invasion of salps provides an interesting addendum."

Rosie gazed toward the hallway and smiled. "I am beat, so I'll accept your offer. What will my neighbours think when I arrive in a limo with a uniformed chauffeur and Spanish flags flapping on the fenders?"

She walked less jauntily than her usual gait, stopped at the door to discuss something with Sergio, waved, and strode to the massive black vehicle. Sergio stomped on his cigarette butt and opened the rear door with a theatrical flourish.

After watching them leave, Jacinta opened Rosie's lab notes. She hummed a tune Tony didn't recognize as she turned the pages. A few minutes later, she cleared her throat, and Tony turned from his fascination with the scene in the tank.

"Miss Rosalind has provided a clear record with observations for each day and reasons for all actions, including the decisions she and Mr. Wilkes made yesterday."

Tony scanned the entry Jacinta was highlighting. "Great student, and she would become a fine scientist. Too bad she won't be attending grad school."

"One must make choices. I trust Miss Parker will make the best ones for herself. But this week, I should reward her superb efforts. Should I engage Sergio and take you, Rosalind, and Mr. Wilkes to a restaurant; the Five Fishermen or Da Maurizio's perchance."

He smiled, imagining the sort of extravaganza Jacinta might organize. "She'd like that, especially rolling up in Sergio's limo, and I'll make sure Tim and I dress for the occasion."

"Fine, we shall go on Thursday. But now, it is late, and Sergio has returned. May we offer you a ride home?"

Ten minutes later, as Sergio pulled Tony's sports bag from the limousine's trunk, Jacinta made a critical observation. "Salps will represent an important factor in your investigation of carbon transport."

Chapter Seven

Monday, August 15, 2022

As Tony rushed past Cuppa Java on his way to the university a week after their Cuba trip, he glimpsed Beth hunched over a large mug. It was a sunny midsummer day, but she was wearing a baggy old sweatshirt. She had her hair pulled into a messy ponytail. Sitting there naked would have been less surprising than this deviation from her normal appearance. He jerked to a stop, hurried inside, and approached the table where she sat dabbing at puffy red eyes. "Have you, you know, been crying?"

"I have."

"And you could start again anytime."

"I might."

"Can I, you know, help?"

The floodgates opened, and tears streamed down her cheeks. "Jeremy left me. He emailed Friday from Paris, saying he wouldn't be coming back—the modern cliché, dumped by email. I'm like, abandoned, pregnant, and no idea what to do. I gotta talk to Mr. Brock, the *Smugglers Cove* director, but I'm like, no energy to call him."

Tony's mouth fell open. Jeremy must be the boyfriend she'd never named. "Pregnant! Does he know you're pregnant?"

"We were making plans together." She sniffed while wiping away tears with a fresh Kleenex. "Now he doesn't even mention the baby."

Time appeared to slow as Tony blinked, eyes bright with tears. He skidded his chair against hers and pulled her close. "Tell me."

"I've no choice," she whispered. "I love children, and I've wanted so much to have this baby. It's a boy. I couldn't possibly abort him."

"So, you'll become a mother, eh?"

She straightened her back. "You make it sound simple. You're right. It's what I gotta do. But I'm like feeling so alone."

"You have family. I know you do."

"They'll support me, but I need to sort it out before I talk to them."

"Friends?"

She shook her head. "The other women in the acting business aren't real friends. We hang out together, but we fight for jobs. Jeremy and I were living in our little bubble, and I let my other friends drift away." She stared out the window, tears welling. "My bubble's burst. I'm like on my own."

"Your true friends will be there when you need them."

Her head and shoulders remained slumped as she gazed through her eyelashes. "And you?"

He almost blurted, 'yeah, I'll be there whenever you need me,' but that was too big a leap. It was too soon for huge commitments. "You need a diversion, and I've never seen the sights outside metro. We could, you know, take your car and visit Peggy's Cove or Lunenburg? Sound good?"

"It'll be hot. How about a picnic at Crystal Crescent Beach?"

Tony's eyes widened. That could lead to the sort of commitment he wanted to avoid. "The nudist beach? I'm not sure we should go to a nudist beach."

She looked up, a tiny smile creeping across her face. "Maybe that's what I need." Her little smile became a frown. "Only teasing, and anyway, only the farthest part is clothing optional."

He glanced toward the exit after making a quick decision. "If you want a picnic, that's what we'll do."

After leaving Cuppa Java, she returned to her apartment. She reappeared thirty minutes later, wearing one of her trademark sundresses with her blond curls blowing in the wind. She was carrying a picnic basket.

Beth drove her blue mica Miata convertible, and neither said much until they arrived at the parking lot for Crystal Crescent's three beaches. At the middle one, she chose a conspicuous spot and fussed with the basket before pulling her dress over her head.

Tony stared, his movie star in a bikini overwhelming his muddled brain. "You don't look pregnant."

"But I'm developing a baby bump." She leaned back, rubbing her belly. "My doctor says it will soon show. This might be your last chance."

"You'll be as beautiful in a few months."

She smiled, lowering her eyes. "Ooh, such a charmer. You've, like, improved my spirits. I'll have a little wine with my lunch. But don't give me a second glass."

Tony poured, then raised his glass.

Beth placed her hand on his. "It's time my knight told me about himself. You've described your work at Dal, never anything about yourself."

"Grew up in London, a south-western Ontario city that's somewhat bigger than Halifax. My parents died in a car crash when I was ten." He paused, sipped his wine, and fast-forwarded over his difficulties coping with the loss of his parents. "I was a good student and interested in sports, but never on school teams. I was lousy at art and music, and I would have been hopeless in a play. After high school, I studied engineering at the University of Western Ontario and came to Halifax for my master's degree."

"Girlfriends?"

Tony smiled. "Never anything serious. My last girlfriend graduated in May and moved to Toronto."

After several minutes of idle chat, three young women appeared.

"Ah, there you are," one said. "We saw your car and came looking for you. Who's the new guy? He's cuter than Jeremy." The others giggled.

Beth scowled. "This is Tony. We're neighbours enjoying a beach day. Tony, these three," she said, pointing to each in turn, "are Jennifer, Amanda, and Theresa. We share the misfortune of being actors."

Jennifer scrutinized their lunch basket and then Beth in her bikini. "It looks like you've been on vacation scarfing too many fattening sweets."

Beth stared at the waves. "An assignment in central Canada. I visited my sister and her family."

Theresa ignored Beth's less than fulsome explanation. She nodded at Tony and winked. "You should bring him to our beach. He'd look good in the altogether."

Beth shook her head. "We're happy where we are."

Theresa made a dismissive gesture, and the trio strutted away.

Beth scowled at their swaying backsides. "They're as bitchy as I said. Wait till they learn I'm pregnant, and Jeremy's left me. Their claws will be flashing."

Tony said nothing until the trio reached a rocky area separating the second and third beaches. One turned and waved her bikini top before disappearing behind an enormous boulder. "So, you normally go to the nude beach, eh?"

"An all-over tan *is* important."

Tony hesitated. He knew very little about Beth's life and her modelling and acting career. "You get parts where it matters?"

"Of course! Imagine a fashion shoot for swimsuits. One can't have ugly white bits. And I've had a few parts with nudity. It's no big deal." She messed with the remnants of their lunch for several minutes. "May I change the subject?"

"We're here to boost your spirits, so your wish is my command."

She smiled. "I have a real cute story about my niece and nephew."

"Fire away."

"Two days before I left, they came to the village to help me find you an apartment-minding present. They described their present jar, one with scraps of paper describing treats they'd get for things like cleaning up their rooms or emptying the dishwasher. We listed things I could do to thank you for looking after my place."

She reached into her beach tote and pulled out a disorganized pile of paper. "Pretend this is your present jar. Pick one now, and if you continue to be my friend, you can choose another whenever you're like, especially good."

Beth fanned the pages like a deck of cards with one protruding. Tony took it. The multi-coloured crayon message said, 'take Tony to a fancy restaurant'.

Beth smiled impishly. "I hoped you'd pick that one."

That evening after dinner, a Mona Lisa-like smile spread across her face as they strolled through the darkening streets. On her front porch, she rewarded him with a warm hug and a long, lingering lover's kiss. Not one of her coffee shop pecks on the cheek.

"Thank you, Tony. You've given back my will to continue. You dumped whatever you'd planned and looked after me when I needed looking after. I won't forget."

She kissed him again and disappeared through her door leaving him standing there dazed.

He wandered to his apartment imagining their life together, making a home for her little boy, and fighting for climate change action. She was smart, beautiful, and really interested in environmental issues. Could he find a role for someone with her talents on the bigger, better, multifaceted ClimateChange&U.ca site he was imagining?

In 2020, the coronavirus pandemic pushed him into climate change research. He soon focused on what seemed like a simple question. Why couldn't humanity address the simple and easily solvable question of reducing the endlessly expanding emissions of carbon dioxide?

At first, Tony directed his ire at climate change deniers on the Christian right. He also railed against people who thought Canada had a God-given right to exploit the Athabasca Tar Sands. During his two years as a graduate student, he added academics who ignored society's problems as they pursued their research interests. Steve Matthews defended their devotion to academic integrity. Shouldn't they also worry about climate change?

Too many people thought climate change was a distant threat they could ignore for many years. Add politicians who spouted platitudes and made aspirational statements while taking no concrete action. Their inertia could kill the world. And industrialists exploiting the environment. They made things worse.

Could I, with Beth's help, use ClimateChange&U to wake people up to the risks? We could make small steps toward addressing the problems.

Chapter Eight

Thursday, August 18, 2022

Steve Matthews' voice pierced the background noise as Tony joined the mid-morning crowd in the oceanography department coffee room. Steve's pontificating wasn't surprising, but Jacinta's reaction was. She was on her feet, doing battle across the table. The dignified Jacinta Lopez towered over the seedier-looking Steve Matthews slouching in his chair like a drug or booze-addled dilettante in a Victorian period drama.

"That is completely unreasonable," she shouted. "You mustn't disparage work based on observations and simple descriptions."

Tony stared from the doorway, surprised by Jacinta's vehemence and the eloquence of her speech. A little excitement improved her English; she'd even used a contraction.

She whipped around and faced him. "Tell Mr. Matthews about our observations."

He understood the conflict's cause. Steve believed the physical laws governing motion and the interaction between particles explained all important observations in oceanography. He disregarded complex biological observations in his efforts to channel Einstein and develop a unifying theory.

Tony sympathized with Steve's perspective. He sought a project that built on Jacinta and Rosie's results but moved into ecological modelling. His goal was a general picture that integrated their results into global biogeochemical models. He wouldn't suggest Jacinta's detail was unimportant, but he wanted to focus on the overall situation, the forest, rather than the trees.

"Jacinta's describing the complexity of the phytoplankton response to lower pH. We need to consider that complexity when we build our biochemical and physical models."

"I disagree," Steve said. "Biological detail doesn't matter. It's the general principle, lower the pH and plankton will grow. That's what we should incorporate into the models."

"No!" Jacinta replied. "You cannot expect plankton with carbonate skeletons to grow as their shells dissolve. We must understand which organisms respond and the biochemistry of the response before you generalizers incorporate anything into your Gaia models and Mother Nature's grand plan."

Steve sneered. "And what about God's plan?"

Tony poured himself a coffee and monitored the discussion. He wasn't interested in arguments about whether Mother Nature or God controlled things, and Jacinta was holding her own. As Steve and Jacinta jousted, he considered his research project. When the squabble died down, he slipped from the coffee room and returned to his cubbyhole of an office.

Tony was hard at work half an hour later when Jacinta swept in. She appeared as calm and composed as ever.

"Are you not having delayed vacation?"

"At loose ends, and Rosie's struggles have me thinking."

"Tell me what you think. I need, how should I say, to calm myself after the discussion with Mr. Matthews."

"To calm down. You should be proud. You answered his criticisms and stayed above the fray when he belittled your religious convictions."

"Ah, Tony, are you now defending my religious beliefs?"

"I'd only criticize them if they confuse the scientific discourse or inhibit attention to important issues."

"Good. Describe your latest ideas as you move toward a project proposal."

Tony glanced at the notes he'd been making. "I start with the competition between various plankton species. Success will depend on numerous environmental factors."

"This is nothing new."

He ignored her mild rebuke. "The diatoms in our experiments grow more quickly than other plankton. This gives them an ecological advantage. And second, they're heavy, so they sink."

She took a piece of chalk and wrote 'more biomass' and 'faster sinking' on Tony's blackboard and circled them. "This generates a problem. Producing more biomass is helpful, but a high sinking rate is disadvantageous."

"Contradictory characteristics of the organisms you and Rosie are studying."

"True, and we should learn more as we progress. Consider your factors individually."

"They grow rapidly at low pH and produce extra biomass from a given amount of nutrient."

Jacinta held her chalk against her first entry. "What does that suggest?"

"They dominate the bloom and displace other organisms."

"And the blooms are persistent."

"Perhaps that's related to a high carbon to nitrate ratio. Could they reapportion nutrients taken up at a more standard ratio to produce carbon-rich biomass as nitrate becomes scarcer?"

"Interesting observations, but very biological. Not aligned with your talents."

"Where does it leave me?"

She added a downward-pointing arrow to her second blackboard entry. "What about the higher than usual sinking rate?"

"More physics than biology, and more related to carbon transport."

"Yes, partly physics and partly biology and important for the global biogeochemical models that interest you."

"So, this could be the basic hypothesis for an interesting thesis topic?"

She backed away from the blackboard and stopped in his doorway. "Work on both ideas and consider the observations we are making. For your project proposal, use the aspects that align with your training."

"And you agree enhanced vertical transport in a low pH environment meets those criteria."

"You must decide."

"Dr. Krueger would have to approve."

She smiled after handing Tony the chalk. "You must convince him your proposition is solid."

"Thank you, Jacinta. You've made sense of the ideas spinning about my head."

After Jacinta left, Tony's brows furrowed as he scrawled across the top of his chalkboard. 'Hypothesis: enhanced production of various plankton at low pH produces enhanced carbon transport to the sediment and enhanced burial of carbon. This slows the trend to lower pH and may even reverse it if the burial is great enough.'

He scowled at his first attempt at a mission statement. It took up most of the board. *Too wordy, but an adequate starting point.*

That afternoon, Tony hurried into Cuppa Java and strode to Beth's favourite place by the window. His heart skipped a beat when she greeted him with the now traditional kiss. No question, his usually suppressed emotional self was winning the battle with his more pragmatic scientific one. When his head cleared, he realized Beth was nattering away.

"Sorry I missed you yesterday and the day before, but Mr. Brock wanted to see me Tuesday afternoon. And Wednesday, we rushed through an extra scene."

He leaned forward, whispering. "Being pregnant isn't a problem?"

She smiled as she twirled a blond curl around her index finger. "Might even help. He wants to weave my pregnancy into the ongoing series. We'll discuss it tomorrow afternoon."

"You'll become a regular?"

"Hope so. Come for dinner tomorrow. I'd love to share the news, and I'd rather it was you than Bernie."

"Bernie?"

"My neighbour, Bernadette," she said as she placed her hand on his. "Not a new boyfriend."

Tony sighed, telegraphing his relief. "When should I arrive?"

"Six. I get hungry earlier and earlier these days." She pulled him from his seat. "Let's go."

He reached back, grabbed his cup, and gulped a final mouthful of coffee before hurrying after her. "Where we headed?"

"The Common."

She led him to the Halifax Common, several blocks of lawn crisscrossed by paths leading to various parts of the city. They lounged on the grass, and Beth described a future that included a staring role for Tony.

After dinner at Dimitri's, a Greek restaurant on Quinpool Road, they wandered home arm in arm like lovers without a care in the world. As they approached her apartment, Beth invited him up.

She pulled her living room curtains across the deck door, put a sultry Diana Krall CD on the machine, and pushed him onto the sofa.

As Ms. Krall crooned 'The Look of Love', Beth reached up and kissed him.

Tony returned the kisses and soon had her dress above her hips and his hands on her breasts. She flinched, and he pulled away. "Something wrong?"

"Sorry, I shouldn't have invited you up. I'm like feeling overwhelmed, but I promise, by tomorrow night when you come for dinner, I'll have it sorted out."

Tony sat for several minutes with his hands in his lap. "I won't, you know, dump you as soon as the baby shows. You realize that, don't you?"

"My mind's in too big a jumble," she said as she dabbed tears welling in her eyes.

They snuggled together until the CD ended. Tony kissed her once more and took his leave. She was almost asleep.

As he traversed the few metres between their apartment buildings, Tony wondered about the previous hour. She'd gone from the brink of a major triumph into a serious retreat. And it wasn't the first time she'd charged ahead only to pull back without explanation.

This time, he had a simple answer. Pregnancy, excitement, and busy days in the film studio had worn her out. *Tomorrow I'll take a gentler approach—flowers, little presents, slower seduction—everything will be perfect.*

When he arrived for dinner the next evening, Beth was pacing her building's porch in another sexy sundress. She looked cool and enticing with her translucent yellow dress with white flowers blowing in the warm evening breeze.

"Come in, come in," she exclaimed before he stepped from the public sidewalk. "I was so impatient I knocked on your door, but you like weren't there."

Tony loped across the few metres of path. "Buying you flowers and a little present." He held up his packages as she reached forward and engulfed him in an embrace.

"I love flowers. Come upstairs, and I'll put them in water. Do you like my dress? It's one of my favourites, too revealing for most occasions, but perfect for tonight."

"Nice. I love your sundresses."

"Come in, come in," she repeated as she opened her apartment door. "Everything's under control. I'll put the flowers in water. Then I must see what's in the box."

He stumbled when the sunlight streaming into the apartment revealed she was naked under the translucent dress. "Hope you didn't wear this dress for your interview."

"Ha. That meeting called for high heels, a push-up bra, and an outfit that accentuates my curves." She tore open Tony's present. "Now, what's in here?"

She held up a glass dolphin with a golden halo. "Oh, beautiful. Are you making me into an environmentalist like Pamela Anderson?"

"Pamela Anderson supports People for the Ethical Treatment of Animals. Brigitte Bardot wants to save the wild ones."

She put the chain around her neck and looked at the dolphin nestled between her breasts. "I love it. Thank you, you are a dear."

"He looks happy sitting there."

"Would he be happier down here?" she asked as she slipped the dolphin inside her dress.

"Don't see him as clearly."

She slid a strap off her shoulder. "I could solve that problem."

His heartbeat raced until he remembered how her flirtatious mood the previous evening had gone so wrong. "Perhaps we should save that for later."

The dolphin remained thinly veiled until bedtime when Beth put on another sultry CD. She shed her dress and lured him to her bedroom after a single song.

Chapter Nine

Thursday, September 22, 2022

The eviction notice punctured the bubble Tony'd been living in since their first night together. It brought him crashing back to earth and revived annoyances like being stuck in classes when he wanted to work on his research project.

Beth shrugged after one look at the notice. "Move in with me. It's the only scientifically credible solution."

Tony smiled at Beth's teasing choice of words. He'd arrived at the same conclusion but worried she might consider it too soon for that logical next step in their relationship.

Two days later, he had a new address. Hopefully, the joys of their new life together would diminish his frustration with the slow pace of university research.

Dr. Krueger appeared in Tony's office doorway on the thirtieth of September. "The focus on courses is difficult, but I can't alter a valid policy nor justify committing funds to unauthorized projects."

Tony glared as he saved the file he'd been manipulating. He couldn't understand the department's rationale for such inertia-generating policies. "Why can't I start the research while I complete these damn courses?"

"We expect you'll spend time in the library. If you describe modest experiments that help define your project, I'll okay them."

"Better than nothing," Tony said as he closed his laptop.

Dr. K waited until Tony looked up. "A reporter asked me about the research you, Jacinta, and Rosie have been conducting. I declined her interview request and suggested she approach you."

The following Tuesday morning, the radio station receptionist introduced Tony to Becky Smith, a freelance reporter specializing in scientific and environmental issues. Older students warned him to prepare for battle with an interviewee-devouring shark, but she appeared young and friendly. He followed her bouncing ponytail to an interview room.

It contained a desk with a few notes and a microphone that Becky sat behind. She faced a comfortable leather chair below a second microphone on an articulated arm. After a few minutes of idle chat, Becky placed large headphones over her ears, a technician adjusted Tony's microphone, and the interview began.

"Good morning. Today's guest is Mr. Tony Atherton, an oceanography student at Dalhousie University. Anyone following climate change debates should know about their exciting research on the impacts of ocean acidification on marine life. Let's start by asking Tony how he became involved in this problem."

She pointed at Tony and nodded.

"It started when I was an engineering student. I designed and built the measurement systems used by the biologists studying ocean acidification in our lab."

Becky smiled as she slowly shook her head. "Explain for our listeners what you mean by a measurement system."

During the next few minutes, Tony described the aquarium control system he designed and the studies Jacinta conducted. He ended with his view on the importance of her work.

"Primary biological production removes carbon from the ocean. It's a natural mechanism for reducing carbon dioxide levels. When the ocean becomes more acidic, greater phytoplankton production should dampen the global trend to ever-increasing carbon dioxide concentrations."

She nodded and mouthed, 'Better.' "You're starting work on a PhD in oceanography. Will you also investigate the biological impacts of acidity?"

Tony smiled. She'd made a common mistake. "Not all oceanographers are biologists. I doubt I'll discover anything new in marine biology."

"So, what will you study?"

"I want to investigate how Jacinta's changes in the plankton affect the ocean's pH. Will the biological changes make acidification worse, slow the increase, or even mitigate harmful impacts by reversing the trend?"

Becky glanced at her notes. "That leads me to two questions related to the current political impasse. First, will natural feedback mechanisms mitigate the impacts of ocean acidification or open the floodgates for engineered solutions? And second, is this mitigation a divine intervention? Let's start with the first question. Will natural feedback mechanisms fix the acidification problem?"

Tony hesitated, trying to develop an answer that would generate discussion of safe topics like feedback mechanisms and engineering solutions. If he was lucky, he might avoid delving into the religious controversy.

"Many biological systems have feedback mechanisms that correct things when they get too far out of whack. A feedback mechanism for ocean acidification is a reasonable suggestion. It's like lemmings, if I may use them as an analogy. Conditions become unbearable before their drastic feedback mechanism kicks in. We may anticipate similar results for natural feedback mechanisms associated with ocean acidification."

"And the second part, can we use the understanding you're developing to manage the problem?"

"Governments may establish mitigation measures based on good engineering. They could be helpful, but we must understand the system far better before we help nature with large-scale fixes."

"You've given us the rationale for conducting your research."

Tony nodded. This was safe ground. *Just avoid sliding into the religion question.* "We can't hope to cure the problem unless we understand it, and the potential hazards the cure may introduce."

"And the question of divine intervention?"

Tony grimaced as he tried to decide what he could say without getting into trouble. He took a deep breath and plunged in, realizing the interviewee-devouring shark he'd been warned about had ambushed him.

"Many people believe in God, but God cannot exist outside their minds. Their belief in God can influence their thinking and behaviour, but it has no physical presence. It cannot impact natural processes or generate feedback mechanisms for ocean acidification."

"We're running out of time. Let's put ocean acidification in the bigger picture of global warming. Some people argue global warming is such a massive problem we must abandon our modern lives and return to a pre-industrial society. Others say our current global warming is a short respite before the next ice age. Where do you stand?"

"The world is warming, and human activities are contributing to it, but the world is always changing, and we shouldn't be against change *per se*. Human activities are causing rapid changes that biological systems cannot absorb. Slowing the rate of change will give us time to adapt to the inevitable changes or counteract them."

When Tony paused for breath, Becky jumped in. "Thank you, Dr. Atherton—"

"Mr. Atherton, the PhD is well in the future."

"Thank you, Mr. Atherton, for your thoughts on this important subject. I must say goodbye to Mr. Atherton and our listeners before my producer cuts us off."

A small light on Becky's microphone changed from green to red as the station technicians transferred to their regular noon-hour newscast.

"You were some good," Rosie said as Tony marched into the lab an hour later. "No wonder Ms. Smith called you doctor at the end. You sounded mature and professional, just like the university prof you'll be in a few years."

"I don't care how I sounded. Did I say anything stupid?"

"Well, you should've declined to talk about religion, and you called God it. I didn't notice any science mistakes. But what do I know?"

"What about Jacinta? Was she listening?"

Rosie shrugged. "Haven't seen her. Tim said he'd listen. Ask him."

Two days after his interview, Tony stopped by Dr. Krueger's office. The professor was on the phone but waved him to a chair. After a minute listening to one side of a heated conversation, Tony pointed to the door. Dr. K shook his head.

Seconds later, he thumped the handset into its cradle. "How did your interview go?"

"Tim and Rosie said it went well. Rosie claims I called God it, which will annoy some people, and Tim told me the lemmings' story is an urban myth, but those were minor glitches."

Dr. Krueger laughed. "Any biologist knows millions of lemmings charging over cliffs is a fallacy generated by the Disney Corporation."

"Shows I've lots to learn," Tony replied, "but I never claimed to be a biologist."

Dr. K's brow furrowed as he gestured toward his phone. "That conversation's related."

"Sounded confrontational."

"Reverend Terrence Goddard," Dr. K said with a sigh. "A religious fanatic who says we shouldn't worry about climate change because God has it under control. His tirade doesn't concern me, but he mentioned your interview. You're on his radar screen and may get a call."

Tony didn't hear from Reverend Goddard, but two others contacted him. One was bad, the other, good. John Springer, a fellow undergraduate from his days in London, Ontario, delivered the first message in a brief phone call.

"A word of warning," he said after identifying himself and reminding Tony of their acquaintance. "Opposition to our stance on greenhouse gas reduction will not be well received."

"That sounds like a threat. Who the hell do you represent?"

"Let's say important people who could ruin your career. And they don't fool around. If you oppose them, they'll squash you." He severed the call.

After staring at a blank screen for several seconds, Tony switched apps and searched for info on John Springer. He found Springer's photo and a short bio in Western's Engineering Faculty yearbook from their graduating year. It helped him remember the big, brash bully who was always engaged in the intimidating pranks engineering students are famous for. Did that explain the odd call? Was he returning to his undergraduate bully tactics, trying to get back at a student who'd done better than he had? At least, Tony concluded Springer hadn't done much since graduating. His bio said Springer left Western for an oil patch job in Calgary, but Tony found no mention of him on social media.

That seemed like the most likely explanation. Springer was frustrated with his dead-end job. He resorted to juvenile antics from his undergraduate years when one of his fellow students appeared on national radio. Best bet, perhaps, but it didn't change Tony's initial reaction. The call was damned intimidating.

The second response to his interview was more positive. It came from Clive Grainger, an entrepreneurial engineer who phoned with an interesting idea.

"Sewage as the nutrient source for a biodigester that uses low pH seawater and your special plankton to produce methane or alcohol. Could be a winner, but I'd need help developing a workable reactor."

Tony stared at the ceiling while he collected his thoughts. "I foresee several problems. Sewage has low salinity. You must add seawater to your reactor to maintain proper growing conditions. That means you'll discharge water." He paused, considering what else he should say. "How will you manage that without discharging diatoms?"

"That's why I called. I need someone to criticize my plans and ask those tough questions. Are you interested?"

"I'll answer questions and comment on your design, and our lab can probably supply diatoms for preliminary experiments. But you'll soon need a reliable source. Maintaining large diatom cultures could be difficult and expensive. Not something I can help with."

"Can't we rely on the incoming seawater having suitable organisms?"

Tony slumped forward, his left elbow on his desk and his forehead resting in his hand. If Clive's understanding of marine biology was that limited, this effort could get complicated. "Not there all year round, and only at high enough concentrations sporadically in the spring."

Clive said nothing for several seconds. "A prototype's a distant goal. I'll include money for diatom cultures as part of my proposal. A local source would be preferable."

Tony paused while he considered the need to consult Dr. K. "I'll read your proposal, provide comments, and check into culturing."

After the call, Tony discovered Clive was a legitimate scientist with an engineering company developing technologies for addressing socially relevant issues. It sounded positive, but Tony couldn't risk getting associated with a loose cannon. Additional digging yielded nothing disquieting.

Tony lacked the necessary understanding of plankton cultures. For that, he needed Marc Lavoie.

Marc started on his PhD in oceanography after earning a master's degree in biology. He was a tall, thin, and painfully shy Acadian from Prince Edward Island. He listened without commenting during most discussions. When he spoke up, his insightful comments demanded attention. His almost obsessive interest in the classification of organisms led to his interest in Jacinta's project. He hoped to turn it into a study of the impact of low pH on biological diversity. *Can I interest him in Clive's project?*

They dropped into the coffee room after a morning lecture. "*Non,*" Marc said after Tony suggested experiments using Jacinta's pennate diatom. "An engineer needs the hardiest species that shows enhanced production."

"But Jacinta's shown her original species responds appropriately."

"True, but it could be difficult to culture, and if one species shows this response, others will too. Your engineer will want one that's cheap and reliable."

Tony's brow furrowed as he stirred his coffee. The damn project was getting increasingly complicated. "What do I tell him?"

"We need time to find the best candidate, and in the meantime, we conduct a small study using your aquaria. I prepare cultures of common phytoplankton, and you measure productivity when they're exposed to low pH."

"That's what Rosie Parker's doing for her BSc project."

"It is! Then you should monitor her results and choose her most robust, easily cultured one."

"And you'll help?"

Marc nodded. He hadn't touched his coffee. Tony knew he was hooked.

Chapter Ten

Tuesday, January 10, 2023

During the Christmas lull in normal university activities, Tony expanded the scope of Rosie's experiments. He conducted studies on hardy rather than academically interesting species.

After Marc returned from his Christmas vacation, Tony produced his results and a summary of Rosie's findings. Marc clicked his pen as he stared at the numbers before drawing a circle around one result.

"This is the best bet for Mr. Grainger. Its growth rate is eighty-five percent of the best one, and it's the easiest species to maintain. Cheapest, too."

"Thought you'd choose that one. Even a stupid engineer knows those little buggers are indestructible. But we should give him a second and third choice in case he wants to conduct comparison studies."

Marc pondered for a few minutes before putting tick marks beside two more results. "These two are nearly as robust and give decent and indistinguishable results."

"Good. I'll write my report and send it off."

Several days later, Tony received a reply with a detailed project proposal attached.

Clive listed him as a junior partner who would bring scientific expertise to the venture Clive had named Algal Energy. They would develop technology for carbon-neutral energy production while reducing other pollution problems. They may even make money.

As Tony struggled with the minefields of departmental policies, climate change politics, and experiments for Clive Grainger, Beth breezed through several months of career resurgence. By Christmas, her contributions to five episodes for *Smugglers Cove*'s second season were complete. In January, she had ample opportunity to rest up for the birth of her first child.

The big day started at 6 a.m. on February second, several days before the official due date. She took a few deep breaths before Tony was completely awake. "You needn't panic; the contractions are ten minutes apart."

He blinked several times as he struggled to get his thoughts together. They had a list of things they needed, and everything except his phone charging on the kitchen table was ready. "We could rest here or get up if you prefer."

"I woke you up too soon, didn't I?"

He sighed. "Awake long?"

"Two hours, but it seems like ages. I need a hug."

Tony put his arms around her. "Something wrong?"

"Sorry, dreaming of things we won't have."

He snuggled closer. "We'll be fine."

"I couldn't manage without you."

She tensed as the next contraction hit her.

They waited for another.

Tony counted until Beth relaxed after her next contraction. "They're getting closer together. Should we get up?"

"I'm like staying here."

"You seem unhappy?"

"Frightened of the pain, and that I'll be a hopeless mother, and you won't like having a baby, and you'll leave me. I'll never get my figure back, and I don't know what else."

"Everyone knows you're great with kids. Remember the fun stories you've told me about your niece and nephew. It'll be better with your son."

Beth sighed. "Whatever."

Tony leaned back, gazing at her tear-stained face and tortured expression.

They rose, showered, and had breakfast. Beth drank tea but ate nothing. After breakfast, Tony tidied the kitchen while Beth checked the hospital bag one last time before phoning her mother. By the time Margaret arrived to drive them to the hospital, they'd tidied the bathroom, the living room, and their bedroom.

Beth contributed to the clean-up activities, pausing during each contraction, but her attitude was fatalistic. She appeared resigned to an unpalatable fate rather than looking forward with joyous anticipation to her son's birth.

By 11:30, Beth's contractions were a minute long and five minutes apart. They headed for the maternity hospital. They signed in, feigning composure they didn't feel, and followed a nurse to a room where expectant mothers prepared for the big event.

When Tony returned from a cafeteria visit, he found Beth and her mother in a birthing room that would be their home for many hours. Lying on a narrow hospital bed wearing a pale blue gown with pink flowers, Beth appeared frightened.

Hours later, a nurse suggested it would be a good opportunity if anyone wanted a bathroom or cafeteria break. She had monitors to attach and measurements to make. Margaret took her first break, and Tony relinquished his post to get Beth something to drink.

"She's dilating nicely," the nurse said when Margaret returned. She stopped at the door. "When I return, it should be time for action."

Shortly after the nurse returned, Beth's water broke, and contractions became increasingly intense. Civility was abandoned, and it became a battle with pain to get the baby into the big bad world. Nothing Margaret or Tony said or did helped as Beth moaned and groaned and writhed during every contraction. Despite her earlier worries about pain, she refused an epidural. Three hours later, it was all over. Michael was lying at Beth's breast, and she was beaming. Her eyes were wet with tears, but the pain was forgotten.

Later, Tony struggled to untangle his emotions as he strode home after declining the drive Margaret offered him. He hadn't once thought of Michael as anything but his child. He'd struggled and panicked and worried during those stressful hours, then rejoiced when Michael emitted his first cry. Sure, he'd worried about Beth, about her health and her happiness. He realized, as he hurried home in the frigid evening air, he was more concerned about Michael.

Winston, a pensioner who lived in a ground-floor apartment, stood in his doorway when Tony entered their building. "Everything good?"

"Everyone's exhausted, but Beth and her son are doing fine."

"She's lucky to have you. That fool Jeremy was a useless, self-centred, pretentious jerk. She's much better off without him."

He looked back into his apartment when his wife called, "Winston!".

He shook his head and turned back to Tony. "Right bastard. You could hear him hurling abuse at her everywhere in the building."

"You suggesting he beat her?"

"Can't rightly say. Never saw any evidence, but no question he was verbally abusive."

Winston's wife appeared in the doorway and dragged him inside.

"It's okay, Mrs. Baker. Beth and Michael are doing fine—seven pounds, four ounces, born at 6:34 p.m."

Tony climbed the stairs and made the calls he'd promised Beth before settling back with a beer. Winston's comments cleared up something bothering Tony for months. Jeremy frightened Beth, and that fear was responsible for the melancholy that frequently overwhelmed her. And in the early going, she thought Tony would also abuse her.

He dumped a can of beans on the stove and downloaded the pictures and video from his camera. She'd buried her fear of Jeremy for several months. *I must keep it that way.*

After their second lecture on the morning after Michael's birth, Tony and Marc paused near their laboratory whiteboard, watching Rosie fuss with an experiment. The Annapolis Valley farm girl hovered over her experiments, treating them like a litter of recalcitrant piglets.

Tony turned to Marc after outlining a series of experiments that would give them jump starts on their research projects. "Will it work for you?"

Marc picked up red and blue markers and started a colour-coded task list down one side of the whiteboard. "Observation of the changes in species composition should help define my future experiments."

"And I can measure differences in biomass accumulation. But I also need settling rates."

"How? Tanks with artificial turbulence won't be realistic."

Tony hesitated. They were brainstorming ideas, and this one needed work. "I could scoop out aliquots after growth is well-established, transfer them to settling columns, and measure how fast they settle."

"Or run experiments until we have measurements for growth rate and species succession, then turn off the turbulence and let them settle *in situ.*"

Tony commandeered most of the board for an experimental flow chart. "Easier to measure growth rate in the aquaria and settling in the columns."

Marc nodded as he added entries to his list, red for Tony's tasks and blue for his.

"Is it fair?" Tony asked as he scanned Marc's list. "I'll gain from your efforts, but you won't get much from mine."

Marc scanned his lists with brows furrowed. "I'll deal with species identification. If you keep the pH under control and look after the other measurements, we'll have a fair split."

Rosie joined them and studied the whiteboard for several seconds. "Weren't the experiments you ran over Christmas a temporary intrusion?"

"We won't get in your way," Tony said while waving his marker. "Jacinta insists she's finished her lab work. And you must soon focus on writing your thesis."

"Yeah, Dr. K won't approve new experiments, but I don't like it. Experiments are more fun than writing a thesis or studying for exams." She paused, glancing at her watch. "Gotta go, lecture in ten minutes."

Marc watched her leave. "Don't be hard on her. She knows you think she should go to grad school, so no point belabouring it."

"I'm not, but what's her future with a BSc in biology?"

"She has it figured out."

"Oh yeah? She's been confiding in you?"

"Nothing weird. She told me about her high school sweetheart and their plans. Education degree at Acadia, then marriage and life running his farm augmented by income from her teacher's salary."

"Okay, Rosie has it planned, but you know what they say about the best-laid schemes..."

Marc laughed as he drew a cartoon mouse perched on one of Tony's flow chart boxes. "The wee sleekit cow'rin tim'rous beastie's plans, they all gang aft agley. My favourite poem."

"Meanwhile, back at our discussion..."

"Jacinta's observations provide a solid foundation for both our projects."

"We let someone else confirm or refute her more controversial ideas, but the primary production increase is established."

"Enhanced growth happens, and changes to the community structure happen," Marc replied. "That gives a biologist like me interesting questions to investigate. You can delve into your geochemical modelling questions and what it means for society."

"But there's a huge unknown. Predation."

"Gives you something to ponder," Marc suggested.

Tony stood for several minutes, tapping the butt end of his felt marker against his front teeth. "But how do I handle it? Jacinta said predation would be an issue when those stupid salps gummed up last summer's big experiment."

"Long-term problem, not for these initial experiments. If we generate anything good in these predation-free experiments, we'll produce a paper."

"And I might learn something that relates to engineering fixes."

Marc laughed as he headed for his office. "Steve Matthews has a point. You appear more interested in engineering problems than academic papers and ivory tower science."

Their experiments and Tony's bent for engineering fed into his commitment to Clive Grainger's methane from plankton project. When Clive announced they had funding from the Natural Resources Department, Algal Energy became a meaningful entity. He described the hiring of several employees and a series of experiments that ranged from lab bench tests to a pilot plant.

Tony was shocked. In five months, Clive had progressed from their initial discussions to a funded project. A mind-boggling contrast with the difficulty he had getting approval for a few preliminary experiments.

A week later, Marc and Tony met Clive and his new assistant, Yusuf Mohammed, for lunch in the Earl of Dalhousie, the Faculty Club's English-style pub. They analyzed Clive's plans and sent Yusuf to his DalTech lab with enough work to keep him busy for months.

Marc left the meeting with a commitment to supply Yusuf with cultures of the robust plankton species Marc suggested. Supplying the quantities needed for bench-scale experiments would not be difficult. And Clive had committed enough funding to the Dal Oceanography group to cover costs for the cultures.

Tony's commitment was greater. Over the next few months, he would work with Clive and Yusuf to merge his new interest in marine biology with his older interest in engineering. Clive's get-on-with-it attitude bolstered his enthusiasm.

They began with reduced pH experiments with no added nutrients. These efforts produced an initial growth rate ten times the maximum rate observed using water at ambient pH.

The time-consuming experiments justified a partial salary from Clive's grant money. That salary eliminated Tony's money worries. While Michael was little, they'd have enough to live on without needing Beth's income. He'd soon learn the importance of that extra financial security.

Chapter Eleven

Thursday, June 8, 2023

By the spring of 2023, Tony's approach to convincing Canadians to take climate change seriously had evolved. He now considered climate change deniers and the go-slow attitude of academics as minor impediments on the road to progress. His focus shifted to industrialists' greenwashing and governments' hollow promises and aspirational goals without any action. But he didn't have time to spar with these new adversaries.

His courses ate up many hours. His experiments with Marc were more time-consuming and puzzling. Work with Clive Grainger swallowed more time and effort but raised fewer questions. Michael was another problem. Tony and Beth, like most new parents, were swamped by one tiny baby's incessant demands.

He'd launched his ClimateChange&U.ca website with features borrowed from the US site. It was attracting interest and presented an opportunity to engage the public in his battle to engage industrialists and governments. He had ideas for features that should bring in even more participants but no time to pursue them. And to make matters worse, John Springer kept hijacking his few free moments.

Eight months after Springer's strange, threatening phone call, Tony no longer believed it was a pigheaded dig at his success. Springer was known for that kind of crap during his undergraduate years, but they ended three years earlier. *How can I explain a continuation of such childish stunts?*

Springer was a follower, not a leader. Someone must have put him up to the call. Who was the puppet master pulling his strings, and what was his agenda? Tony found nothing on Springer's life after he moved to Calgary in the summer of 2020 to work in the oil patch. The guy had become a wraith, invisible on social media or technical publications associated with the oil industry.

The absence of a social media profile was suspicious. And it made finding the person or organization using Springer impossible. Tony abandoned Facebook, Twitter, and other social media searches and returned to questions related to his research project. *If I had something new to report, would that draw Springer into the open.*

On the afternoon of June eighth, Beth's lilting alto voice wafted through the doorway as Tony trudged up the stairs to their second-floor flat. The silly lyrics and unfamiliar melody improved his spirits.

Beth shifted Michael to her other breast as Tony stepped into their apartment. "Something's wrong. Proverbial bad day in the office?"

Tony hesitated, surprised he'd telegraphed his frustrations. "Lab work has left me with a meddlesome problem."

"We haven't discussed your work for ages, and I'm like missing my oceanography lessons."

Tony sighed, relieved Beth assumed his concern reflected science problems. Until very recently, her fears he would abandon their little family generated most household tension. Laboratory problems were trivial by comparison.

He spent several minutes explaining his difficulty understanding how nature could supply the nutrients needed to support enhanced growth. He concluded, "without a viable mechanism, my embryonic research project's in trouble."

Beth ignored his final remark as she settled the now contented baby in her lap. "We should discuss these subjects more often. They'd keep me from focusing on dirty diapers. But why did you arrive home carrying the weight of the world on your shoulders?"

"Frustrated by the slow pace of academic research."

She settled the sleepy baby in a cradle before joining Tony on the sofa. "Slow compared to the work in Dr. Grainger's lab?"

"Yeah. Problems of academic versus pragmatic science keep coming up, but I'm more worried about the government's attitude." He didn't mention Springer and the aggressive opposition from many industrialists. This was not the time to worry Beth about those concerns.

"That's like your ClimateChange&U website. You'll never get away from the conflict between academic and pragmatic research or individual response to climate change and governmental inaction."

"You've been checking the site," he said as he strode into the kitchen and opened the fridge. Preparing dinner was his job, and it was time he got on with it. *But Beth's reaction to the website's important, something I mustn't ignore.*

She hoisted Michael's cradle and followed. Beth lowered it onto the kitchen table, where she gently rocked him while continuing their conversation. "I need something to occupy my mind. Your website's a good starting place. But I'm like feeling left out. Why haven't you told me about it? I mean, you started the Canadian site last fall, that's nine months ago."

"Not much to discuss, and it wasn't live until midwinter. I'm, you know, following the American protocols and collating the carbon usage data anyone submits."

"But it's growing, isn't it? You're getting lots of data?"

He gestured with the paring knife he was using to peel and dice vegetables. "Growing nicely."

"You know I'm interested in environmental problems. I may lack the technical knowledge, but surely, I could help.

Tony hesitated, surprised because she was already busy with her career and baby minding. But hell, if she had the time, it presented a golden opportunity to push forward his new focus on pigheaded governments and industries. "You suggesting we work on this together?"

"I see synergies, but I'd need to understand the science."

"We could marry scientific reality with implications for society," he replied before searching the fridge for leftover chicken.

She leaned over and kissed him as he emerged with his sought-after plate. "Good. You already appear happier. And I can turn you into an activist."

"And I can improve your understanding of the underlying science."

"Deal," they said in unison as they high-fived one another. Michael joined in with a wail and a massive burp.

Six weeks later, Beth returned from the Smugglers Cove studio in tears.

She collapsed on the sofa. "The show's cancelled. Mr. Brock pulled the plug. It's done, finished. We have five episodes in the can, but they're dust. I'll be lucky to recover any salary."

"Can't they sell it to another network?"

"I'm sure they've tried."

He gathered her into his arms. This could be a huge crisis for their fragile relationship, and he was unsure how to approach it. "What about your other projects?"

"One appearance in another Drug Squad episode. And I no longer have an in with Justin Kilburn, my link to the local fashion photography business. I'll never work with him again!"

"What happened? A problem with the pregnant woman book?"

"That project's fine, and Justin's good at producing them."

"The impresario of naked women pictures, eh," Tony said, telegraphing his dislike for the photographer he considered little more than a pornographer.

She pushed away from his embrace. "You don't like him, but his reputation as a fashion photographer is solid, and his art books are successful."

He snorted. Would this discussion generate new revelations about why she'd been subconsciously unhappy when he first met her? "What went wrong?"

"Nothing. My pregnant mum photos are an interesting thread running through a photo essay about love-making, pregnancy, and birth. Problem was his attempts to involve me in his next project."

"His next project?"

"One day, when you and Marc were real busy."

"What happened?"

"He asked me if I wanted in his new project. I like agreed without asking questions."

Tony stared as he struggled to find the correct words. He'd never met Justin Kilburn, and until tonight, Beth always said good things about him. Now, his gut reaction appeared vindicated. But how did these revelations mesh with her failed relationship with Jeremy? "And..."

"Photos to illustrate a book his friend's writing about BDSM."

"What! Bondage and sadomasochism?"

"I backed out, and he got upset."

"Models must pass on projects."

"They got all belligerent. I feared his assistant would take out her anger with whips and stuff."

Tony jumped from the sofa. "You mean you'd started working on this?"

"They were showing me what they wanted. Anyway, after some histrionics, they let me go. They were real scary."

"This is intolerable!"

"Calm down. It's okay." She reached up and tugged on his arm. "It like happened months ago, and it's dealt with."

"Why didn't you tell me?" he asked as he resumed his seat.

"Yeah, right, and have you storm out with vengeance on your mind. My problem, and I solved it without getting you and Michael upset. I shouldn't have mentioned it, but with the Smugglers Cove cancellation, it slipped out."

Tony pushed damp strands of blond hair from her face and pulled her close. Despite living together for months and cooperating on raising her child, their careers were pushing them along separate paths. He understood her desire to deal with her problems, but she'd been overwhelmed.

"What now?" he whispered as he envisaged a light at the end of the tunnel.

"My prospects are lousy, but me turning into a stay-at-home mum with no income wasn't in our plans."

"Don't worry. I'm earning enough to keep us going. We'll be a team working together."

"Like being married?"

Tony sighed. Marriage seemed like an outdated idea, but they needed to solidify their commitment to each other. "Closer, more honest with each other. An opportunity to develop your role on ClimateChange&U. It will keep you from obsessing about your work situation and help make a better tomorrow for Michael. And for us, an enduring life together."

As summer rolled by without improvement in Beth's prospects, Tony's turned to ideas for enhancing her role on ClimateChange&U. They needed interviews with sympathetic public figures and other human content to complement the scientific reports, technical advice, graphs, and statistics that dominated the site.

Beth had contacts in the Halifax arts community and exuded confidence in front of a camera. With her sense of drama and growing understanding of environmental material, she could become a more dynamic interviewer than Becky Smith, the woman who interviewed Tony sixteen months earlier. And Beth would bring sex appeal to the site.

Beth was less than enthusiastic when Tony presented his plan.

"I'm no journalist. I wouldn't know where to start."

"You've twisted interview questions until you were posing your own. Take it one step further, and you're the interviewer."

She shook her head and stared into space. "It can't be that easy."

"Interview someone you're comfortable with," Tony said. "Anyone, even a low-profile person who's pro-environment. Discuss what they're doing to fight climate change."

Beth looked up, smiling. "I have the perfect person. I'll need a camera operator and a set. Your problem?"

Details, details, we'll sort them out. I needed buy-in, and I have it.

Beth's transition to website interviewer wasn't entirely smooth sailing. One chilly November evening, as fall turned into winter, she was sitting on the sofa with her laptop open when Tony entered their apartment. He threw his jacket on a chair and leaned down to help Michael with wooden blocks he was stacking into a tower.

Beth poked her computer screen with her index finger. "I can't deal with this guy's nasty, vindictive attacks. He threatens us using statements like 'the wrath of God will descend upon you'."

Tony peered at her screen with his hand on the sofa arm. "Who? Does he sign his name?"

"The Reverend Terrance Goddard."

"Oh, him."

She glanced up, wide-eyed. "You know him?"

"Ages ago, he had a run-in with Dr. K. He's irrelevant, a crazy windbag from a fringe church with fifteen congregants."

"I'm like sure it's more than fifteen," she said as she slammed the laptop shut. "Because it's local, I can't ignore it."

"Don't imagine he represents all Christians. His band of misfits isn't recognized by other churches."

"But they claim to represent the perspective of real Christians."

"Hogwash," Tony said as he knelt beside Michael and helped with the unstable tower. "Thousands of our contributors are churchgoers. Jacinta's devoted to her church and has conservative views, but she's a dedicated environmentalist. And what about Rosie?"

"How should we handle him?"

Tony shrugged before abandoning the tower-making efforts. "I'll look at his comments and point out the scientific fallacies in his arguments. Same for other deniers, refute their arguments on a case-by-case basis."

"And the ostriches who refuse to consider the problem? They're an even bigger problem."

Tony hadn't lumped noisy climate change deniers like Reverend Goddard in with those who lacked the will to join the fight to reverse global warming. "We provide scientific evidence for climate change in simple terms anyone can understand. What else can we do?"

"You've presented the logical scientific stuff, but we need social and political arguments to reach the fence-sitters, the people who aren't swayed by your scientific arguments. And Goddard scares me. Something he does is gonna bite us."

Tony shook his head as Michael demanded more help with his latest creation.

Beth laughed, looking down at Michael's monstrosity before completing her thought. "We gotta fight like dogs to save the environment. If we don't, the world Michael faces when he's our age will be the sort of hell I wouldn't inflict on anyone."

"Not even Reverend Goddard?"

"Not even Reverend Goddard."

Chapter Twelve

Thursday, December 7, 2023

On a chilly December day, Tony and Marc learned they passed the comprehensive knowledge exams that were a prerequisite for the submission of PhD project proposals. That afternoon, Tim Wilkes dragged them to the Muse for celebratory beers.

He raised his glass after filling three from their standard pitcher. "To the successful candidates whose project proposals are undoubtedly ready for submission."

Tony set down his glass, wondering if Tim, like Steve Matthews, was planning to raise objections to his embryonic proposal. "Ready to go. Builds on productivity measurements that expand Rosie's work and the efforts I made subsequently. I need better measurements for settling because my initial ones don't work. Big problems are predation, decomposition rates in sediments, and availability of nutrients."

"You've known predation was an issue since Jacinta left Rosie in charge of the experiment with the salp infestation," Tim said.

"What about Rosie?" Marc interjected. "Anyone heard from her?"

"E-mails," Tony replied. "Married, living on their farm, and doing education at Acadia."

"And your solution to the predation problem?" Tim asked.

"I can generate extrapolations based on the present-day ocean, but no way to confirm them."

Tim turned to Marc. "Where do you stand?"

"Less advanced because I don't have many relevant results. But it's on track and may even help answer Tony's predation question, and we'll find common ground on the nutrient question."

Tim topped up their glasses. "Good luck, guys. Here's to your ongoing collaboration." He took a large swig. "Once I finish this glass, I'm back to my thesis writing. The rest is yours."

During the following weeks, Tony drew flowcharts for his proposed model of phytoplankton growth and sequestering. Tim provided ongoing commentary. One of his favourite themes was the predation problem Rosie encountered when Tony and Jacinta were in Cuba.

Marc strolled in as Tony completed the last of the changes generated by Tim's comment. "Looks like you've lost interest in sediment decomposition rates."

"My current thinking is predation is the critical problem."

Marc scowled. "Why?"

"It's the critical process for getting material to the sediments. What happens in the sediments can be a separate investigation."

"They're linked."

Tony pointed to the whiteboard. "That's why I've developed two flow charts with arrows joining them." He stopped and drew a large circle around the left-hand side of his diagram. "I'll focus here in the water and move to the sediments later." Tony looked around, noticing Marc's furrowed brow. "Something wrong?"

"Yeah, man. You're missing what's happening in the aquarium annex. Natural blooms that I grow out at low pH are too persistent."

Marc's comment reminded Tony of their observations in Cuba and the longevity of Jacinta's low pH blooms. The unusual longevity of the blooms was a persistent feature, something he shouldn't ignore. "Something that affects my models?"

"Predation will speed up transport of material to the sediments. But the only way to explain the persistence is a feedback mechanism that returns nutrients to the water column."

Tony picked up an ugly puce-coloured marker. He stared for a few moments with his nose wrinkled before using it to triple the size of the arrow for chemical transport from the sediments to the water column. He wrote 'nutrients, see Marc' beside it using the ugly colour before he turned to Marc. "What's the deal?"

Marc smiled. "We need to re-establish the synergies we discussed before developing our proposals. You may not realize it, but you need my results for the release of nutrients from the sediments beneath my blooms. And I need help controlling the chemistry in the damn sediments."

During those early winter months, Jacinta Lopez had been a wraith spending hours holed up in her office or the library. In February, she submitted her three-hundred-page dissertation and returned to Spain for six weeks. In late March, she was back in Halifax for her thesis defence.

Her oral got off to a rocky start when a curmudgeonly professor proclaimed to his neighbour, "I hope she won't badger us with a sermon about God. We shouldn't tolerate such claptrap."

Jacinta bit her lip, and Dr. Krueger jumped to her defence. "If you will keep such churlish thoughts to yourself, you'll see that Ms. Lopez is here to defend her work using scientific arguments."

Jacinta gave Dr. K a wan smile as the chairman quickly brought the meeting to order. "Committee members and then members of the audience," he said while staring at the professor, "will have opportunities to ask questions once Ms. Lopez completes her dissertation."

She highlighted the discovery of the unexpected structural form of Nitzschia in the experiment she conducted in the Aquatron tank in May 2022. Discussion of her observations filled the crucial chapters. She invoked a recurrence of an ancient genetic response to explain the structural change. It was a contentious choice, but Jacinta provided well-developed arguments. The examining committee found no serious fault with her presentation.

After her successful defence, her uncle hosted a reception at the Spanish consulate. It included Jacinta's student colleagues, her professors, and numerous people from Halifax society. Tony and many fellow graduate students clustered in one corner, but Beth and several outgoing students mingled with the distinguished guests.

When people were leaving, Jacinta cornered Tony. "I wanted to thank you for the help you provided me over the past three years." She stopped and turned to Beth. "He treated me like a professional. The other students behaved too informally."

Tony held up a final glass of bubbly. *Funny how our testy relationship whenever religion was mentioned could seem benign in retrospect.* "Least I could do, treating a visitor how she wanted."

"I must also thank you for your patience when we discussed religion. Dr. Krueger insisted I avoid religious comments in my thesis. I would appreciate one last chance to discuss the boundary between science and religion before I leave. Perhaps we could dine together."

"Come to dinner at our apartment," Beth suggested.

*****

Two days later, Beth greeted Jacinta at their building's front door. She was reminded, as she had been whenever she saw the composed and elegant young woman, of her irrational fears early in her relationship with Tony. In those early days, she'd been convinced Tony would favour first Jacinta, then Rosie when he learned about her pregnancy. "Come in, please. Let me help you with your parcels."

"Thank you. I have flowers and a little present for your baby."

"Our apartment's upstairs. If we leave Tony alone too long, he'll start experimenting with dinner."

Beth described the apartment's features as they climbed the stairs and stepped into the kitchen.

"Hello, Jacinta," Tony said, turning from the stove. "Small, isn't it?"

"Not different from young couples' homes in Spain."

"May I fetch you a glass of wine?"

Jacinta paused after a sip from the glass Tony offered her. "I like that; it is like a favourite from home. Is it Canadian?"

"Nova Scotian. Our wineries can make good wines, but the less expensive ones are a crapshoot."

"It is no different in Europe; we have many mediocre wines." She reached into one of her bags. "Here are two nice Spanish ones, one red and one white, from my uncle's cellar. He insisted I bring them for you. Keep them for another occasion, and tonight we can enjoy your selections." She stopped and looked around. "When do I see the baby?"

"He's sleeping," Beth replied. "But he'll wake up soon enough."

They drank wine and sampled Beth's crab cakes until Michael woke. Later, Bernadette took Michael for a stroll. Jacinta, Beth, and Tony enjoyed their roast lamb with mint sauce and roasted potatoes—Beth's favourite meal—without interruption.

After dinner, Jacinta raised the subject of religion in science.

"I wrote and defended my thesis without describing how God inspired me. Dr. Krueger insisted on this, and it makes everyone in Canada more comfortable."

"The source of your inspiration doesn't concern me," Tony replied. "It's your reluctance to champion conservation and mitigation."

"But I do not avoid conservation. God, through His teachings, instructs us to be frugal."

Beth scowled. Jacinta's description didn't jibe with the opinions expressed by critics on ClimateChange&U. "I thought the churches claim carbon dioxide won't cause harm. Christians can enjoy their lives without worrying about the future."

"That's the doctrine of evangelicals like Reverend Goddard," Tony suggested.

"It is not our view," Jacinta responded. "We should apply church doctrine to the modern situation like many enlightened priests are doing. When we do that, we conclude excessive use of fossil fuels causes hardship. With faith and dedication, we will discover the correct path before we generate a catastrophe."

Tony reached for the wine bottle. He held it up for Jacinta and Beth, but they declined. He filled his glass and left it handy. "Your church leaders should promote conservation measures. That's what I'm advocating. Serious attention to conservation by individuals, industries, and governments while we determine the best ways to mitigate the harm global warming causes."

"Conservation is entrenched in Europe. You must sell your conservation mantra here in North America."

Beth sighed. The pig-headed attitude of American politicians who insisted climate change was not a problem poisoned the discourse. Canadian government actions weren't much better. "Europe's ahead of North America on energy conservation, but you and your European colleagues could stress its importance. Communication is global, and we'll hear your message in North America."

"I will add my voice to those advocating conservation," Jacinta replied. "We have reached the point I always reach with Tony. We agree on the goal, and often the mechanism, but not the motivation."

"On that, we'll never agree," Tony interjected.

Jacinta smiled before turning to Beth. "Thank you for a wonderful evening. I hope you will visit us in Sevilla whenever you convince Tony to vacation in Europe."

Tony stood and took Jacinta's hand as she rose from the sofa. "Should I order a taxi?"

She shook her head. "There is no need. Sergio will be waiting."

*****

On Wednesday, March twenty-ninth, Steve Matthews stood alone, staring as rain from an early spring storm pounded on the coffee-room windows.

"Something wrong?" Tony asked when Steve failed to respond to his greeting.

Steve turned and approached a table. "How goes the epic battle with the acid ocean? Heard from Jacinta?"

"Not yet. She doesn't start work until May, so perhaps she's on vacation."

"But the paper you're writing together is on track?"

Tony hesitated after pouring his coffee and dumping a loonie in the tin. Steve clearly had something on his mind. Something that made him far more subdued than his usual argumentative self. "Jacinta's paper, with Rosie and me as supporting crew. It's been submitted."

"Which leads to your project based on enhanced sequestering of carbon in a low pH environment?"

"I haven't submitted my proposal," Tony said as he placed his coffee mug on Steve's table and pulled back a chair. "I've passed the ideas by Dr. K. He's onside, and so is Dr. Wharton."

"You'll be investigating a scenario that might explain how plankton production generated fossil fuel deposits in the Cretaceous?"

"Cretaceous and much earlier periods when many coal fields formed. Atmospheric CO_2 was higher than current levels in those periods, so oceanic pH was lower. But why are you winding me up?"

"Don't get snippy. I'm interested in what my colleagues will do after I leave."

Tony sipped his coffee and grimaced before placing his mug on the table and tearing open another sugar packet. He stirred it in and took another sip. "You planning to submit your thesis?"

"I've suspended my studies. Going home to help my mother rescue the family business."

"You're kidding! Can't they hire management specialists if your family members can't cope?"

"My brothers aren't incompetent. They're marketing-oriented. They need someone to handle engineering and production."

"And *you'll* do that?"

"Yeah, Mr. Tony Atherton, Master of engineering. I studied engineering before I arrived here."

Tony paused, thinking Steve was the antithesis of a typical engineering student. "No idea you were an engineer. But my question stands. Can't you hire engineers?"

Steve shrugged his shoulders. "The family firm needs me, and I must do my part. I can't expect my mother to do it all."

"What happened to your father?"

"Don't go there."

"Sorry, shouldn't have pried. When will you leave?"

"Soon as I complete the course I'm taking. If we get the company functioning, I may return."

By May, when the less hectic summer term began, Steve had joined Jacinta amongst the newly departed graduate students. Tim would soon join the exodus from Dr. Krueger's climate change research group. Tony and Marc would have a hard time filling the void.

Chapter Thirteen

Wednesday, May 8, 2024

During one of Tony's routine visits to Clive Grainger's DalTech lab, Yusuf Mohammed pointed to a graph while describing his most recent results. "Eighty-two times as much biomass as the baseline number Mr. Lavoie provided for ambient seawater."

Tony paused while he deciphered Yusuf's numbers. Eighty times a baseline value seemed like a phenomenal growth rate. "In a static aquarium?"

"All experiments are static. Seawater with standard inoculate of phytoplankton, adjusted to 7.5, and varying amounts of high nutrient discharge from a sewage lagoon."

"A more dynamic system should increase your production rate. In this set-up, you must see rapid growth and a levelling off as plankton limit light penetration."

"That is correct," Yusuf replied as he shuffled through his stack of graphs. "Growth starts slowly, shoots up, and levels off."

"And the design we discussed last time for a flow-through system?" Tony asked.

Clive led them to another room. "Show him."

Yusuf spread his arms to encompass a maze of tubing connecting two large glass tanks to a continuous centrifuge. Tony stepped up to the first tank. "Plankton culture already adjusted to pH 7.5 and treated sewage in the second one?"

Yusuf nodded. Tony moved on to peristaltic pumps that regulated the flow from the tanks to glass tubes underneath ultraviolet lamps. He raised his eyebrows when he noticed the solenoid attached to the valve that diverted the flow to the centrifuge.

Yusuf explained. "We divert the flow when light penetration drops to a predetermined level and separate the biomass using the centrifuge. In an operational plant, we'd send it to the digester."

"Another development since you were last here," Clive said as they walked from the laboratory to Clive's office. "Dr. Pedro Gomez from a university in Havana, Cuba, called. He suggested you fill me in on an interesting application he may have."

"Pedro Gomez," Tony replied as Clive messed with his espresso machine. "I can guess what interests him."

"He said you'd understand. A bay with inputs of acid and nutrients. It has enhanced phytoplankton production."

"Sixteen months ago, we spent a week there making measurements. Interesting for us because it allowed us to study a bay with low pH. What's your interest?"

Clive passed Tony a small cup with the thick brew his machine generated. "He wants us to join forces in a full-scale plant that skims off excess production and converts it to methane."

Tony stared at the cup, took one sip, and placed it on the corner of Clive's desk. He drank lots of coffee but hadn't developed a taste for espresso. "Hang on. That inlet had high biomass compared to natural environments, but nothing like Yusuf's experiments."

"The plant won't rely on the successful completion of Yusuf's work. A different application using ambient water with enhanced production. It processes much larger volumes than any plant we'd build."

Tony's brow furrowed as he considered potential objections. "They'll push large volumes of ambient water through concentrators and return the water to the bay?"

Clive nodded. "They'll direct the concentrated biomass to a digester as per our concept."

"They'll generate minimal reductions in acidity. Wouldn't stopping the discharge of acid waste be better?"

"That's Cuban politics. No political will to clean up the acid, but they'll go for this plant. They'll improve water quality and generate methane. It will power their plant with the excess sold to other industrial users like the bay's sugar refinery."

Tony paused, staring at his tiny coffee cup while gathering his thoughts. "So, you plan to go ahead?"

"I plan to continue my discussion with Dr. Gomez unless you tell me their science is flawed. If they're successful, it will enhance our chances for commercializing our project."

"Give me copies of his proposal and any supporting documents. I'll get back to you."

Tony returned to his lab, impressed by the progress Yusuf made in a few months. And Clive's eagerness to crash ahead with a full-scale commercial application at such an early stage was hard to believe. Another illustration of the clash between the almost glacial speed of academic research and Clive's get-on-with-it-before-they-knew-what-they're-doing attitude.

After reading the Cuban material, Tony realized the negotiations between Clive and Pedro's company were more advanced than Clive implied. Tony found no technical flaws but wondered why the project was being considered.

Well-connected Cubans, Maria Consuela's family amongst them, backed the project. Were they following the path of evolving eastern European countries like Russia and Ukraine, with oligarchs taking advantage of economic chaos to carve out industrial empires? Were they misusing World Bank and UN agency funds for curing environmental problems in third-world countries? This project would cure nothing. It would reduce some negative effects without tackling the underlying problem.

Tony's worries about Clive's disregard for basic environmental stewardship grew as he dug into the new Cuban project. Clive's eyes narrowed when Tony expressed his reservations.

He was standing in his book-strewn office, fussing over his espresso machine. It was a standard ritual for Clive. As soon as Tony entered his office, he strode to his machine. "They can reduce biomass in the bay and sell the methane they produce. If they neutralize the water they return to the bay, they'll have a win-win situation."

"Their proposal rejects neutralizing the water as too expensive. Truth is, it would reduce the biomass they're harvesting."

Clive passed Tony a small cup with the thick coffee. "What's your point?"

Tony sipped the bitter brew and set his cup aside. "They claim environmental improvement is a prime motivation, but improvements will be minimal. They should divert organic waste from the sugar refinery and acid from the scrubbers to a plant like we're developing. That would remove pollutant inputs, and the bay would recover."

"No political will for the scenario you describe, and our technology isn't ready for export."

"And no easy money to extract from the World Bank."

Clive shook his head. "Your cynicism is bad for business. Everyone needs government support to get projects like these off the ground. That applies here in Canada, but it's even more critical in smaller countries."

"I suggest well-connected backers of this project are after the World Bank money. The project is secondary, and I doubt they have any concern for the environment."

"You're being unreasonable. Money's tight. Everyone must grab the opportunities they uncover. Unless we think the project's harmful, we keep quiet."

Tony finished his coffee and returned the demitasse cup to its saucer. "Won't do much good, but it shouldn't do additional harm."

"Then keep quiet. Little return for us, but examples of closely related applications will be useful in our efforts to secure venture capital."

Not the greatest, Tony thought as Clive droned on. *I'm posting articles about corporate greenwashing on ClimateChange&U. I want to lure John Springer into the open, but I'm also worried about corporate honesty. Is Algal Energy sinking into those murky waters?*

As summer rolled into fall, Tony incorporated his data into global ocean climate models. He spent hours in the library, expanding the biological understanding he'd gleaned from his courses. He often tested his ideas by bouncing them off Marc Lavoie and Tim Wilkes in the Muse.

One afternoon, Tim looked up as Tony approached their table with several large rolled-up printouts. "Hey, how goes it with our new world, Ptolemy."

"Why Ptolemy? Because I have maps rolled up like ancient scrolls?"

Tim laughed as he unrolled one. "Ptolemy was the world's first map maker, and that's what you've turned into, our cartographer extraordinaire."

Marc, always the purist, objected. "Ptolemy wasn't the first cartographer. He was a mapmaking pioneer who wrote a treatise on the subject."

"Whatever," Tim replied. "What do you have?"

Tony chugged some beer and set the glass aside. "The best estimates I can find for global distributions of my fifty species."

"These give you overestimates of the real distributions because your data merging routine causes too much spreading in directions perpendicular to major currents," Marc said as he rolled out several additional maps.

Tim picked up on Marc's observation, pointing to areas like the Sargasso Sea, where Tony's concentrations were unreasonably high. He suggested a way to solve the problem that displayed an in-depth knowledge of Tony's modelling approach.

"Thanks, guys," Tony said. "I can do that. It's computer manipulation, no need for additional digging in musty old textbooks."

After Tim returned to his never-ending thesis writing, Marc displayed Tony's remaining charts using empty glasses and various other objects to hold them flat. He took a pencil and drew shapes on the charts, nodding as he admired his artwork. "This will work. If we ignore the places where your extrapolations spread into barren waters, you can see the pattern."

Tony rearranged the charts to show the flow of high concentrations of various species from tropical to subarctic waters. They gave a distorted picture of the oceans because the maps weren't all drawn to the same scale. The distinct patterns that emerged reminded him of the geometric shapes in cubist drawings. "You're right. It looks good."

Marc nodded. "It won't be easy to parameterize this given the spatial and temporal variability in primary production, but I can see the picture you're developing." He looked up, smiling. "Should we call you the new guru of global plankton distributions?"

"Give me a break! First, Tim says I'm a modern-day Ptolemy, and now you suggest I'm a plankton distribution expert. I need advice on the best way to estimate productivity in a low pH environment, not stupid accolades."

Marc sat back, savouring his beer as he scanned Tony's array of charts. "Sorry, didn't mean to sound facetious. They're interesting and... useful. You can use them, along with satellite data, to approximate the biomass of your various species in the present world. Then use your factors for biomass enhancement at low pH to scale things up."

"That's too easy. No one will accept it."

"I disagree, start simple and add complexity as necessary."

During the following weeks, Tony revised his pictures of global distributions and growth rates for his fifty prolific plankton species. By summer, he had solid pictures of present and future abundance using calculations he could defend. He applied his estimates of settling rates to determine the removal of carbon to the sediments. He then attributed discrepancies between predicted and observed distributions in the present-day ocean to predation and calculated factors for removal by predation. The final step was the application of these factors to his future ocean distributions. *Voilà*, he'd achieved his primary objective, an estimate of sedimentation in a low pH ocean.

His laboratory work was only one aspect of two successful years as a PhD student. His unconventional personal relationship with Beth Manville was, perhaps, even more successful. They continued to lead rather separate lives, and the baby born months after they began living together wasn't his. But they'd developed a strong bond, held together in part by the expanding role she'd assumed on ClimateChange&U.

ClimateChange&U was the second part of his *raison d'être*. It embodied his commitment to convincing the public to take a more proactive approach to addressing climate change. Beth's efforts to engage fence-sitters with her celebrity interviews were wildly successful. She was getting flack from climate change deniers on the Christian right, but they could live with that. His articles on corporate stonewalling were attracting negative attention from the oil industry. So far, they hadn't brought John Springer or his handlers from their caves. Perhaps his presentation at the fall meeting of the American Geophysical Union in San Francisco would do that. He was playing with fire but couldn't resist the challenge.

79

His AGU paper would be the first time he presented his results to international experts. Would they accept them? Or would the holes they shot in his arguments return him to square one? *Could that, or another problem lurking on the horizon, destroy the comfortable life he and Beth were developing together?*

Chapter Fourteen

Thursday, December 12, 2024

Tony was in an upbeat mood as he prepared for an interview on the penultimate morning of the American Geophysical Union meeting. His paper had been well-received, and he'd heard many positive comments about ClimateChange&U.

As he strolled from his hotel past Union Square to San Francisco's Moscone Center, he noticed jewellers and upscale clothing boutiques decked out for Christmas. *Should go shopping somewhere more offbeat. May find the perfect gift for Beth.*

Tony joined delegates scurrying through the convention centre's main lobby. He scanned the area to get his bearings and joined the stream heading past the media centre. When he saw the sign indicating interview rooms, he separated from the crowd.

The interviewer, Ms. Samantha Loveridge, introduced herself, thanked Tony for agreeing to participate, and turned on the video recorder. She so completely epitomized his image of a young California blonde vying for a job as a television news anchor that he was momentarily distracted. He shook his head, dislodging the inappropriate stereotyping, and focused on her words.

For several minutes, she asked questions that allowed Tony to describe his work. Then she switched gears.

"I'll leave the details of the science aside and mention the implications of your hypothesis for society."

Tony hesitated. He'd hoped to describe interesting opportunities for field biologists to investigate natural low pH marine environments, work that may help him in the ongoing development of his models. "I can't talk about the effects on society. I can only identify potential environmental impacts if our observations are correct."

"Describe that world."

Tony held up his right index finger. "We'll see an ocean that doesn't support organisms with calcium carbonate skeletons. No coral reefs and large changes in the planktonic organisms dominating community structures." He paused for a breath. "Losing coral reefs will change the physical habitat for organisms that hide within the corals. We can't predict the impacts of such ecological changes."

"Scientists have already discussed these problems."

He nodded before adding his middle finger. "We've observed another major ecological change that favours certain phytoplankton and produces masses of organic matter with a different chemical composition. We don't know the ramifications of this change any better than we do the disappearance of calcium carbonate skeletons. My calculations suggest it will dampen or even reverse the trend to lower pH."

"You're suggesting at least one positive effect and others you can't predict."

Tony shook his head before dropping his hand in his lap. He didn't want to appear badgering. "Calling it positive is misleading. It should reverse the pH trend and lower carbon dioxide levels, but we can't sit back and wait for nature to solve the global warming problem. Before this mechanism kicks in, habitat destruction will be extensive, millions of species will go extinct, God knows what else."

She smiled. "Sounds like you're heading toward societal responses."

"Society, not scientists, must decide how we respond. Our job is to describe the scientific basis for the environmental changes we anticipate. Before natural reversal of current pH and CO_2 trends occurs, we'll see sea-level rise, higher water and air temperatures, more extreme weather, and many ecological changes."

"Your scientific understanding will guide society..."

Tony returned her smile. He understood where she was heading. "My ideas on how society should respond are no more important than yours or the next guy's."

Ms. Loveridge's smile gained a distinctly mischievous edge. "Okay, with that caveat, what should we be doing?"

Tony took a deep breath and launched into the need for individuals to reduce their use of fossil fuels. He suggested the nebulous long-term nature of the problem would limit government action unless individuals led the way.

Ms. Loveridge shuffled her papers, and Tony noticed she now had a screenshot from the ClimateChange&U website on top. "Are you suggesting we should be like modern-day Thoreaus foregoing our pleasures and leading minimal lives?"

Tony rolled his eyes. She'd latched onto a common misconception. "If we commit to the small things, we can reduce our carbon dioxide emissions by twenty or thirty percent without adversely affecting our lifestyles. We should expect lifestyle changes, but not enormous ones, and some would be improvements. And it can lead to positive action by governments and private industry. Climate change is not an insurmountable problem, but it needs long-term commitments."

"Anything else in your formula for society?"

"Research is crucial to guide us as we move forward."

"Your early training was in engineering. What about large-scale engineering solutions?"

This was an interesting development he hadn't anticipated. "Medium rather than large scale engineering solutions are feasible. They should contribute to the solution, but we must tread carefully."

"We're running out of time, and there's one other topic I want to mention. One of your colleagues said God has a plan to save us from climate change. What's your reaction?"

Tony recoiled, he hoped not too visibly. Samantha's drastic change in direction when little time remained was not fair. His only option was to defend Jacinta's integrity while leaving his views unstated. "Dr. Jacinta Lopez Martinez conducted the experiments my research builds on. She's a devout Catholic and finds inspiration and guidance from her beliefs, but she never claimed she was following a plan God laid out for her. It doesn't matter if we attribute the changes to simple physical, chemical, and biological forces, or God's will. We must help nature deal with the stress we're putting on her by pumping so much carbon dioxide into the atmosphere."

"We should leave it there. Thank you, Mr. Atherton."

General circulation models describing the ocean/atmosphere system using the basic laws of physics and chemistry were the topic for the final climate change session. The talks resurrected a problem worrying Tony for some time. The pH related effects he'd been modelling wouldn't occur for seven or eight decades. Would another overwhelming impact of climate change disrupt the oceans on a shorter time scale?

Several talks described a warmer ocean choking off deep water formation and changing the dynamics of large ocean currents like the Gulf Stream. This would produce a more stagnant ocean with less latitudinal heat transfer. Could he integrate the effect of pH he'd been modelling with these impacts? And if he did, what impact would it have on the calculations he'd been making? Or conversely, what impact may his observations have on the global circulation modellers' calculations. He considered these questions as he listened to the day's final talks.

Friday morning, Tony discovered his phone was off when he returned to his room after breakfast. He stopped in the hallway, turned it on, and read his messages. The first, a text from Dr. Krueger, said <don't talk to Reverend Goddard>.The second was a call from Beth asking him to phone ASAP.

She picked up on the first ring. "So glad you called. That bastard Goddard's press release caused chaos."

Tony glanced over his shoulder, worried about someone overhearing his conversation. "Not concerned about that jerk. I can defend my position against anything he says."

"It's not your science; it's what he's said about us. He's calling you a Satanist and me a whore."

"Nothing new," Tony interjected, wondering what was really bothering her.

"Justin insisted he deleted the photos from when he tried to talk me into that BDSM project, but Goddard has them."

Tony hesitated as Beth drew her breath in little gasps. "That is new. I'll get home, and we'll sort it out."

"Those photos will ruin us," she wailed, her efforts to avoid crying abandoned.

"Please, calm down. I'll call the airline and arrange something. What did he actually say?"

"He said anyone who interferes with God's plan is a Satanist. Vicious things about our lifestyle. That you're living in sin with a loose woman."

Tony snorted as he engaged his room key. "That garbage will screw him, you'll see."

"It's those damn photos. They give his story credibility. And he wants to destroy our website."

"Fuck that. I'll get home, and we'll figure it out. Until then, relax. And don't talk to anyone."

Thoughts of little shops in Chinatown and fancy San Francisco jewellery stores were forgotten as Tony struggled to discover the quickest way home.

Michael squirmed from Beth's arms when they greeted Tony in the baggage claim area at eleven Saturday morning.

Beth released her grip on the wriggly tyke when Tony grabbed him. "Guess he missed you. The overnight flight wasn't too awful."

"Seemed like a minimal sacrifice. Okay, now? Yesterday's problem resolved?"

"Murky as hell. We can discuss it on the bus."

On the bus, Michael stood in Tony's lap with his little fists latched onto the window frame. The traffic, and forests and lakes they were driving through, would entertain him.

"Many hits on the items I posted on the UN Climate Change conference," Beth announced, "and some interesting comments."

Tony was proud of Beth's efforts to expand the scope of ClimateChange&U. He generally encouraged her, but right now, they had more pressing issues. "Does this lead us to Goddard?"

"Indirectly. Broader scope means broader readership. We're attracting a different sort of criticism from climate change deniers. Goddard is an extreme example."

Negative comments from deniers were an inevitable consequence of Beth's success. They'd discussed the problem *ad nauseam*.

Tony leaned over to comfort Beth, causing Michael to squeal. When he had Michael resettled, Tony tried to link Beth's unhappiness with Goddard's comments. "Saw Goddard's comment on your editorial. Nothing to worry about, and, in a screwy way, it indicates your success raising important issues."

"I thought you might be too busy."

"Always check for reaction to your postings."

"I wouldn't have overreacted to Goddard's stupid comment if Dr. Krueger hadn't contacted me."

"What's his problem?"

"He and his lawyer want to challenge Goddard."

Tony held up his hand. He needed a moment to consider this twist in the narrative. "The lawyer's Kurt someone or other?"

"Kurt Bayer, like the aspirin manufacturer."

"He's a high-profile civil liberties lawyer. They'll be after Goddard for something unrelated to his climate change rants."

"They asked for our communications with Goddard. I said you'd get back to them. And Goddard calling me a whore and you and Dr. Krueger, Satanists, was real threatening."

Tony shook his head while trying to find a positive spin. "Focus on the reaction to your articles on the climate change conference. You're on a roll."

"But Tony," Beth said as Michael crawled into her arms. "We can't ignore these critics."

"I disagree, but we can discuss that later. What about those photos?"

She growled playfully as she enveloped Michael in a bear hug, but quickly turned her attention back to Tony. "This morning, Justin told a reporter he had a commission to produce the illustrations and hired models to play the various roles. He insisted the photos were simulations done with professional models."

"Not quite true, is it? Doesn't explain your photos."

"He slid over the fact mine aren't in the book. But the reporter described it as an acceptable project for a photographer and his models. It looks brighter this morning."

"Still happy I rushed home. I'd have been a basket case as I wandered around San Francisco waiting for my flight."

In their apartment, Michael scurried about showing Tony the pictures he'd drawn and his latest Duplo monstrosity. Beth sat at the table after Michael returned to his toys on the living room floor. She slumped forward with her chin in her hands and watched Tony munch the grilled ham and cheese sandwich. "Everything was good until my call messed up your week?"

He used a Kleenex to dab tears escaping from her eyes. "AGU talks are hard because they're so short. Ten minutes to tell your story, and if you run over, the session chairman cuts you off."

"Did you get arguments from the audience?"

"Positive reaction, and my talk was before a break, so the discussion could continue." He smiled, thinking about one listener who made a really good suggestion about streamlining one aspect of his model. "Everything was pretty good."

"And the interview? Honour, wasn't it, to be chosen?"

He sighed. "Yeah, I suppose, and the interview went fine. They're posted on the conference website, but how many people watch them? They can't have much impact."

After a Sunday afternoon strategy meeting with Dr. Krueger and Mr. Bayer, Tony paused in the park where they often brought Michael. Several aspects of the meeting bothered him. He gestured toward a bench and sat before Beth could object to an unnecessary delay.

She remained standing, but Tony wasn't dissuaded. "Can you believe all the lawyerly bafflegab Mr. Bayer used? Did he have to use words like notwithstanding and hithertofore?"

"I don't think he ever said hithertofore. Is that even a word?" she said as she sat next to him. "Anyway, he was describing material he'll present to his lawyerly colleagues."

He turned and grabbed her hands. "Probably true, and my mind may still be fogged after my overnight flight, but, you know, none of this makes sense."

"No?"

"Crackpot minister spouts garbage about two insignificant people, and suddenly a high-powered lawyer is looking after our interests at zero cost."

"Goddard also attacked Dr. Krueger, and Mr. Bayer's Dr. Krueger's lawyer. Perhaps they like see defending you and me as the best way to defend Dr. K."

Tony slouched forward on the bench. "Why does Dr. K have a high-profile lawyer with a reputation for representing plaintiffs in social action cases?"

Chapter Fifteen

Tuesday, December 17, 2024

At 10 a.m., Kurt Bayer led Dr. K, Tony, and Beth into the Halifax courthouse lobby. The crowded scene with reporters and cameramen jostling for space surprised Tony. *Is Goddard more notorious and newsworthy than I realized?*

The crowd settled rather quickly, and Kurt launched into his pitch. "We've called this meeting to set the record straight by challenging the false statements Mr. Terrance Goddard made against my clients. First, I will respond to the allegations about Dr. Krueger and Mr. Atherton's scientific endeavours. Then we will address the libellous accusations he's made against Ms. Manville. This will include a signed affidavit by Mr. Justin Kilburn, a professional photographer who offers a credible explanation for photographs central to Terrance Goddard's libellous contentions. After these statements, we'll answer questions."

He paused, posing for the cameras before challenging the accuracy of Goddard's accusations against Dr. K and Tony. Nothing in that attack was particularly newsworthy.

"Next," Kurt said as he gestured towards Beth. "Mr. Goddard called Ms. Manville a whore because she's an actress—another archaic and completely inappropriate use of words. Mr. Goddard must retract his statement and apologize to Ms. Manville or risk legal action. Ms. Manville is a successful professional model and actress. She's starred in three television series filmed in Nova Scotia."

Tony watched Beth as Kurt described Goddard's vile words, wondering how she would react to the public presentation. She stared stone-faced as Kurt continued.

"The same goes for photographs of Beth when she was pregnant with her son. They're legitimate art photos produced by a professional photographic artist for a beautiful book on pregnancy and childbirth."

Dr. K began distributing single sheets of paper to the reporters after Mr. Bayer nodded in his direction. "As Heinrich distributes copies of Mr. Kilburn's affidavit, I'll address the most contentious of Terrance Goddard's libellous statements before we entertain questions."

As Kurt presented his version of the story behind the BDSM photos, protestors from Goddard's church pushed into the phalanx of reporters. They distributed handouts with their side of the story while making *sotto voce* comments about Beth's transgressions.

Before Kurt opened the floor to questions, the protestors commandeered a space where they unfurled a banner in plain view of the cameras. Bayer ignored them as he pointed to a reporter, asking him to state his name before posing his question.

"Thank you. John Carter, *Chronicle Herald.* My question is for you, Mr. Bayer. Why did you hold this impromptu press conference rather than going to court?"

"To clear the air and present our side of the story. We also wanted to give Mr. Goddard an opportunity to retract his allegations and offer apologies."

"Do you think he will?" Carter persisted.

"That's up to him, but after hearing our rendition of the facts and reading Mr. Kilburn's affidavit, Mr. Goddard should realize his position is untenable."

"And why do you persist in calling him mister, not reverend?"

"Because he's not a minister. He has no qualifications from a recognized theological school."

Mr. Bayer pointed at another reporter.

"Michelle Harvey, Daily News. Ms. Manville, what is your reaction to the photos Reverend Goddard produced?"

Beth stepped forward. "The pregnant mother and mother and child photos are beautiful. Mr. Kilburn's book is a wonderful chronicle of pregnancy. The job paid reasonably well, and he made a beautiful book."

Another reported jumped up. "Cheryl Cudmore, CTV News. Ms. Manville, are you going to let Mr. Goddard call you a whore without taking legal action?"

Tony saw the tension developing in Beth's shoulders and tried to step forward to comfort her, but Dr. K placed his hand on Tony's arm. "She'll be fine."

Tony watched as Beth took several deep breaths. "Goddard being a stupid Elizabethan prig and calling me a whore because I'm an actress is pretty minor. I'd be happy if he apologized, and someone like you explained it to the public. The bondage and beating photos are another matter. More considerations and more people involved. We must set the record straight concerning those photos."

Michelle Harvey waved her hand. "That's right, Ms. Manville. You answered my questions about the baby photos, but not your reaction to the others. And we've discovered that your photos are not in the BDSM book."

"I'm unhappy with those. I'm like working with Mr. Kilburn on the baby project, and he asked me if I was interested in his new one. He didn't hide the fact there would be some pain, and I agreed to a test." Beth paused as she fought back tears. "The pain was too much for me, so I declined his offer. I thought they'd destroyed their test video."

Hoots of derision from the protestors greeted this last assertion. One protestor strode forward and thrust a sheaf of photos of women in bondage at Beth. Others passed copies to anyone who would take them.

"Those aren't me," Beth screamed as Reverend Goddard appeared from nowhere, sporting what appeared to be an assault rifle. He rushed forward, unleashing a volley. Beth stared open-mouthed as her favourite dress erupted in red.

"Paintballs," Tony yelled as he threw off Dr. K's restraining hand and forced his way into the line of fire. He felt several impacts before security personnel took down Goddard. When Tony looked around from his protective stance, he noticed the smug smile on Kurt Bayer's face.

Within minutes, the courthouse teemed with cops. They carted Terrence Goddard away, herded his disciples into one meeting room, and Tony and Beth into another. As Tony helped his traumatized partner into their refuge, he glanced across the lobby at the main doors.

Bayer was already outside, holding court with the gaggle of reporters. Tony considered Kurt's smug expression when Goddard opened fire and wondered what he might now be saying.

But Tony had more important problems. Beth was disoriented and in pain. The paintball markers launched from several metres caused considerable damage.

A policewoman helped Beth into a chair. "An ambulance is coming. It will take you to the hospital, where they will assess your injuries and provide treatment. And you, sir," she said, turning to Tony. "Do you also need medical attention?"

"I took a few hits," Tony replied as he turned his back. "They aren't too bad."

"At least three separate impacts. We'll need your jacket to make an accurate assessment, but the thicker cloth probably protected you from injury."

Beth tried to stand but slumped back into the chair. "They're like real painful."

Tony turned to face the constable with his body rigid, and his chin thrust forward. "The paintball marker looks like an assault rifle, and they can inflict serious damage. How did he get past courthouse security carrying a bloody weapon?"

The next morning, Tony sat in their living room staring at the Christmas tree and other holiday decorations Beth erected while he was in San Francisco. They owed

Michael the best possible Christmas, but Tony couldn't put the previous day's events behind him.

Mr. Bayer had demolished the accusations made by Terrance Goddard's band of misfits. And Goddard shot himself in the foot with his paintball stunt. But Beth had paid a price, and he couldn't dispel the idea something important remained unanswered.

A few minutes later, Beth followed Michael into the living room and gingerly lowered herself to the floor. They began working on a Duplo tower.

"Mummy," Michael exclaimed when his creation collapsed. "Not helping."

Tony slurped the last of his coffee and crawled onto the floor to take over as Michael's engineering assistant. He gazed at Beth after he resurrected Michael's tower. "You okay?"

Beth leaned against the sofa. "Me? Covered with bruises and confused by Justin's affidavit. What could be wrong?"

"What doesn't make sense?" Tony asked, trying to ignore her sarcastic tone.

She dabbed at moist eyes with a Kleenex. "I assumed he leaked the photos to Goddard. But his hastily prepared statement made him sound confused and puzzled. If he'd orchestrated it, wouldn't he have a better explanation ready?"

"You suggesting someone stole the photos?"

"Why would a burglar steal them?" she asked.

"What if Goddard sent him?"

"Goddard wouldn't know they existed." Beth paused, drumming her fingers on the floor. "The culprit must be Morgan, Justin's assistant."

"Why?"

"I never trusted Morgan. It's not because she's tight with my onetime lover. There's something mean and devious about her."

Tony shook his head. He didn't want to sink deeper into a love triangle quagmire. "Should we suspend construction of Michael's extravaganza and make breakfast?"

"Hey, Michael. Daddy's right. It's time for breakfast. Should we have pancakes?"

"Pancakes," Michael exclaimed before looking at Tony. "Daddy, make pancakes?"

The doorbell rang after Michael and Beth returned to his Duplo extravaganza. A few minutes later, Tony followed Dr. Krueger into the apartment.

"I was returning from another discussion with Kurt and decided to deliver my news in person."

"And you should stay for coffee," Beth suggested.

"If it's not too much trouble."

Tony refilled their coffee maker as Dr. Krueger joined Michael's town-building efforts. When Tony brought out a tray with three coffees and juice for Michael, Dr. K withdrew from the construction site.

"The police have charged Goddard with assault, and he's being held while they pursue additional charges."

Tony pushed a car he found in the Duplo bucket to Michael before turning to Dr. K. "He has a history of supporting various right-wing causes, disappearing when it gets too hot, and rising phoenix-like from the ashes. He could do it again."

Dr. K shook his head. "Goddard's been charged with a serious crime, not a misdemeanour. And other charges are pending. Kurt insists he won't make this disappear. We'll be done with him, once and forever."

Beth brought a plate of biscuits from the kitchen. "Do we know about these additional charges?"

"He's been a vocal opponent of progressive views on social issues like abortion, family planning, and same-sex marriages," Dr. K said after pausing to admire a complicated creation Michael insisted on showing him. "He's also supported right-wing groups that claim the right to defend their property. His followers are no better than *Burgerwehr*, vigilantes."

Tony offered a biscuit to Michael and took another for himself. "I can believe that after seeing the way they behaved yesterday. Those paintball-game sites seem like thinly disguised places for training illegal militias. What happens next?"

Dr. K shifted as he repaired Michael's latest creation. "We leave the assault to the police, but we must decide if we should pursue further action on character defamation."

"I just want it to go away," Beth replied.

"You shouldn't face more personal attacks like the ones Goddard made last week, but he and others will continue to attack our science."

Tony put his arm around Beth's shoulders. "Shouldn't worry us. Climate-change-denying crackpots will always exist."

Dr. K struggled to his feet. "It won't shut them up, but sensible people will realize how misguided they are." He headed to the door after nodding at Beth. "Thank you for the coffee. Give our little battle with the forces of intolerance a week to settle, and in the New Year, you'll find it's ancient history."

Beth returned to the early morning discussion as Tony prepared their evening meal. "I figured out what was bothering me about Justin's affidavit."

"Let's hear it?"

She hesitated as Michael stumbled over, demanding she picks him up. Tony kicked over his step-stool, and Beth stood him on the top step. "Morgan hovered in the background whenever Justin was shooting. She fetched things and helped arrange lighting. Always there, but usually invisible."

"The artistic genius's trusty assistant, helpful but not interfering."

She nodded, but her pained expression told Tony she was unhappy. "That damn BDSM stuff was different. He looked toward Morgan for guidance, or maybe even approval. He was following her orders."

Tony placed his paring knife on the counter well away from Michael's reach and transferred his cutting board's contents to the wok. "Could it be something you've imagined to explain Kilburn's recent behaviour?" he asked as the veggies sizzled.

"It's real," Beth replied while shaking her head. "And it helps me put everything behind me with no niggling doubts."

Tony added extra oil and stirred frantically for a few seconds to keep dinner from sticking. "That's important. I had a similar reaction to my doubts about Kurt Bayer's interest in our problem. Once I realized what sort of shit disturber Goddard was, I understood Kurt's perspective. It wasn't about defending our interests, and climate change was a minor issue."

Beth nodded before lifting Michael into his high chair. "And the press conference? Was it a theatrical production Kurt staged with me cast as a siren luring Goddard to his doom?"

Interlude

Summer, 2049

I arrived at Michael and Vanessa's house above Pemberton Meadows for the second time in thirty hours at 7 p.m. on May twenty-ninth. I'd been on the road for sixteen hours but only travelled 150 kilometres. That meant I'd averaged less than ten kilometres per hour. My ponderous pace had a silver lining. Our modern, super-efficient electric vehicle had high-efficiency photoelectric cells embedded in its roof. They generated enough power to drive at that speed during bright sunshine without depleting its batteries.

At Pemberton, the convoy continued northeast toward Lillooet and the highway to northern BC. I alone turned off and headed northwest into the Pemberton Valley. When I reached Michael's, I had a bite to eat and fell asleep on their porch. I remained dead to the world until Alice woke me on Sunday morning.

During the following weeks, the skies became hazier, and the smoky smell more pervasive. I helped clear combustible material from an extensive firebreak west of the town. The residents of nearby Mount Currie made similar efforts across valleys to the south and east. I suspected these valiant efforts were futile.

As spring turned to summer, we expanded the firebreaks separating Pemberton and Mount Currie from the encroaching fires. By August, we had impressive areas scraped clear of anything combustible. Our efforts were successful. We limited the damage behind the firebreaks to a few fires. These were contained before they harmed either town. September brought heavy rains to our part of British Columbia, and the fires retreated. Knowledgeable firefighters rejoiced, convinced we'd won the battle.

I had no role in the summer's other major effort. Experienced mountaineers explored escape routes from the upper Pemberton Valley to the coast. Warmer weather and retreating glaciers made it possible, but I couldn't imagine escaping the flames through the mountains.

A route for trade and communications, however, would be in everyone's interests. I applauded an effort that demanded skills far more specialized than mine.

In October, they abandoned trail-building in the mountains. They'd mapped a route to the head of the Toba Inlet and made plans for cutting a serviceable trail after the winter snows melted.

At the mouth of the Toba River, our trailblazers encountered a group of refugees. They'd arrived in a ragtag armada from points south and constructed a serviceable anchorage and several log cabins. They planned to overwinter there and establish a permanent settlement in an enclave that had been spared by the initial wave of forest fires.

During my early days in Pemberton Meadows, I set up my shortwave radio. I began broadcasting messages to anyone who could receive them and listening for messages coming my way. I had no trouble pulling in Bill Robertson on Haida Gwaii, but not my contact at our monitoring site at Tofino. It was much closer, but I heard nary a peep from them.

I heard from Ham radio operators in Alaska and across Canada's north. I received sporadic messages from Iceland and various locations in northern Europe. No messages arrived from North Americans living south of Pemberton.

By the 2040s, shortwave radio was an almost forgotten technology. It was only used by survivalists and old-fashioned nostalgia buffs. Most thought modern devices ended shortwave radio's usefulness. The complete absence of anything but very local radio signals on other bands proved them wrong.

Many modern technologies depended on centralized infrastructure support. They would go silent if that support was disrupted. Others should have been more durable. The silence was an eerie reminder of how alone we were.

I couldn't fathom the absence of shortwave messages from anyone south of about 55°N. Less than two percent of the world's population lived north of fifty-five degrees. Why didn't I hear from the other ninety-eight percent? Was the destruction far worse than I imagined? Had electromagnetic pulses destroyed all electronics? Had fires like the ones spreading northward from Seattle ravaged most of North America? How many survived from the continent's most populated areas?

We had few data to draw on. Refugees escaping Seattle said huge explosions wracked the city. Were they caused by terrorists targeting fuel depots or power stations? Or did they plant bombs in strategic locations? If so, they must have been huge. Could they be the newest generation of portable nuclear bombs terrorists were rumoured to possess?

Fires that started in and around Seattle were very persistent. Some said they persisted by feeding off each other. Others suggested terrorists started new fires that spread the conflagrations.

No one mentioned climate change. The technological fix that kept global warming in check for fifteen years failed in the 2040s. Rapidly increasing temperatures caused tinder-dry conditions and more frequent thunderstorms. An obvious factor everyone ignored. They believed the climate change problem had been solved. It was a bill of goods, but too many believed it.

The fires and Beth's fate trapped somewhere in eastern Canada dominated our thoughts, but Bill Robertson's monitoring data yielded another important observation. Despite the often-hazy conditions, temperatures during that first month spiked to the highest springtime levels ever seen on Haida Gwaii. Bill's controlled measurements were confirmed by our less rigorous ones in the Pemberton Valley. It was much hotter than normal.

The haziness meant solar radiation must be down. Did the extra heat come from burning the forests and fuel in depots and power stations? Otherwise, we needed an external source like heat produced by bombs designed to produce more heat than blast. To understand these observations, I needed to revisit results from my thirty years of research.

Decades earlier, I found the 2024 AGU meeting demoralizing. My study of the effects of low pH on marine productivity was well-received. It generated a positive response from several experts. But it had a flaw. Low pH wouldn't have an impact on climate change for seventy or eighty years. Other aspects of global warming would cause the turmoil we feared long before acidification became the overriding problem. I knew acidification was important, but my enthusiasm waned as other issues hogged the limelight. I toiled in the trenches determining how each new revelation would affect acidification. My absence from the cutting edge describing the next critical issue was demoralizing.

Beth experienced no sophomore slump. Once she put the Goddard fiasco in the Halifax courthouse behind her, she charged from one success to another. In the process, she helped me overcome the lethargy I experienced after completing my thesis. We shifted our focus from my preoccupation with ocean acidification. Our broader perspective included other climate change issues, the fight to convince society to address the problems, and her growing political ambitions.

I collaborated with Marc Lavoie, Achara Zhu, and a little later, Olivia Grange. They were biologists. Marc's focus was nutrient supply for low pH phytoplankton blooms. Achara was more field-oriented. She studied high productivity blooms in the present-day ocean. Olivia focused on predation by zooplankton, minute animals that fed on phytoplankton.

I was an engineer turned oceanographer with an interest in mathematical models. Together, we made a formidable team. As we dug deeper into the problem, we learned that ocean acidification was the one climate change problem that wouldn't go away. When others realized this, we'd be back in the limelight. In the meantime, we trudged ahead, laying the groundwork for our big comeback.

By the summer of 2027, when we reach the end of the second part of my saga, public reaction to climate change was hardening. Confrontations were becoming more frequent. A major upheaval in the world's approach to climate change management was imminent. It would unleash the forces that destroyed civilization.

Part Two

Cruisin' to a Crisis

Chapter Sixteen

Saturday, February 1, 2025

Michael's second birthday party rocked. At least, Tony presumed it rocked as much as a party for six toddlers could rock in a small apartment. He'd been banished to his university office while Beth and Bernadette orchestrated everything. He returned at four thirty to help clean up the mess.

Michael grabbed Tony's hand and dragged him into the living room. Michael's friends had departed, but he remained hyperactive. "Play!"

"Slow down, my little man. You can show me your new things, but we must tidy everything before dinnertime."

Tony slid to the floor as he surveyed the situation. The place appeared less chaotic than he expected. Beth joined him as he collected toys the party guests had strewn about. "Everything went okay?"

"Yeah, great. Bernie's a marvel with little kids. I entertained the mothers. One was Sandra, the pushy New Democratic Party activist, but Gwen kept her in line."

"Gwen Mulholland, the mother of Michael's cute little girlfriend?"

Beth laughed as she tossed pieces onto Tony's growing mountain of Duplos. "Emma's mother. She's like contributing data to ClimateChange&U."

"Why so?"

"She's so knowledgeable she must be a contributor."

Tony dumped a handful of Duplo bricks in their tub. The reference to their website was surprising, and the implication it was becoming a larger factor in Beth's consciousness, encouraging. "Funny topic for a kid's birthday party."

"Sandra started harping on politics and environmental policies. Gwen mentioned the website to shut her up."

After carting armfuls of toys to shelves in Michael's bedroom, Beth watched Tony from Michael's doorway. "The discussion reminded me of our pre-Christmas trip home from the airport. Should ClimateChange&U use the next federal election to start a campaign pushing for real action?"

"Can we, you know, avoid picking sides?" Tony asked as Michael climbed onto his back.

"We'd need a non-partisan approach, stating the facts, and insisting it's time for meaningful action regardless of which party wins."

He rolled over, holding the now squealing tyke above him at arms-length while considering ways to keep this conversation going. "How will you convince them?"

"Reiterate ClimateChange&U's standard mantra. Global warming is real, sea level will rise, and extreme weather events will become more violent and frequent." She tipped her head to one side, gazing at Tony with a furrowed brow. "Then we'll say individuals, various industries, and many lower levels of government are making improvements. We'll finish with the need for national government action."

"We've always said that."

"In dry scientific language. We need to be more aggressive using words everyone understands. I'll take a stronger stance, and you'll back me up with the facts."

Tony held up his hand as Michael scampered off to find something in his room. That afternoon, he'd learned something important. "Small glitch that could affect your plans."

"What?"

"The US government shut down ClimateChange&U.com."

"Can they do that? Isn't free speech protected by their constitution?"

"In theory."

"Their government can't arbitrarily shut something down. They must have reasons."

Tony rolled his eyes. For years, American presidents had been playing fast and loose with the rules, and Congress wasn't much better. "They listed bullshit reasons that fit their nativist thinking. They accused ClimateChange&U and a bunch of other websites of subverting suburban family-oriented attainment of the American dream."

In the evening, Michael finally fell asleep after Tony read him three stories and Beth two more. She closed his door and plopped onto the living room sofa beside Tony. "You'd think any kid as wound up as he was today would've fallen asleep over his dinner."

Tony laughed as he rose and headed for the kitchen. "Maybe he'll sleep in tomorrow morning."

"Fat chance, but what does the American government action mean for us?"

He turned away from loading the dishwasher. "In the short term, very little. Our government's fighting with the Americans over so many issues. We won't follow their lead on this one. I say we move ahead as planned."

"You accept my new approach?"

He abandoned the dishwasher and plugged in the kettle. Tea had become part of their routine from the days of Beth's pregnancy. Making it would give him a few moments to consider his response.

He carried the teapot, cups, and a plate of cookies leftover from the party into the living room. "The disconnect between a public keen to address the issue and governments incapable of action has been obvious for years—"

"Not all the public."

"All our public. The people who participate in our website are onside. If you broaden our attack, you'll be taking on climate change deniers and other public critics."

"We can't win with the deniers," Beth said as she reached out to swirl the tea. "We must target the fence-sitters, people who should agree with us but can't overcome their inertia."

Tony sat back with the tea Beth poured. People sympathetic to their cause but unable or unwilling to join the fight were becoming central characters in Beth's approach to ClimateChange&U. Tony agreed the uncommitted were a demographic they must attract but worried a blunder at this stage may chase them away. "Tackle your issues separately. What's the big issue for your anti-government campaign?"

"Governments. When you dig into provincial government initiatives, they're often as bad as the feds. We're over halfway from the Paris Accord signing to the target date for reductions Canada and other countries agreed to." She paused as she stirred milk into her tea. "We've hardly dented the problem. Provincial and federal governments insist we'll reach our goals, but no one, not even their bureaucrats, thinks it's possible."

"What's the major stumbling block?"

"The oil and gas industry and the efforts by the feds and the western provinces to boost production and export of fossil fuels."

Tony reached for his backpack and rummaged for a paper he passed to Beth. "Massive government subsidies for expanded production of heavy oil are central to their push."

She scanned the paper before handing it back. "We should focus on that?"

"Important, but we need more issues. Write an editorial on the subject, and it wouldn't hurt to feel out your interviewees, see if they'll say something provocative. But keep your focus broad."

"And the reluctant public?"

"Figure out why they don't buy in."

"Fear," she said as she grabbed a cookie. "Fear of living without something important, fear of losing their jobs."

He nodded, feeling himself drawn in by Beth's enthusiasm. She was onto something important, but they must avoid overexuberance and exaggerated claims. "Jobs are key. They link the public skeptics and the government ditherers. Everyone's worried about impacts on employment. You can weave it into your climate change tapestry."

"Sounds like you're laying out a major campaign, more than providing a climate change focus for the next election. What's your role?"

Rabble rouser and devil's advocate. He needed to keep her engaged without letting her say anything indefensible. He must also avoid making his meddling obvious. "I'll continue to manage the technical side of the website and compile and assess input we get from citizens—"

"And provide scientific rigour for my stuff."

He smiled. Keeping his ulterior motives hidden may not be too hard. "That too, but I'll focused on getting my thesis written and finding a postdoc. Much easier than convincing governments and millions of citizens to do something they're uncomfortable with."

*****

Ten days later, Beth's efforts to bring the climate change battle to the federal government were in full swing. Other aspects of her life, especially plans for a second child, were progressing nicely. Tony's rapid acceptance of the idea when she raised it suggested he'd harboured similar goals. It was now a done deal with the baby due in August.

She'd allowed enough time for the idea of a political campaign to germinate. Gwen suggested catchy graphics highlighting the time when the world passes the Paris Accord's two-degree warming threshold. Experts agreed this limit was creeping closer, not receding into the indefinite future as it should if humanity had the situation under control. If Tony developed a website feature publicizing the date when global temperature increases would pass the threshold, she could launch her campaign.

She tackled the problem that evening after Michael fell asleep. "We must show how bad a job everyone's doing."

"Bad in what sense?" Tony asked.

"We aren't making progress extending the date when global warming hits various thresholds."

"And you want to publicize this looming failure?"

She smiled. "Something that shows how the time until we reach these lines in the sand gets closer whenever we get an update on our so-called progress."

Tony's brow furrowed as he extracted graph paper from his backpack. He drew a vertical line near the left edge of his page. "Years until critical warming on the Y-axis and date on the X-axis going from 1900 to 2050 might be interesting."

"The inverse of the temperature or carbon dioxide trend," Beth suggested.

"Close, but the trend line would intersect the X-axis. It may not provide the catchy visual you're seeking. And I foresee a problem."

"What?"

"We've focused on Canada and what individuals can do to help our country meet its UN-mandated targets. You're talking about the global response, not just Canada's."

Beth stared at Tony's rough graph. She jotted a few notes in the margin before responding. "We need to invigorate efforts ClimateChange&U has made to push toward the reduced emission goals our government agreed to at various international meetings."

"That's our mission," Tony said. "Don't want to lose sight of it."

"But we can't forget we're one part of a worldwide effort."

Tony held up his hand, fingers spread, palm facing outward. "You're talking politics and social engineering rather than science. Are we qualified?"

"We must attract thinkers in these fields to our cause." Beth jumped up and began pacing the room. She paused by the coffee table, jabbing his plot with her finger. "But first, we need a strong image to catch people's attention."

"Our equivalent to the Atomic Scientists' doomsday clock from decades ago."

"Exactly."

Tony scratched away on another rough graph. "A comparison of projected temperatures based on government promises versus projections based on actual reductions in CO_2 emissions. That might make an interesting plot."

"Illustration not plot," she said as she checked his handiwork. "We must engage the non-scientists."

Tony sighed as he completed his graph. "I'll work on your scientific foundation, but you must proceed with care."

"Fine," she said as she struggled to contain her annoyance at his scientific caution. They had an important opportunity, and they must accept the inherent risks. "Generate a good way to illustrate our conundrum, and we'll incorporate it into our political campaign. I'll even test drive it with my interviewees."

Her first opportunity to broach her new approach came several days later when she interviewed Hunter Mayhem, a leader in the Toronto visual arts scene. He was a radical thinker, critical of recent federal governments.

"Frustrating," Hunter replied when Beth asked him about government policies. "The public sympathizes with your concerns, but governments focus on their short-term priorities."

"How do we get them to extend their focus from four years to twenty or thirty?"

"I can almost sympathize with the government," Hunter said after Beth described Tony's efforts to illustrate society's apparently inexorable march to climate catastrophe. "They have many short-term pressures and an obligation to keep our fiscal house in order."

"But we've proven the importance of a longer-term view of climate change, and millions of Canadians are making an effort."

"A few years ago, artists launched something similar centred on the country's semicentennial celebrations. It's been a struggle, but we're making progress."

This was interesting, but how could she spin it into a rallying cry for her listeners. "Advice for us?"

"My response, given my reputation as a radical socialist, will surprise you."

"Surprise me."

His eyes twinkled as he placed his hands on his chair arms and started to rise. Was he about to live up to his reputation for outlandish behaviour by intentionally misunderstanding her invitation?

"Careful," she said. "The camera's like running."

He laughed as he settled into his chair. "The government must keep its books in order. Ignoring this leads society into a black hole. But they have resources to deploy. The trick is ensuring they spend that money wisely."

"And how do we convince governments to spend money on long-term problems rather than short-term priorities and wasteful publicity stunts?"

"We need governments led by thoughtful people with a long view. We seem compelled to vote for charismatic individuals who do nothing."

Beth nodded. They were on a roll, and she needed to maintain the momentum. "Like Trudeau, but surely not Harper or O'Toole."

"Harper came across as more serious, but he wasn't committed to the environmentalist's long-term objectives. You need serious, environmentally conscious leaders with the courage to stick to their principles. The ideal government would embrace these worthwhile objectives while keeping the financial house in order. Not an easy task."

"The Green Party's not the answer?"

"Would they support culture?" Hunter asked. "Would they be fiscally responsible?"

"What's the answer?"

"Numbers. Politicians will only act when voters unite behind action on an issue. ClimateChange&U represents the right approach. Serious but measured consideration of an important issue with proof you reflect the views of large numbers of voters."

Beth sat back after Hunter Mayhem departed. His ideas may have done more to spur her ongoing efforts than to encourage her listeners to take more active roles. He'd provided no immediate steps they could take, but their conversation did give her several ideas. The looming election campaign would be an opportunity to test them.

Chapter Seventeen

Saturday, March 8, 2025

When Canada's latest minority government fell, Beth's ClimateChange&U election strategy was ready to roll.

Tony had exceeded her fondest hopes, creating an animated display depicting the time until the world reached two critical global warming thresholds. In one panel, a family fought sea level rise, extreme weather, and forest fire hazards in a two-degree warmer world. Two clocks anchored a moving banner that scrolled below the family pictures. It claimed the hypothetical family would manage if the warming threshold was never breached. The first clock provided the current best estimate of when the world would reach that point. The second showed their current speed as the hurtled toward the brink. Clickable links provided graphs of how the two parameters had changed over the previous decade.

Panel two depicted four-degree warming, the scientific consensus for change that would produce irreversible damage. The pictures showed a bleak future, and the banner gave no reason for optimism.

They posted the feature within an hour of the official election announcement. While waiting for public reaction, Beth drafted an editorial describing their nonpartisan advice.

China could reduce carbon emissions by government edicts and economic management policies they imposed upon people and industry. Canada, the US, and other free enterprise democracies couldn't pursue that option. A price on carbon was their best choice.

The more progressive parties might accept a cap-and-trade system that permits government regulation and influence on the free market economy. They could pick winners and losers, limit the overall emissions, and siphon off resources for their favourite green energy solutions.

This approach would be anathema to the free-market-loving Conservatives. But why wouldn't they adopt a carbon tax policy like the one enacted in British Columbia? It generated substantial carbon emissions savings, and in 2017, the federal government endorsed that approach. Carbon taxes would address a social necessity, but corporations wouldn't encounter additional regulations. And revenues from the carbon tax would provide fiscal room to lower other taxes. The secret was a tax that wasn't burdened with endless escape clauses—special exemptions and other provisions that blunted its impact.

"Will it like work?" Beth asked Tony the morning after they implemented his animations. They were sitting on a park bench watching Michael play in a giant sandbox.

He paused, scratching his chin before responding. "You have a starting point for your election campaign. It will take some tricky wordsmithing to make your points while maintaining political neutrality."

A puzzled expression clouded her countenance when she looked away from watching Michael's shenanigans. She failed to see where Tony was heading. "I planned a few large posts, but I could do a series a few days apart. Five weeks so two posts a week provides ten opportunities. But it's like the most complicated thing I've attempted. Can I do it?"

"You always ask that question," Tony said as he rose from their bench. "How many failures?"

"Some haven't worked out as well as I hoped, but no terrible failures."

"That's your answer. You can, you know, do it. But take it slow. Use the first post to pose the question and develop your arguments over the next few. You'll have opportunities as the election looms nearer to hammer away at your main points."

Beth kicked at the sand under the bench while Tony checked on Michael. *It can't be that easy.*

"Gwen," Beth said when Tony returned. "She has a master's degree in political science, and she like got me going on this. She'll understand what I'm trying to say and help me make it clear."

Tony smiled. "Our readers like your simple prose, and they'll understand what you're saying."

"But this is complicated. Gwen can help."

"Ask her, but write the articles in your style. And I'll provide postings on our countdowns to two and four degrees."

Tuesday afternoon, Beth was watching Michael from her favourite bench when Gwen arrived with her two small children. Emma scurried off to play with Michael. Gwen, with Jon in her arms, sat next to Beth.

"I liked your political post," she said as the baby twisted, reaching toward Beth. "Will you hold him for a sec?"

"I've always loved babies, and it never hurts to stay in practice."

"Hoping for another one?"

Beth smiled. "Working on it."

"Good luck. But I hope it doesn't take you away from your website. You're doing good work, a real improvement on the exaggerated comments we usually hear."

Beth's smile became a laugh. "Compliments always welcome. And my latest post builds on things you said during that birthday party conversation with Sandra. You can help me with my follow-ups."

"Really," Gwen said as she retrieved her baby. "I studied political science, but with marriage and babies, I haven't pursued it."

"Playing Lizbet on *Kiddie's Korner* and my acting career overtook my plans for an education."

"My sister's kids thought Lizbet was way cool. What else did you do?"

Beth gazed heavenward, remembering those heady days when she and Bernadette worked all day and partied all night. "Seems like so long ago. Some modelling and acting in a series that got cancelled. Since then, the local scene's been abysmal. Tony's website and Michael have become my focus."

Gwen placed a hand on Beth's arm. "But acting gave you an inside track for your celebrity interviews."

"I started interviewing local actors and musicians, people I understood. Then I got requests to interview environmentally conscious strangers in sports and other fields. A little web searching gets me the background info I need."

"Your latest project sounds more like editorials than interviews."

Beth looked up as Michael and Emma rushed from the sandbox to slides and other playground equipment. Gwen resettled paraphernalia associated with babies and small children on a sunnier bench near their children. Beth helped Emma climb a kiddies' slide while Michael waited impatiently at the bottom.

She turned toward Gwen as Michael scrambled up the ladder. "Editorials and I need help getting the political context right."

"What's worrying you?" Gwen called out.

"Start with the Conservatives. They're a known entity. Explain why, from your political science perspective, they won't put a price on carbon."

"You want their politician's perspective?"

Beth returned to the bench once the kids established an acceptable sliding protocol. "Exactly."

"The Conservatives have a minority government. Their job's simple. They must add twelve seats to form a majority."

"Okay, no surprises there. Where does it lead you?"

"They can develop a platform that solidifies their base and offers enough inducements to gain the twelve seats. Or, they can develop a more adventurous platform that retains their base while appealing to a broader spectrum of voters."

Beth stared into the distance, using her forefinger to draw an imaginary flowchart. "The first would be the cautious conservative approach they've signalled for their campaign. Low taxes, reduced debt, good economic management, growth based on resource industries. The second is the more adventurous approach I'm looking for."

"They've gained over the last few elections, and the other parties don't appear ready to wrest power from them. Targeting those twelve seats is their best bet."

Beth grimaced, struggling to get her head around Gwen's cynical view of politicians' motives. "Different situation for the opposition parties."

"Not that different. They must eat into the Conservative Party's base, a group that's against taxes and debt. Hard to sell a bold new policy that tackles climate change without increasing taxes or debt."

"But a carbon tax can be revenue neutral."

"The BC Liberals were first. They're really a conservative party. Conservatives might convince the electorate they're serious if they introduce a revenue-neutral carbon tax because they've established credibility on tax reduction, but not the other parties. If they promise to offset new taxes with tax reductions, no one believes them. The Liberals must live down the blatant cynicism of their carbon tax with offsetting rebates and the massive spending after the pandemic."

Beth frowned while shaking her head. Gwen seemed to be forgetting their subsidies to the oil industry and the money they lost buying a pipeline company. "Where does that leave me?"

"Exactly where you were before we started this conversation. Put forward your ideas, but don't expect any party to suggest anything similar."

That didn't sound very promising but probably reflected the grim realities of political life. "And you'll help me describe the situation?"

"Definitely," Gwen said as a scream from the kiddie slide distracted them. She rushed to console Emma. "Getting away from constantly worrying about kids will be fun."

The election campaign unfolded as Gwen predicted. Climate change seldom surfaced as a critical issue in battles fought over government debt and a few contested seats. On election night, the television's talking heads provided few real insights. The outcome remained unclear when Beth went to bed after midnight.

The next morning, Michael woke at the crack of dawn. After preparing Michael's breakfast, Beth sat back with a cup of tea. As she scanned the results on the online news channels, her head cleared.

Their efforts to influence the election results failed. The Conservatives won their coveted majority while offering nothing but platitudes on climate.

In a discussion the previous evening, one party insider in Beth's Halifax riding offered a different take on their climate change conundrum. "The PM heard your message and is receptive. Don't expect immediate action, but by the end of our mandate, you'll see something positive."

Were those words bromides designed to sideline ClimateChange&U? Or were insiders convinced the PM's position would shift? Beth sighed as she considered her strategy. Abandoning her quest was not an option, but her approach needed more thought.

It was too soon for frontal attacks on the national government. Better to return to celebrity interviews focused on personal commitments to the cause. From now on, she would seek her interviewees' views on actions, or lack thereof, from big government and big industry. And her editorials could keep the issue from falling off the table.

"You okay this morning?" Tony asked when he finally surfaced. He'd stayed up watching the election results until two thirty.

"Yeah, fine. We couldn't expect anything different."

"But I can't help wondering why environmental issues were so low priority. Those damn commentators had hours of empty time to fill, but, you know, they hardly mentioned climate change."

"I blame the Green Party. They focused more on defeating the Conservatives at any cost than pushing their agenda."

Tony laughed, thinking back to a previous Green Party leader who'd taken a similarly short-sighted approach. "Suggesting voters support Liberal or NDP candidates with a shot at defeating Conservatives cut their candidates off at the knees. It must have lowered the Greens' total vote count."

"And a bad omen for us."

He nodded as he poured his morning coffee. Beth may have converted to tea drinking, but he couldn't get a jumpstart on his day without his coffee. "Their popular vote dropped by three percent. That makes our job of pushing for climate change action more difficult."

"But we can't quit. We must keep trying!"

"Greens must rethink their approach to campaigning," Tony said as he smeared raspberry jam on his English muffin. "Must go. My thesis won't write itself."

"How's it going? I've been so preoccupied with the election, I haven't given it, or our future, much thought." She rubbed her belly in an unconscious action, then smiled at Tony.

"Good. Drafted most chapters, and I'm confident I won't need further lab work. I've also had a positive response from the climate modelling group at U Vic. A postdoc's available if we want it."

"But we do, don't we?"

"Looks like the best fit for me. I can integrate what I've done with a general circulation modelling group focused on climate change. And there should be opportunities for Algal Energy in Victoria. They still have pipes dumping raw sewage into the ocean."

It offered an opportunity to maintain the political pressure in a province with a stronger interest in environmental issues. And she mustn't forget the fence-sitters she'd been targeting before the distractions generated by the election. *If we're to succeed, they like must become key players in the unfolding drama.*

Chapter Eighteen

Tuesday, April 15, 2025

Tony munched his muffin as he walked to the university. They'd hardly mentioned their plans during the thirty-eight-day election campaign. Beth had been preoccupied with the election, but he'd found time for his studies. Progress toward his PhD and a postdoctoral appointment at the University of Victoria were evolving nicely.

Victoria was a beautiful city. Two years living in that west-coast mecca would be an adventure. And they'd still be in Canada, where Beth could use ClimateChange&U to beat governments and industries into submission. The demise of ClimateChange&U.com was a pain, but it hadn't caused them serious trouble. He had several research interests he could pursue, ones that may even unify his ideas. It was the right choice. They'd make it work.

Their conflict-free decision to have another baby showed they were a much more committed couple than it sometimes appeared. They'd lived together for two-plus years and were raising Michael together, but Beth always appeared defensive. He'd discovered the cause and worked to mute the effects of an abusive partner. But could they ever completely resolve the problem? *One never knows with relationships, but I'll keep working on it.*

Algal Energy Inc. was running smoothly. Their algae were an ideal source of organic matter for conversion to methane because they grew rapidly and digested easily. Yusuf Mohammed was making great strides investigating the conversion efficiency.

The company's Cuban clients had their World Bank money. They were proceeding with construction of a production plant. The Cuban operation contributed to Algal

Energy's bottom line, but it left Tony feeling uneasy. It used the natural environment, a large bay on Cuba's north coast, as an incubator to produce plankton in low pH waters. Would these well-connected Cubans expand their business by encouraging pollution of other bays with nutrients and acid?

ClimateChange&U's longer-term issues also weighed on Tony's mind. They had dedicated followers but weren't attracting new ones. An unwavering fraction of the public refused to accept the need for action on climate change. Governments remained incapable of action. University researchers refused to abandon their ivory tower detachment. The religious right continued to oppose proactive policies. They had many opponents, but they'd survive.

Tony whistled with a bounce in his steps as he climbed the stairs to their third-floor lab. They had many long-term issues to deal with, but his short-term prospects appeared rosy. The sight of a glowering Dr. Krueger waiting outside his office extinguished his happy mood.

"Something wrong?" Tony asked as he lowered his backpack onto a lab bench.

Dr. Krueger nodded, the furrows in his brow softening as he did so. "My office? It's not something we should discuss here."

Tony followed, relieved when he realized Dr. K's scowling was at least partly for effect. But what was his problem? After several years of tacit approval, had someone objected to his commitments to Algal Energy? Had something he and Beth published on ClimateChange&U generated waves? Or had the Goddard fiasco resurfaced? Most likely that bastard Goddard, Tony thought as Dr. K closed his office door behind him. He rotated his computer monitor so Tony could see the screen.

"I received this message from Pedro Gomez," Dr. Krueger said as he scrolled through his emails. "You remember him?"

"Yeah. Prof at Havana's polytechnical university. He organized our Cuban sampling trip."

"And my concern evolves from that trip."

"Is this about the methane plant Cuban industrialists are building?"

"Correct. Maria Consuelo's involved, and they have business ties with Algal Energy."

"Whatever happened to her?" Tony asked. He'd neither seen her nor thought about her proficiency in English since returning from Cuba.

"She transferred from Oceanography to the School of Environmental Management. She graduated last year with a master's degree."

"Makes sense. Her family's behind this plant. She can develop a useful role."

Dr. K nodded. "Her father and uncle are principals in the firm, but I'm worried about Algal Energy."

Tony rose and stared through Dr. K's office window before turning to face him. "Because I'm a junior partner in that company? I'm not involved in the Cuban operation. I raised objections, arguing they were abdicating responsibility for basic environmental stewardship."

"That's what Cuban environmental groups are saying. Pedro Gomez is trying to avoid having his university dragged into this fight."

Tony resumed his seat and read through Pedro's email. "What do you want from me?"

"What's your company's role in the Cuban development."

"None."

"But you're listed as a partner that received payments from the World Bank financing."

Tony fidgeted for a few seconds before responding. "We agreed to advise them on the enhancement of plankton production at low pH and signed a licensing agreement for the use of our incubator design."

"They're using technology you developed from research done here at Dalhousie?"

He shook his head before describing the Cuban operation. "They copied Clive's design but only use our incubators as holding tanks. They use none of our technology for enhanced phytoplankton production, nothing that builds on research in our lab."

Dr. Krueger said nothing as he drew a flow diagram on a sheet of newsprint. He looked up. "In the scheme you've described, the bay becomes the incubator for enhanced low pH production. The rest of the operation is standard technology for separation of solids and conversion of biomass to methane."

"Correct, and they return the low pH seawater to the bay. They skim off biomass—biomass elevated by organic matter and nutrients inputs from the sugar refinery and acid from other industrial discharges."

Dr. Krueger scrolled through additional emails. "That suggests Dalhousie's in the clear. Our research into enhanced plankton production is not a factor in any environmental degradation."

Tony stared into space while scratching his chin, reminded of Carlos, the environmentalist, and his efforts to track down the acid source. "It's perverse, isn't it?"

"Why so?" Dr. Krueger asked.

"Cuban oligarchs with close ties to the government are making money by exploiting the pollution caused by discharges to the bay. If they followed our advice, they'd neutralize water they returned to the bay. That would increase the ambient pH. But it could shut off the enhanced production, killing the goose that's laying their golden eggs."

Days later, Tony met with Clive Grainger and Yusuf Mohammed in Clive's office. After they dealt with their formal agenda, Yusuf returned to his laboratory. Tony described his meeting with Dr. Krueger.

"I'm also disappointed," Clive responded. "Our income would have been much greater if they used our technology. But I don't see what's worrying Dalhousie. You checked their proposal and concluded it wouldn't harm the environment. Are they questioning that conclusion?"

Tony shook his head, annoyed with everyone's disregard for proactive options. "My original assessment was sound. They won't harm the environment, but they aren't doing anything positive either."

"Aren't they removing excess organic matter and nutrients?"

"Only ones added by the discharges from the sugar refinery. They're doing nothing to solve the real problem—the addition of acid. They could reduce it by neutralizing their discharge water."

Clive rose and leaned forward with his hands on his desk. "For Christ's sake, Tony, be realistic. First, this isn't our problem unless they use our technology to make matters worse. And second, neutralizing the discharge isn't in the company's interest. The pH of water they return to the bay is higher than the inflow pH, so we cannot accuse them of adding to pollution levels."

Tony stared, wondering if Clive was hiding something important? "Where'd you get that information?"

"From their environmental impact reports."

"Why haven't I seen them?"

"Because they send me masses of information, all in Spanish. Since they aren't using our technology, none is relevant to Algal Energy. You have better uses for your time than struggling through reports in Spanish."

"If I'd seen the reports, I'd have been in a better position to answer Dr. Krueger's questions and present our company's perspective."

Clive raised his eyebrows and stared at the ceiling. "I'll dig them out," he said before a large sigh. "But we must focus on two things. First, selling our ideas to a company that will develop an industrial-scale plant based on our Eastern Passage pilot, and second, finding marketable ideas in Yusuf's work. Saving the Cuban environment is not our concern."

Tony walked away with three short reports on environmental conditions. They were written by Maria Consuelo. From them, he'd learn what Maria had been doing since she left Dalhousie. He shrugged and shifted to a more serious problem. Clive seemed unmoved by environmental problems in Cuba. Was he another cynical businessman who played the environment card when it suited him but ignored those concerns when it didn't? A bad sign that could have repercussions.

John Springer accosted Tony on the way to his office. His once-imposing undergraduate colleague had gained twenty kilos. He now looked more like the Pillsbury doughboy than the college babe magnet he once was.

Tony smiled. *Bloody sight less intimidating than the image I had six months ago when he phoned with his threatening message.*

"What do you want?" he asked.

"Cool it," Springer said before pointing at a nearby coffee shop. "In Halifax for a meeting. I've searched you out to offer some friendly advice. Back off from your anti-oil stance, or you'll regret it."

Tony placed his mug on the coffee shop table. "This isn't a game played by business tycoons looking for quick profits. Our civilization won't survive unless we freeze carbon emissions. We can't succeed without serious reductions in the burning of coal and oil."

"That's what you environmentalists say. You can't expect the Canadian oil industry to bear the brunt, cutting back while the US and other countries expand production."

Tony hesitated, sipping his coffee while he gathered his thoughts. "Fine. I can understand your perspective. But it's not a fight you have with me. It's a fight with the federal government to get them to demand more even-handed reductions by all countries."

"Bullshit! Your lot wants complete elimination of coal, oil, and gas burning."

"Study my bloody website! I support mining and burning of metallurgical coal. Likewise for oil and gas. We don't see elimination of oil and gas burning for decades. Canada has a role to play as a supplier of that energy." He paused for breath and an opportunity to gauge Springer's reaction. "We need new approaches, ones that eliminate coal for heating and electrical generation as soon as we can. We must reduce oil and gas burning when we have viable alternatives. And get those damned pipelines to the west coast built. If we can supply countries like China and India with oil and gas that gets them away from coal-burning, we're doing the world a favour."

"And what will you do for us?"

"Support your need for pipelines. Give you credit for concrete actions to eliminate thermal coal and use oil and gas more responsibly. Support your efforts to convince the feds to push for fairer environmental policies at the international level."

Springer tossed his empty paper coffee mug in a nearby trash can. "I'll see what I can do, but you better start giving our side a better shake." He stood and strode away.

Tony sat back, wondering if the discussion accomplished anything. He still didn't know who was pulling Springer's strings, and he ended with another veiled threat.

The biggest problem, energy-intensive exploitation of the Athabasca Tar Sands, was never mentioned.

Global warming would play havoc with ocean circulation patterns. Ocean acidification would generate massive phytoplankton blooms and, eventually, global cooling. These fates were a dead certainty if people didn't reduce carbon emissions. Would Canadian hydrocarbon producers and the federal and provincial governments take serious action? *Not bloody likely.*

Chapter Nineteen

Saturday, May 17, 2025

Tony and Beth took Michael to Crystal Crescent Beach on the first day of the Victoria Day weekend. The unseasonably hot weather reminded Tony of the mid-summer day almost three years earlier when he realized destiny brought them together. He'd just learned she was pregnant with another man's child, but he refused to abandon her. Now, she was carrying his child, and they had rambunctious and hyper-independent two-year-old Michael to contend with.

He'd seen many changes during those three years. He'd started as a carefree university student who saw his involvement in high-profile climate change research as an adventure, an opportunity to experience his fifteen minutes of fame. The thesis he was now writing described work on an important environmental issue. The crisis it predicted, however, wasn't sufficiently imminent to attract the attention he thought it deserved. His work had become something he railed against earlier in his career. An academic study interesting for its biological and evolutionary insights, not its immediate impact on society.

They laid their towels and picnic basket on the surprisingly busy beach, and Michael staked out a nearby area for the sand sculpture he insisted on making. Beth settled back to get some rays while Tony and Michael ventured to the surf zone. Moments later, they struggled up the beach with watering cans full of water and their young engineer-to-be began constructing his masterpiece.

"Thesis writing's going okay?" Beth asked after Tony abandoned the construction site. He could watch from a few metres away.

"Second draft's done and reviewed by Dr. K. I've studied his comments. Nothing I can't handle."

"No time-consuming return to experimental work?"

He laughed. A valid question that plagued him for months, but one he could answer without reservation. "Several recalculations and additional background reading, nothing serious. One month for the next draft, then the committee has to review it before I produce a final copy. Defence could be in mid-summer."

"When the baby's due."

"Yeah, maybe better to drag it out."

Beth punched his arm. "You want me to postpone the birth of your daughter. Not happening, buddy."

Tony smiled while shaking his head. She'd fallen right into his little trap. "My thesis defence. It probably won't happen until September."

"Then what?"

"U Vic. Their climate modelling group has accepted my proposal and has funding to cover it for one year, probably two."

"So, we'll stay in Canada for your postdoc. That'll be a huge boost for our ClimateChange&U efforts and my ambitions."

Tony sighed as he watched Michael struggle with his building project. Why was she belabouring this? They both knew staying in Canada was their preferred option, one that was never in doubt. And he was happy to be putting some distance between himself and Clive Grainger. He'd never reconciled himself to Clive's approach to the development in Cuba, and a recent crisis at their Eastern Passage pilot plant had annoyed him. Clive gave Yusuf the job of managing that facility, but he'd proved incapable of managing problems with the pilot plant staff. Fixing the problem became Tony's responsibility when he needed to focus on his thesis.

"Our best bet," he said without elaborating.

"But you're uncertain. I like thought the U Vic general circulation modelling group was top notch."

"I hope they can, you know, maintain their reputation after one prof retired and their leader abandoned science to become a politician."

"He led the BC Green Party to electoral success and significant influence. But that was several years ago. Isn't the group broad enough to keep the momentum going?"

"Hope so. My timing may be shit if they've lost their spark."

"But you're committed?"

"As we've said, it's our best bet, eh?"

Michael dropped his three watering cans beside Tony. "More water."

Beth nodded toward their lunch basket. "Okay, little fella," Tony said. "One more trip to the shore for water, then a few more minutes making..." He pointed at Michael's construction site.

"Giant snake," Michael exclaimed with arms spread wide.

Tony stood, collecting the three cans. "Let's see if you can finish your snake before Mummy has our lunch ready."

"Help me?"

"Let's go."

Four hours later, they drove back to Halifax in a car signed out from the local car share service. Beth waited until the econobox lulled Michael to sleep. "Victoria should be fun, and remaining in Canada makes our website easier to manage. Also good for journalistic prospects I'm working on."

"Something new in environmental advocacy?" Tony asked, thinking of her happiness when her actress job was going well. "I thought you might resurrect your acting career."

She shook her head, animating blond curls that still belonged, in Tony's view, before a camera. "I'd rather focus on our environmental concerns. I've been looking into national newspapers and other media outlets that might carry a climate change column. Something that allows us to reach a greater audience."

"Someone's biting?"

She nodded. "We're at the squabbling about money stage. If I'm not too greedy..."

"Your success is important to me and everyone else. Broadening the reach of ClimateChange&U makes sense."

"That's my thinking. Use it and other channels I can develop to push a climate policy that's independent of the US."

An eagle or a large hawk circling above the forest's edge distracted Tony. He refocused on his driving but didn't abandon his train of thought. "The United States has become more inward looking and nativist. They've abandoned their eighty-year-long reign as leaders of the free world and shifted to bilateral trade relationships with strange bedfellows like China. The deals often beggar their long-time friends and allies."

"Canada's been hit especially hard."

Tony considered the policy ramifications as the hawk once again swept across his field of vision. "We've suffered from US bullying tactics starting in 2018 with massive US tariffs on imports of iron and aluminum. Renewed restrictions on lumber and oil imports followed, and endless other buy America policies. The Americans have ignored long-standing free-trade agreements whenever it suited them. We're no longer great buddies with them and following their lead on every issue."

A lightning strike lit skies darkening since they left the beach. Thunder, followed by a sudden downpour, showed how close the strike had been. Visibility dropped to zilch, and Tony pulled onto the shoulder.

Beth stared at huge raindrops bouncing off the car's hood. "Wow. When I was younger, we never got downpours like this."

Tony snorted. "Common enough in Central Canada and especially the south-central US. More proof climate change is no far-off threat. We're already living it."

"Reminds me of the days when we first met. You were so enthusiastic about ocean acidification and the low pH blooms you were generating. Now you think it's a non-issue, its impact so far in the future we needn't worry about it. Couldn't it become an issue sooner than you thought?"

"Worldwide coal consumption keeps going up, and that shortens the time frame for those climate change impacts. But it also moves up the date for other equally traumatic impacts, like reductions in deep water formation as temperatures increase. Refocusing on how they affect phytoplankton dynamics is my best short-term option."

"Short term like during your tenure at U Vic, but what about the longer term?"

"Faculty position somewhere, and if that doesn't work out, another postdoc."

Beth sighed as the deluge continued. "I can't help thinking we haven't seen the last of your low pH super-plankton. What if we experience the crises you're describing in your thesis before these other problems hit us?"

"Could happen. More likely, we'll discover various impacts interact in ways we haven't anticipated. That should motivate scientists researching all aspects of the problem."

"But what will motivate Dr. Tony Atherton?"

"Been thinking about that as I developed my U Vic proposal. They're interested in ocean circulation models and how global warming will affect the large-scale vertical and horizontal circulation. Major focus is wintertime sinking in polar and subpolar areas like the Labrador Sea."

"Presumably, global warming will mean less sinking."

Tony nodded. "Because colder water is denser than warmer water and more prone to sinking. A lot of other considerations, but that's the critical feature."

Michael started fussing. Beth reached around and freed him from his car seat. She lifted him to the front and bounced him on her knee. "Okay, but where does your acidic ocean and enhanced phytoplankton productivity come into this?"

"They're interrelated. Climate change affects plankton productivity, but increased productivity will affect carbon budgets and climate change. It's what they hired me to do—investigate how we incorporate changing plankton productivity into the global circulation models."

"And?"

"Carbon emissions cause global warming and that leads to many problems including disruption of the global scale ocean circulation."

"Things like the Gulf Stream. That's like not a trivial consideration."

"True, but carbon emissions cause higher carbon dioxide concentrations and that leads to ocean acidification, another phenomenon that will have serious consequences."

"Okay, but this isn't new. We've been over it many times."

Tony looked up as the deluge suddenly ended. He waited for Beth to settle Michael into his car seat, and they resumed their homeward journey. "The experts suggest changes in currents like the Gulf Stream will force society to act before acidification becomes an overriding issue. What if that conclusion's wrong and we adapt to the circulation changes?"

"That's where you'll focus?"

"Think so."

"And for me and our ClimateChange&U website, this idea should motivate us to keep fighting for serious responses from governments. If we can't convince governments to act, we'll be in big trouble."

Tony smiled as some idiot pulled out to pass them. They were already travelling ten kilometres per hour above the speed limit. He relaxed because it would be easier to consider Beth's comments if he didn't have a speed demon sitting on his back bumper.

Her words put their objectives into perspective. During the past year, she'd bounced back from a religious nutcase's very public attack on her lifestyle and their environmental efforts. The attack inspired her, spurred her on to greater and more varied efforts to promote climate change awareness. He'd let the problem, one that should have affected Beth much more than it affected him, fester, adding to doubts that surfaced at the AGU meeting. His vision became cloudy, his goals lost in a Nova Scotia fog. He felt like a failure, investigating something whose impact was so distant it was irrelevant.

It was time to cast those feelings aside and integrate everything he learned about the impacts of climate change on global ocean circulation with his understanding of the pH related ecological changes. And together with Beth, he could incorporate that understanding into their battle to convince governments they must act on climate change.

Chapter Twenty

Thursday, September 11, 2025

Hannah was born on Friday, July twenty-fifth, and Tony defended his PhD thesis on Tuesday, August twelfth. He charged through the final departmental requirements and began packing their possessions. Ten days later, the moving company collected the pod Tony loaded for shipment to Victoria. They spent the next week living from suitcases at Beth's family home in Dartmouth.

On Labour Day, they flew west to visit Beth's sister in Toronto, then winged their way to Victoria. Flights over the Rocky Mountains are spectacular introductions to Canada's geographically isolated westernmost province. The descent into the lower Fraser Valley with Vancouver nestled at the river mouth provides a jaw-dropping introduction to the scenic wonders of British Columbia's south coast.

"Amazing," Beth said as they emerged from the Coast Mountains near Hope, BC. Tony had flown to Vancouver several times, but it was Beth's first trip to the west coast. She glanced toward Tony as Michael struggled to snag the best view through the jet's tiny window. "Much more intense than pictures or videos."

The stopover at Vancouver's Sea Island airport was brief. Within thirty minutes, they were aboard a tiny Dash 8 turboprop for the hop across the Salish Sea. A taxi dropped them at the garden apartment Beth rented sight-unseen before they left Halifax. Ground transportation from the airport to their apartment in Victoria's Mount Douglas neighbourhood took longer than the flight from Vancouver.

Michael scurried from room to room, slamming doors as he went. Beth cradled Hannah as she surveyed the empty apartment. "Good, don't you think?"

"I, you know, worried about the video they sent, but it gave a realistic picture, and the apartment's brighter than I imagined."

She glided to the patio doors at the back of the apartment. "The garden's bigger than I thought, and the green space behind, nicer. It's like our private playground. I can sit outside with Hannah, and Michael can play."

Tony nodded as he considered the logistics. "The pod should arrive tomorrow. We'll have three days to get everything shipshape before I start work on Monday."

"Real good." She swished an imaginary sword. "We'll soon be slaying BC's climate-change-denying dragons."

Beth's enthusiasm persisted as they settled into life on Canada's *left* coast. Michael adapted well to his new environment. The west coast's Mediterranean climate made baby-rearing and other aspects of everyday life easier. By comparison, Tony struggled to get this new phase of his professional career off the ground.

A problem Jacinta Lopez identified years earlier when salps overran an experiment reappeared shortly after he started work at U Vic. He had no measurements of predation by salps or other zooplankton in a low pH environment. His efforts to generate useful measurements at Dal failed, and he'd resorted to extrapolating present-day results.

He needed measurements of predation at various pHs, but the University of Victoria had no mega-scale aquaria. At one time, the nearby Institute of Ocean Sciences had large seawater enclosures floating in Patricia Bay. That mesocosm facility was no longer active. He must devise an inventive solution that didn't need massive tanks. He'd tried but failed to generate a cure during his PhD studies. Could he do better this time?

Tony hoped Marc Lavoie might produce mutually beneficial experiments, but Marc abandoned Dal before he completed his PhD. He took up residence at the Bermuda Biological Station. The tiny tropical island laboratory had a new name, the Bermuda Institute of Ocean Sciences, and a higher profile, but it lacked facilities for complex experiments.

Marc wasn't forthcoming when Tony asked him about the move. "A suitable change of pace with facilities I need," he'd said without elaborating.

Work on projects he promised to do for Milton James, the professor funding his year-long visit, proceeded more smoothly.

"That's why we moved here, isn't it?" Beth asked when Tony expressed faint praise for his efforts. "You wanted to pursue new avenues of research and generate some papers."

"Yeah. After two months, I have the fodder for one paper and promising preliminary results for two others. Milton's up for tenure next year, so he'll push for quick publication."

"What's the problem?"

"The papers will support my efforts to find a permanent job. But they don't help my research into plankton transport in the low pH ocean lurking in Earth's future."

"For God's sakes, Tony. A year ago, you came home from San Francisco convinced other problems were more important. You're getting a chance to work on them. Follow the new path for now and return to the low pH problem after you land a faculty position."

"After the AGU, I focused on problems with more immediate impact, and the work here contributes to that effort. Last spring, I spent six months writing my thesis. I worried about the effects of lower pH and decided I'd downplayed their importance. What if we're overestimating the impacts of higher temperature, and we find ourselves in a low pH, high productivity world?"

"Humour me. What will we experience?"

"It could produce dramatic removal of oceanic carbon, drastically lower global temperatures, and a new ice age."

"Important stuff, the integration you've been talking about. Can't it wait until you're established in your new job? Then you can make like Albert Einstein and develop your grand unified theory. You can bring together the impacts of global warming and ocean acidification."

Beth envisaged a bright future for Tony's research, but the public's waning enthusiasm didn't improve his frustration. A national survey showed an increasing number of citizens accepted climate change was bad for people and their environment but thought they were powerless. Their response to questions about government action was similar. Canada's population was too small to impact the global situation. The poll claimed thirty-five percent of the respondents held these views. That was five percent percentage points higher than the previous year's numbers.

The survey confirmed impressions he'd developed while managing the ClimateChange&U website. Their original disciples, individuals committed to reducing their carbon footprints, were a significant part of a national effort. The environmental activists Beth attracted with her interviews and editorials were another small group. They'd never attracted the defeatists who felt their efforts were meaningless. That group, more than the climate change deniers, must be the key to fighting climate change, but they hadn't found a strategy that engaged them.

Despite Beth's best efforts to lift his spirits, Tony's melancholy extended through Christmas and into January. In February, glorious early spring weather with cherry trees flowering along residential streets finally lifted his spirits.

On Saturday, February seventh, Tony, Beth, and their two kids strolled along Victoria's inner harbour waterfront. They walked past the Empress Hotel and the Royal British Columbia Museum to Beacon Hill Park. After a mandatory stop at a children's play area, they approached Finlayson Point and the rocky beach to the east.

As Beth helped Michael clamber over the enormous driftwood logs that littered the beach, Tony stared at the Strait of Juan de Fuca.

"Well, Hannah," he said to the baby sleeping in the baby sling wrapped around his chest, "Looks pristine. Hard to believe there's so much fuss about sewage discharge."

Michael charged up, with Beth trailing behind. "Mummy says we can get ice cream."

"What do you think," she said, pointing at the jumble of bleached logs. "Like crazy, letting these logs pile up on the beaches."

Tony shrugged. Logs on beaches hadn't penetrated his preoccupation with climate change. "The coastal forestry industry has always transported logs in huge sea-going booms. Losses are inevitable, and they end up on beaches. It's how it is, and as pollution goes, not a serious problem."

"Nothing like climate change or the local sewage problem. Like, how's that going. Making progress selling Victoria on Algal Energy's methane production technology?"

"Not great," Tony said as they followed Michael up the path from the beach. "Sewage treatment in Victoria has been controversial, and the fuss over their much-delayed McLoughlin Point plant is too recent. Our proposal could bring a pollution-reducing and money-making spin to the problem, but there's no interest."

"Bad timing, or something seriously wrong?"

"Timing, and Clive's lost interest. I don't know what's with him. He was enthusiastic before our westward migration, but now, the project's fallen off his radar screen."

"Odd, don't you think?"

Tony kicked a stone off the path. "Rather like he's forgotten this was to be our second avenue to commercial success."

"And the plant for the Eastern Passage Sewage Treatment facility?"

"Also languishing, but that's more understandable. The regulatory hurdles are daunting."

Beth sighed as she grabbed Michael's hand before he approached a busy road. "It's like our other initiatives. We get bogged down in government inactivity and red tape."

"Yeah, really. Inertia's a serious foe. Individual action by contributors to ClimateChange&U expands, but government policies don't change. And Algal Energy's progress appeared unfettered at first, but now it's bogged down. Causes of this inertia vary, but it's always out there, impeding progress."

*****

The developments that weighed so heavily on Tony's mind didn't discourage Beth. She'd overcome the trauma of Terrance Goddard's attack and developed a new interest in influencing the political process. In Victoria, she began contributing a weekly environmental awareness column to a prominent online journal. With this new endeavour, child-rearing, and her ongoing commitments to ClimateChange&U, she was busier than ever. Her dedication to the environmental cause never wavered. She remained convinced that, with dedication and persistence, they could vanquish their enemies.

The evening of their stroll along the Victoria waterfront, Beth returned to progress with Tony's various work-related activities. Except for one evening in November, he'd been uncommunicative since they'd arrived in Victoria. She'd now given him ample time to acclimatize. It was time to get their partnership working again. He needed her help fending off the strange uncertainty he always felt about his research work. She needed more commitment to their environmental activities.

"How's progress with Dr. James?" she asked as she sat beside him. "It can't be bogged down in government inactivity and red tape."

Tony set aside the laptop that was his almost constant companion. "Chugging along. First paper's accepted, and the others are ready to submit. And they accepted the paper I submitted before defending my thesis." He tapped his computer case. "Get these two finished, and I'll be set to apply for the faculty job UBC's posted."

"University of British Columbia in Vancouver, wouldn't that be something? Great city, great university, we couldn't ask for anything better."

"You sure? Super expensive, and don't you miss the east coast?"

She sighed, leaning her head on his shoulder. "A long way from family, but the west coast weather is unbelievable, and I'm like loving living here by the Pacific Ocean. It's warmer in midwinter than the Atlantic is in summer. And I'm being paid for the columns I'm writing. The guy who runs the site is a pain, but he pays his columnists, including me, and I'm a beginner."

Tony turned and hugged her. "Hardly a beginner. Your experience doing interviews and editorials for ClimateChange&U makes you an old pro."

"Rank beginner or old pro. Vancouver's a huge dynamic city, a mecca for environmentalists. Perfect place with endless opportunities for an environmental activist to snag a paying gig. But what about you? Would UBC let you return to your acidic ocean?"

"I'd be independent. New profs get start-up funding. It's up to them to generate productive projects. I don't anticipate trouble establishing collaborations, attracting students, and developing interesting projects."

"Collaborations. Reminds me of you and Marc working together." Beth paused as she considered their interaction, sometimes squabbling like siblings but apparently enjoying their confrontations. And she suspected they inspired each other. "Is he still a student?"

"A Dal student, finishing his PhD, but he buggered off to Bermuda to make measurements he considers critical. I've had some emails, but he's being mysterious."

Beth sighed, slumping down into the sofa as memories drifted over her. "Bermuda. Wonderful place. My parents took my sister and me there when we were teenagers. My first experience with somewhere exotic. Maybe Marc's having an exotic adventure with a dusky, Bermudan beauty."

Tony shook his head. "Not Marc, but he's been enigmatic, saying he's making important measurements but not describing them, and hinting they'll also be important for my work. Doesn't sound like he's dallying on Bermudan beaches."

"Spoilsport," she said while thumping his shoulder. "I hope he has plenty of time for dallying on beaches."

Chapter Twenty-One

Tuesday, March 17, 2026

On St. Patrick's Day, Marc's message popped up when Tony opened his office email. The subject line read <Chemical dissolution of silica DOES maintain low pH diatom blooms>.

Marc's words reminded Tony of the days when they collaborated on data collection for their PhD projects. Their final collaboration investigated the persistence of diatom-dominated blooms long after the silicate necessary for diatom growth should have disappeared.

During those weeks before he focused on model construction and thesis writing, Tony argued contamination of their experiments with silica dissolved from aquarium surfaces extended the blooms. Marc fought for chemical dissolution of silica from the frustules of diatoms that died and settled to the bottom.

Persistence had been a concern from the initial experiment in 2022 when Jacinta observed elevated production in diatom blooms at low pH. The problem remained unresolved when Tony abandoned experimental work to focus on his thesis. Marc continued his quest.

Tony opened the email.

<Greetings from the Bermuda Institute of Ocean Sciences, St. Georges, Bermuda. How are Beth and the family? Enjoying life in Canada's western paradise?

Been studying low pH plankton blooms in a completely plastic mesocosm deployed in the inlet near the institute. Shallower than I'd like, but adequate to follow bloom development.

I see chemical dissolution of silica at the bottom of the enclosure. It maintains diatom growth in a low silicate environment.

I'll call later, five AST, and we can discuss. Hope you can take the call.
Marc>

Tony returned from lunch at ten minutes before one. A call from Marc, even one with evidence his explanation had been correct, was welcome. Anything that rekindled his interest in phytoplankton dynamics in a low pH ocean would help him counter the funk he'd found himself in for two years. He was making progress, establishing a solid reputation and an extensive Curriculum Vitae. That would help him find his coveted academic posting, but the excitement he felt during 2022 was missing. *Beth's tried her best to inspire me, but she hasn't succeeded. Would Marc's new results do the trick?*

The phone rang, and Marc addressed his overriding concern after a minimum of small talk. "I have measurements that show how we maintain high diatom productivity at low pH. Shells and organic matter settle to the bottom where conditions rapidly become anoxic. Silica dissolution continues, so it must be a chemical process that proceeds at pH 7.5 and zero oxygen."

"Bermuda, so tropical waters but generally devoid of excess nutrients."

"Shallow inshore waters, so adequate nutrients, including silica. I've been adjusting the pH and inoculating the system with native diatoms acclimatized to low pH, but no added nutrients. The blooms are less vigorous than the ones we generated at Dal, but they follow similar patterns."

"So, you have experimental evidence for a mechanism that explains the predominance of diatoms. Sounds good. I foresee bigger and better things on your horizon."

Marc hesitated, then cleared his throat, a sign he was less than pleased with Tony's facetious compliment. "I've been studying your thesis. I'll send you a synopsis of my observations and the relevant data. You must consider their impact on your models of plankton productivity in the low pH ocean we'll see in not too many years."

Tony hesitated when Marc ended the call several minutes later. He'd always been quiet and reserved, but easygoing. Now he seemed overly jumpy. *Is he simply wound up in his latest results, or is his mysterious venture from Halifax to Bermuda more significant than I assumed?*

The following morning, Marc's package with masses of raw data, reams of observations and calculations, and a synopsis of his ideas waited in Tony's inbox when he fired up his computer. By noon, he'd developed an basic understanding of the status of Marc's experiments, where he hoped to take them, and the role he envisioned for Tony.

On a bench in a greenspace within the university's ring road, Tony perused a printout of Marc's synopsis. He pondered the significance of his friend's observations as he munched rabbit food he brought to fend off lunchtime hunger pangs. Marc's experiments employed mesocosms containing ambient seawater from the waters of St. George's Harbour. He adjusted the pH to 7.5 and dosed them with diatom species he wanted to study. That meant the mesocosms contained natural assemblages of phytoplankton and zooplankton. If they survived the pH shock, they'd be active during his experiments. Could he use this system to study predation by salps at low pH?

Tony pulled out his phone and sent Marc an email before leaning back with a carrot. After crunching the damn vegetable, he searched his Tupperware container for something more substantial. All he found was a chunk of Swiss cheese and a small piece of Polish sausage. He chomped on carrots and celery accompanied by the odd bite of cheese and sausage and dreamed of Halifax and the donair shop within walking distance of his Dalhousie University office. That's what Victoria needed—a donair shop he could walk to from his office. Not good for the healthier west coast lifestyle Beth was pushing, but an adopted Nova Scotian couldn't live by sushi alone.

Marc's reply appeared as Tony pondered unhealthy dining choices.

<Difficult as hell. Consider all the biological and physical factors that influence sedimentation. You'd need to specify each one.>

Jesus, Marc, Tony thought as he marched back to his office, think like the biologist you are, not a bloody mathematical modeller. Take your mesocosm, spike it with your diatom, let the bloom develop, and introduce salps. See how effective they are at transporting biomass to the bottom. Then repeat the experiment after reducing the pH in the mesocosm and compare the results of the normal pH and low pH experiments.

He'd flesh out his arguments and send Marc another message. This might become the protocol he needed to estimate the impact of salps and other zooplankton predators on sedimentation at low pH. *Finally, I've got something that sparks my interest in the old problem.*

By four thirty, he'd learned what he could from Marc's missives. He put them aside and turned to his ongoing search into the life of John Springer. He soon realized this was his lucky day. He'd finally found a link on Google—Albertan Autonomy listed Springer as a participant in their founding convention. Tony checked their website. The newly formed group, not an official political party, favoured right-wing libertarianism and provincial autonomy. A perfect fit with the garbage Springer'd been spouting.

At five thirty, he shut down his computer and headed home with a spring in his step. Albertan Autonomy was a fringe group with a few hundred members. No way a fringe party in Alberta could make good on Springer's threats to end his oceanographic career. Just like their undergraduate days, meaningless blather from a pompous ass.

Three days later, Tony arrived home in a fog that was more befitting Halifax's cold, damp springs than Victoria's balmy climate. Should he be happy because his family would soon have a large nest egg, or sad because the work he'd put into Algal Energy had been for naught?

Tony entered their garden from the common area and found Michael perched at his child-sized patio table, drawing furiously. He glanced up from his task. "Making pictures for my book. Mummy helps with the words."

"Good for you. When you're finished, can I read it?"

He hunched over his page. "When I'm done."

"I'll wait," Tony said while tousling Michael's hair. "Where's Mummy?"

"Inside, with Hannah."

Hannah's crying greeted Tony when he stepped inside. He found Beth rocking her cradle with one hand as she cut vegetables with the other. The erratic rocking was not calming their baby. Beth looked up. "Is Michael okay?"

"Drawing pictures, very intent."

"And you, you like, don't appear so good," Beth said as Tony lifted Hannah from her cradle.

Tony sighed, thinking Beth could invariably read his mood in a nanosecond. "Surprising news. Not sure what to think. You want it now, or should I keep it for later?"

Beth smiled. "If you can juggle entertaining Hannah, keeping an eye on Michael, and telling me your news, go for it."

Tony walked back and forth as Hannah became sleepier. Finally, she fell asleep, and he returned her to her cradle.

He fetched a canister from a cupboard and turned to Beth. "Noodles as usual?"

"Yeah. Stir-fried veggies, leftover chicken, and noodles. Now, get on with it. Tell me this news before Michael comes in."

"Clive sold Algal Energy to an American oil company."

"Why would they want your company?"

"I suspect they're most interested in improvements Yusuf made to the primary digestion process."

"The digestion of the algae? Are they interested in turning algae into biodiesel?"

Tony paused while he dumped noodles into the now boiling water. He couldn't fathom Clive's or the US company's thinking. "They may be more interested in applying the basic principles to the digestion of higher plant life."

"That would be positive, wouldn't it? Making hydrocarbon fuel from renewable sources rather than fossil fuels."

"If they're on the level. But is it like the big car manufacturers' venture into electric cars decades ago? They did some development, then buried everything. Set the electric car industry back years."

She waved her knife after dumping sliced-up vegetables into their wok. "Oh Tony, don't be so negative. It could be a positive development. But what does it mean for us?"

"No more salary, but we'll be paid for our share in the company."

"But how much? The valuations on your company never made sense."

"They were total guesswork," Tony said as Michael arrived in the kitchen trailing crayon drawings that were escaping from his hands. "Clive tells me they'll offer us between one and two million for our share."

"One to two million dollars! Jesus, Tony, that's a fortune."

"Right on cue because I had an unofficial call telling me UBC will offer me a professorship. Housing costs in Vancouver are beyond absurd."

Her knife clattered when it hit the counter. "You trying to give me a heart attack. You come in looking like some piece of detritus the cat dragged in when your pockets are bulging with your dream job offer and two million dollars. That's like, beyond wonderful!"

Chapter Twenty-Two

Thursday, May 7, 2026

After two months without communication, Tony received a Wednesday afternoon email from Marc. <In Victoria scoping out employment opportunities at the Oceans Sciences lab in Patricia Bay. Could we get together tomorrow afternoon before I fly to Halifax on Friday morning?>

Tony replied immediately, suggesting Marc head for his office or his apartment whenever he was free. He refocused on his project, anticipating a follow-up email.

Typical bloody communication with Marc, Tony thought as he checked his email for the third time on Thursday afternoon. He'd sent an open-ended message because he'd forgotten how literal-minded Marc could be. Without a direct question or request for a response, he'd probably arrive without warning.

At 4:15, Marc entered Tony's open doorway, scanned the room, and settled into the one available chair. He flipped a USB flash drive onto Tony's desk. "Data from successful mesocosm experiments to measure nutrient cycling from the water to my low pH phytoplankton blooms and back to the water column after the blooms settle to the bottom."

Tony's brow furrowed as he tried to remember where their last conversation ended. "The experiments we discussed two months ago?" he asked, hoping Marc would put his results in context.

"Those and follow-up studies I conducted after we talked. Also, results of experiments to answer comments from reviewers of the paper I prepared."

Tony plugged the drive into his computer.

Mark described the range of measurements as Tony waited for his computer to process the first data file. "Key observation is the positive relationship between nutrient release from the bottom and strength of the sustained bloom."

"After the initial response to pH alteration and injection of your inoculant?"

"Exactly. The results leave no doubt. Nutrients released from the decomposition of material settling from the blooms sustain them."

Tony stared for several minutes at Marc's first file. The large table summarized results from forty-seven experiments with blooms that weren't dominated by diatoms. *Masses of data but no context. He's waiting for me to figure it out.*

"Little silicate regeneration when the bloom's dominated by organisms that don't need silicate," Tony said when he looked up.

Marc smiled as he straightened his shoulders. "Critical! It solidifies my contention I'm seeing true cause and effect, not chance covariances."

Tony nodded as he pushed back from his desk. "I agree. Pretty telling observation."

He walked to a corner where he'd stored a rolled-up map of the world's oceans beside a filing cabinet. He unrolled it on his desk and weighted the corners.

"Ptolemy strikes again," Marc said, reminding Tony of a discussion years earlier with Tim Wilkes in Dalhousie's graduate student pub.

Tony sloughed off the reference to easier times at Dalhousie. His brain was digesting an important research idea, and he didn't want to lose the thread. "We have a well-established dynamic in shallow seas and coastal shelves that produces enhanced biological productivity."

Marc nodded. "The Grand Banks of Newfoundland being the example everyone quotes."

"If we imagine this happening in a low pH environment, we have an endless loop of enhanced productivity with regeneration at the sediment feeding back into more enhanced productivity in the photic layer. We could pump down incredible quantities of carbon."

"That's your mechanism for enhanced CO_2 removal in a low pH ocean. Where's this going?"

Tony turned to the whiteboard behind his desk. He sketched the flow diagram he'd used in his thesis for the cycling processes. "That's what I argued in my thesis, but nutrient availability limited the enhancement. You're now saying there's no limit in waters shallow enough for your dynamic integration of phytoplankton productivity and nutrient resupply."

Marc nodded as he stared at Tony's map. "You should add upwelling areas. That's another mechanism that supplies an almost unlimited quantity of nutrients."

"Look at my map—"

"I'm looking at it. Take the continental shelves, add broader shallow seas like the North Sea and areas of oceanic upwelling."

"The area's small compared to the ocean, but if the mechanism's sufficiently strong, I could pump huge quantities of carbon from surface waters into the sediments."

Marc laughed. "Sounds like a modeller's dream come true. You should go for it."

"There must be a limit. How many times can I recycle the same nutrients? And leakage. I must include leakage of precious nutrients."

"Horizontal transport away from the shallow areas and incomplete nutrient regeneration from the organic material trapped in the sediment. Volatility of ammonia, probably other limiters. You'll see losses, but can't you develop algorithms for the various loss terms?"

Tony jumped up, strode to his window, and stared at the lushness of springtime in Victoria. "I'm missing something. These processes occur in our present-day ocean. Primary productivity will be greater in our low pH ocean. What magnifies the removal?"

When he returned to his desk, he noticed the time. "Christ, it's five fifteen. Beth will kill me if I don't drag you to our place for supper and a natter about the good ol' times at Dal Oceanography. You have time, don't you, and no commitments for this evening." Marc nodded, so Tony continued. "We can wander to our place, letting these ideas develop. Later we must return to this. I see massive potential, but I'm missing an important factor."

They strolled to Tony and Beth's garden apartment through the leafy splendor of springtime in Victoria. Tony imagined Bermuda's leafy splendor, thinking Marc may have been more impressed if he'd arrived from wintery Halifax instead of subtropical Bermuda.

"Victoria's beautiful," Marc said as he gazed about, "but it suffers from Bermuda's problem. Island dwellers invariably get isolation phobia."

"Ever-increasing air travel must dampen that phobia."

Marc stopped, staring with one index finger raised. "I don't believe it. The big advocate for everyone doing his bit to reduce carbon emissions is pushing more air travel."

Tony shook his head as he waited for Marc to catch up. "Just saying air travel, something that isn't affected by water, should reduce your island phobia. The solution for reducing carbon footprints is reducing our urge to travel. It doesn't matter if it's travel by car or by plane, we must travel less."

At their apartment, Beth dominated the conversation, pestering Marc about his life in Bermuda. She mentioned memories from her family's one visit fifteen years earlier. When she added questions about his girlfriends, Tony shifted the conversation to the reason for Marc's visit to Victoria.

"Dissertation's drafted, and Dr. K agrees I won't need additional lab or fieldwork," Marc replied. "Revisions, yes, but should have it completed by August. Not interested in a teaching position, so I'm investigating research labs outside academia."

"Like the government's Ocean Sciences lab in Pat Bay," Tony said. "It's a fisheries department lab, so government policy and the departmental mandate restricts its scope. Not the opportunity for open-ended research you would find at a university."

Marc nodded. "Borne home by this morning's discussions in the Patricia Bay Lab. Something like Bermuda's Institute of Ocean Sciences may be better."

"Or a research professorship at a US university. They don't have the same teaching responsibilities."

"What's wrong with a regular professorship like the one Tony will have at UBC?" Beth asked.

Marc's eyes drooped as he shook his head. "Nothing. It's me. I don't want to teach."

Michael interrupted with a demand for attention. Marc helped him finish a kiddies' jigsaw puzzle as Beth fed Hannah and Tony prepared dinner for everyone else.

After dinner, they took Michael to the public library. Tony and Marc found a quiet corner near the children's section where they could watch Michael while discussing their research interests.

Marc initiated the discussion. "Helping Michael assemble his jigsaw puzzles gave me time to consider your comments before we left your office."

"Something that makes carbon cycling in a low pH ocean different from cycling in the present-day ocean?" Tony asked.

"Exactly. Enhanced primary production produces enhanced predation by copepods, salps, and other zooplankters. That leads to increased activity up the food web."

"The only difference being increased rates compared to the current environment."

Marc nodded. "Now turn to the removal terms. Increased production of all kinds yields increased transport of organic material to the sediment. Then what happens?"

Tony hesitated, glancing at Michael as he chewed on Marc's question. He was obviously onto something, but Tony hadn't figured it out. "We get regeneration of nutrients and decomposition of organic matter back to CO_2 or burial. Why is this fundamentally different?"

"Consider the decomposition term. Turning organic matter to carbon dioxide requires oxygen, but we have no process that increases the supply of oxygen. In fact, we'll see less oxygen in the warmer, low pH ocean."

Tony smiled. The various threads were finally weaving themselves into an appealing tapestry. "I get it. Increased transport to the sediments. Slower decomposition than in the present ocean, so more anoxic sediments formed more rapidly and more burial of carbon. Predation's not important. I expected some critical revelation about predation."

Marc shook his head. "Two things are important. First, the system churns more quickly. Second, decomposition of organic matter cannot keep up with increased sedimentation. Predation is an important component of the mechanism that increases the churn rate, but slower decomposition's the key factor."

"How do we tackle it?"

"We?"

"Yeah, we. It's what you're on about, isn't it? Once you defend your thesis, you'll need a new focus. You're not telling me you plan to abandon this and head in a different direction."

Michael appeared and dumped a stack of children's picture books in Tony's lap. "Mummy says you should look after these."

Tony sorted Michael's six books into a stable pile and placed them on a table. "And what will you do?"

He pointed toward a nearby enclosed play area.

"Okay, off you go. If you need anything, we'll be right here."

Michael scampered away, and Tony turned to Marc. "Well?"

"Interesting, and the mesocosm I built in Bermuda could be useful, but I'd need funding. That's the issue. I'm not interested in a tenured faculty position, but I need money for a postdoc level stipend and operating costs."

Tony sighed as he watched Michael in the glassed-in play area. "I have a tenure track faculty position at UBC starting in September. I'll have start-up funding to establish a lab, but I can't use it to fund work in Bermuda." He paused, wondering about Marc's attitude. He was as full of good ideas as ever, but he seemed to lack commitment to taking the steps toward positions that would let him pursue them. "I'm working on an initial funding proposal. Our discussion will help me finish it." Another pause while he considered how he could write Marc into his proposal. "You could aid your cause by applying to the National Science and Engineering Research Council for a postdoc. If you got one, you could write your ticket, take it to Bermuda or wherever you wanted. I could find money for travel costs related to our collaboration." And maybe some operating funds, he thought but said nothing. *Better not suggest something I can't deliver.*

Chapter Twenty-Three

Thursday, August 27, 2026

Tony read the message before the morning coffee break on the final day of the Third Annual Southampton Climate Change Conference. <Sir Gareth of Penarth requests the pleasure of your company at his club on Friday afternoon to discuss your ocean acidification research.>

Tony turned to British colleagues who were also waiting in the coffee queue. "Either of you know a Sir Gareth of Penarth?"

"You joking?" one asked. "He's one of Britain's richest citizens. Bit reclusive, owner of an influential bank, a man of substance. Why do you ask?"

"Received an invitation to meet him tomorrow at his London club. You think it's a prank?"

He shrugged. "Does the message give you a means of contacting him?"

"Phone number, says the switchboard will put me through immediately when I give them my name."

"Check the bank's website. If the number's legitimate, it should be there."

Tony looked ahead at the slowly moving queue. "Thanks, guys. I'll forego coffee and check this out."

At two thirty, he rushed to the Southampton train station. He'd presented his papers, one on Tuesday and the second on Wednesday. He received helpful advice on both, plus some useful comments on their ever-changing ClimateChange&U website. The last session, the one he was cutting short, wasn't particularly interesting. He couldn't keep his thoughts from wandering to the strange invitation he had from an icon of British Aristocracy.

On the train to London, Tony pieced together the four hours of rapid-fire events that would upend the remaining days of his trip to the UK. They began with his ten thirty call to Sir Gareth. The initially frosty receptionist melted completely once he mentioned his name. He had a brief conversation with Gareth of Penarth, who insisted the sir was an honorific he didn't normally use and a longer and more involved series of conversations and text messages with his executive assistant. They resulted in a reservation at the five-star Connaught Hotel in Mayfair and revised and upgraded tickets for his trip to Halifax on Saturday. First-class all the way, with everything covered by Sir Gareth's investment bank.

In Waterloo Station, Tony hesitated at the entrance to the Waterloo Underground Station. During a normal visit, he'd take the underground to the closest stop and walk to his hotel. But this wasn't a normal visit. He strode to the taxi canopy and hailed a cab. Fifteen minutes later, the black London hackney carriage dropped him at the Connaught Hotel.

Inside, the reception desk clerk apologized for only having a room, not a suite, available on such short notice, but Tony was relieved. A room in a five-star hotel would be more luxurious than he deserved. Minutes later, he whisked up the elevator to his room, where he read the introductory letter Sir Gareth left for him. He hung out his dress slacks and blazer and decided which of the hotel's four eating establishments best suited him for dinner. He chose the simplest-looking one.

Friday morning, Tony visited the Tate Modern Art Gallery and bought presents for Beth, Michael, and Hannah. He had one beer and a light lunch in an English pub and returned to his hotel. At four, a minicab waited outside. It transported Tony to Sir Gareth's gentleman's club in the City of London.

Sir Gareth stood and extended his hand as a club porter escorted Tony into an old-fashioned sitting room. It had fireplaces, stained wood panelling, and overstuffed burgundy-coloured leather armchairs. "Dr. Atherton, I presume."

Tony smiled and took the chair Sir Gareth indicated without commenting. What could he say? Did anyone know how Dr. Livingstone responded to Stanley's greeting?

Sir Gareth held up his glass of what was probably single malt scotch. "What's your preference?"

"You know, I'm a country boy from Ontario. Anything more exotic than Crown Royal on the rocks would be wasted on me."

A waiter who'd been hovering nearby disappeared after the slightest nod from Sir Gareth. He immediately turned to business.

"I assume you're curious about the reason for this meeting. The effort I've made to bring you here shows I'm not joking. It's my job to convince you I'm serious about accomplishing meaningful climate change action and that you must join our fight."

Tony remained leery. "If you've followed our website, and I'm sure you have, you'll know that my partner Beth Manville and I are committed to that fight."

Sir Gareth nodded as the waiter placed Tony's drink on the table beside his chair. "Well aware of your contributions to the site and the success of Ms. Manville's efforts to bring your message to the public. I'm also familiar with your research, although sometimes I struggle to understand the details. Next week you'll begin a distinguished career as a professor of oceanography at the University of British Columbia."

"A very junior assistant professor and how successful is undetermined."

Sir Gareth smiled. "Self-effacing Canadian, eh. I'll leave the pursuit of academic excellence to you, but we can find synergies in our combined battle with climate change."

Tony sipped his drink while he tried to fathom the direction the conversation was heading. Sir Gareth described climate change research sponsored by wealthy industrialists. But the august banker was a leading example of a human sub-species that was frugal by nature. An introduction to a research foundation didn't justify the sum Sir Gareth devoted to this elaborate meeting.

"You're looking puzzled," Gareth said before signalling the waiter. "Replenish our drinks, then I'll explain."

The server reappeared almost immediately with two generously filled glasses. When he withdrew, Gareth began. "A consortium of European industrialists and bankers has developed a mechanism for stabilizing global temperatures. This initiative isn't an altruistic undertaking. It's a pragmatic development to alleviate a bane of modern business. Uncertainty and unpredictable events are profit killers for all but a few modern dot.com companies. Global warming causes more uncertainty than any other factor. We must stop it."

"Answer should be simple—reduce carbon emissions."

"Scientists have been saying that for forty years, and the message hasn't resonated. Our campaign will stabilize global temperatures, but we'll need help reducing carbon emissions."

"What sort of help?"

"Help with convincing the public of the need for further action, and ongoing scientific research into the disruptive impacts of increasing carbon emissions."

"You want buy-in from influencers like Beth on ClimateChange&U."

Gareth shook his head. "No coercion. Acceptance of the commonalities in our goals and a realization we're fighting on the same side."

"And on the science side?"

"Most of the recognized impacts of climate change are related to global warming. We need research on other impacts of carbon emissions."

"Like ocean acidification and the effect it has on coral reefs?"

"And the research you've been doing on changes in phytoplankton productivity. Results that help define when these factors become serious concerns are critically important. We'll provide funds to researchers pursuing these goals. And if ClimateChange&U needs funding, you'll know where to turn."

Sir Gareth rambled on for the next hour, describing a scenario where wealthy industrialists would control global temperatures without halting carbon emissions. When questioned, he refused to describe how they could control temperature without halting emissions. It was clear he understood the linkage and that controlling carbon emissions was the critical problem. He insisted, however, they must tackle temperature first.

Later, they had dinner in the club's formal dining room. Sir Gareth shifted the conversation to other topics and said nothing more about climate change. Tony returned to his hotel trying to be open-minded about Sir Gareth's effort to tackle climate change but very concerned about the secrecy surrounding his method of doing so.

Saturday evening, Beth, Michael, and Hannah greeted Tony in the arrivals area of Halifax's Stanfield International Airport. He was a day later than planned but arrived bearing gifts and stories of his meeting with an English aristocrat.

"No problem," Beth said when Tony apologized for their lost day. "One more day sitting in Halifax waiting for the flight that wings us westward to our very own house. And hey, I gotta hear about your meeting with a British lord."

"He's not a proper lord. The knighthood's an honorific conveyed on him for service to the country. But he's immensely wealthy and lives a very luxurious lifestyle."

She met Tony's efforts to explain Sir Gareth's intentions with puzzled frowns. Not surprising, as Sir Gareth had not been forthcoming about his intentions, and Tony's understanding was murky, at best.

Beth asked the critical question. "Why wouldn't this strange group of industrial bigwigs tackle carbon emissions instead of temperature? Everyone knows carbon emissions are the problem, and we have technologies for trapping carbon."

"I asked that question but received no answer." Tony paused, shaking his head as he remembered Sir Gareth's efforts to deflect his questions. "A problem with the entire conversation. He conveyed his message, well, two messages, but wouldn't provide details or properly answer questions."

"The two messages being?"

"His mysterious group will resolve the problem of ever-increasing temperatures, and he understands carbon emissions are the real problem."

"Sounds like a wily politician or a carnival barker selling snake oil. He does or says something to gain your confidence, then presents his solution without explaining how it works."

Tony nodded. "It was rather like that, but I hope he's on the level. I checked into his bank's climate change research funding. It's real, and there's some mention of expanding the program. Could be a major benefit for people like Marc."

"Can't he get funding from NSERC?"

Tony paused while Beth backed her mother's car into the family driveway. "Difficult. The National Research Council's geared up to support university research, but Marc insists he isn't interested in an academic appointment."

"I remember that from his visit to our place in Victoria. I didn't understand his reasoning."

"Neither did I, but he's adamant."

"Okay, so Sir Gareth of Penarth, snake oil salesman extraordinaire, may benefit Marc, but what does he mean for us?"

Tony chuckled, intrigued by Beth's fixation with her snake-oil salesman analogy. The debonair Sir Gareth he met the previous day looked and behaved nothing like a carnival barker. "Nothing for you or ClimateChange&U until we know what his consortium is doing. We now know they exist. We should keep our eyes open and our powder dry."

"And for your research?"

"Same story. I don't need funding, and I have no intention of changing the direction of my research. If anything, my conversation with Sir Gareth convinced me I should keep going."

Beth smiled. "Maybe the snake oil salesman succeeded. He convinced you to keep working on a problem that suits his interests."

"That's what I planned, anyway. He's had no material effect other than to spur me to try harder to generate more collaboration with Marc."

Monday morning, they caught an early flight to Vancouver. The closing for their first house was that afternoon. Only thirteen-month-old Hannah treated the event with equanimity. She remained calm, but Tony, Beth, and Michael couldn't hide their nervous anticipation.

They landed at three and took a taxi to their lawyer's Tenth Avenue office. After completing the paperwork, they were proud owners of their first home.

They arrived at the empty house at five, carrying the luggage from their trip, three air mattresses, three sleeping bags, and Hannah's paraphernalia. They'd camp out in their Point Grey house until their furniture arrived from Victoria. Happy homeowners in an upscale neighbourhood thanks to the nest egg delivered by the sale of Algal Energy.

Tuesday, the faint yellow glow of a glorious new day greeted them through uncurtained windows at six thirty. Hannah cried, and Michael demanded breakfast. Their new life as happy homeowners in Vancouver had begun.

Chapter Twenty-Four

Tuesday, October 27, 2026

The federal government produced numbers showing minute improvements in carbon intensity for April to September. Beth stared in disbelief at the press release. A tiny reduction in carbon emissions per unit of GDP in a year with robust GDP growth meant the actual carbon emissions were much higher than a year earlier. It was a disaster, an unspoken admission Canada wouldn't reach its Paris Climate Accord target by the 2030 deadline.

She could base this week's editorial on ClimateChange&U on the government's futile attempt to hide their failure by focusing on intensity. Her missive would write itself. She'd have it finished before Tony and Michael arrived home from the childminder. And her debut on the environmental affairs programme on national television in early November? These disappointing results and the government's ham-fisted attempt to downplay them were manna from heaven. She'd build them into a killer exposé.

Beth's life was charging ahead at breakneck speed. Her reinvigorated existence started with Michael's instant acceptance of his new home. Mothers at his Victoria playgroup predicted a difficult transition, but he loved his new group. And the grandmother who often cared for Michael and Hannah with minimal notice was a godsend.

Mrs. Findlay's case was an interesting one. She'd moved in when her daughter abandoned her husband and two young children to go chasing adventure. She stayed rent-free in her granny suite after her son-in-law remarried. Her grandchildren had left the family nest, but she remained. She now cared for neighbourhood children to earn spending money.

"Good. Go with it," Tony said after reading Beth's editorial. "Another example of government's inability to grasp an opportunity and run with it."

"It is, isn't it," Beth replied as she extracted half-eaten cookies and other debris from Michael's tiny backpack. "From 2020 to 2024, we made progress on reducing emissions, but now, we're back to our inadequate pace."

"Progress was an anomaly, generated by reductions in economic activity and especially travel during the coronavirus pandemic." He sighed, remembering the disruptions the pandemic caused. "We're back to normal with a kick from government incentives to recover from lost opportunities."

"Strengthen my last comments to emphasize that point?" Beth asked.

"Wouldn't hurt. But just those last sentences. Don't mess with anything else."

The following morning, she revised her editorial's last few sentences and posted it on ClimateChange&U. She moved on to her first segment on national TV. It required more effort, and she only had two weeks to prepare it. She'd already developed a plan in consultation with her friend, political scientist Gwen Mulholland in Halifax. Yesterday's announcement caused some rethinking, but nothing she and Gwen couldn't handle.

"Already working on it," Gwen said when Beth phoned. It was 7:45 in Vancouver but 11:45 in Halifax. "I've revised our questions for interviews you haven't yet conducted and generated a few follow-up questions for ones we've completed. Sent it to you a few minutes ago. Surprised you don't have it."

"Odd," Beth replied before grabbing her computer and checking her inbox. "I checked, and it wasn't here. Now, I have it."

"Network's been slow this morning. Nothing important, just part of doing business across a continent. Have your morning coffee, read my suggestions, make your changes, and get it back to me. Cheers."

Beth checked on Hannah, grabbed her coffee, and read Gwen's message. It was thorough, requiring few changes. She'd feed her toddler, make the changes, and relax. Life was unfolding as she hoped.

She had lingering worries about Reverend Terrence Goddard and other anti-climate change rabble-rousers. And the significance of Tony's meeting with Sir Gareth in a posh City of London gentleman's club remained unresolved. They were minor concerns, inevitable hiccups associated with running a controversial website. They'd deal with them if and when they reared their ugly heads.

A response to her latest editorial on ClimateChange&U was the most recent example. One John Springer claimed he spoke for Albertan Autonomy. He attacked her appeal for renewed effort to reduce carbon emissions, claiming Albertans had a God-given duty to exploit their hydrocarbon resources. The reference to God reminded Beth of Terrance Goddard's attacks, but Springer's arguments were economic, not religious. By five thirty when Tony arrived home, they'd received four more nasty posts from Albertan Autonomy.

"Do you know anything about it?" she asked before he removed his jacket.

"The Springer posts?" When Beth nodded, Tony continued. "I knew him when we were students at Western. He's a jerk, a pig-headed bully. He barks when some idiots in Albertan Autonomy poke a stick up his ass. They're no more worry than Goddard and his gang of idiots."

"Not so," Beth replied as Michael scampered into the room. "My producer called this afternoon, saying she was being pressured to pull my first segment on our environmental affairs show. It's like not even finished yet, and someone's pressuring the network bosses to pull it. That's gotta be serious."

Tony hoisted Michael onto his shoulders and headed for the kitchen. "What's everyone want for dinner?" he asked as he pulled a wine bottle from the fridge.

"Salmon," Michael squealed as he slithered off Tony's shoulders. "Mrs. Finlay gave us one when Mum picked me up. She says we can have it with pasta."

"It's been gutted, but still has its head and tail. Shouldn't be too much work," Beth said before getting back to her concerns with Albertan Autonomy. "They may not be large, but they must have influential friends."

"They're a fringe group of Libertarians. They may have supporters in Alberta but not in Ottawa or here in BC. If your producer has any g—, courage, she'll stare them down."

"Hope so, but businessmen with mysterious agendas like these guys and your Sir Gareth of Penarth worry me."

*****

Sir Gareth's motives also worried Tony. Unlike Beth, he didn't accuse Sir Gareth of pulling a massive con job, selling completely ineffective snake oil that solved nothing. The man's refusal to explain how he'd save the world from global warming undermined Tony's trust. But he wasn't ready to accuse Sir Gareth of pulling a fast one on the world for nefarious purposes.

He welcomed Sir Gareth's funding of Marc Lavoie's project proposal. Marc now had resources for a three-year-long project to investigate critical biological processes in a low pH ocean. The results would feed into Tony's work by providing data they could use to parameterize several important linkages.

Sir Gareth's claim they could control temperature without constraining carbon emissions was harder to accept. The only practical mechanism was carbon capture, something governments and industry always rejected. Did that suggest they had another process that would be more palatable? That may explain Gareth's interest in ClimateChange&U and its potential as an influencer of public opinion, but it wouldn't explain his interest in climate change science. And if they had so much political power, why didn't they apply it to carbon emissions?

And he said something more disconcerting. He suggested his industrial colleagues were committed because it would expand profits. How could a temporary temperature constraint expand profits? The business was too damn nebulous and ill-defined. He couldn't trust Sir Gareth of Penarth if he wouldn't be more forthcoming.

He was only seven weeks into his first term as a professor and busy learning how to handle his teaching assignment. He'd reviewed Marc's project proposal and purchased equipment he'd need for his research lab. He devoted leftover minutes to papers summarizing his graduate student and postdoctoral research. Integration of impacts of warming on circulation and acidity on primary productivity drove those efforts.

At home, family and ClimateChange&U swallowed the snippets of free time he found. Improving the energy efficiency of their house became a sidelight that allowed Tony to live the energy-saving life he'd been advocating for homeowners on their website. That left little time to dig into Sir Gareth's motives.

Wednesday, November eleventh, brought a welcome change of pace. The Green Party hosted a family-friendly Remembrance Day celebration at Brockton Point in Stanley Park. Beth felt she couldn't miss a major event focused on increasing interest in public action to reduce global warming.

They made it into a family outing. If it became boring for Michael, Tony could take him and Hannah to see the Brockton Point totem poles or the aquarium.

When they arrived half an hour before the scheduled start, the field was jam-packed. They came by bus, so they, unlike many participants, weren't struggling to find a parking space in an area with scattered parking. Beth approached the event organizers, looking for comments she could use on the website. Tony searched for ways to distract Michael and Hannah.

Michael noticed a face-painting booth. He dragged Tony in that direction. Soon Hannah had little red hearts painted on her cheeks, and Michael waited for his turn. The trouble erupted as a teenage girl finished painting an elaborate scene of rocket ships, planets, and stars on Michael's face. Young gladiators' hooting and hollering in an area roped off for novelty races didn't drown out the angry confrontations beyond them.

Tony, with Hannah in her stroller and Michael firmly in hand, rushed toward protestors disrupting a previously peaceful meeting. They met Beth striding toward them near the finish line for the sack races.

"Strange," she said after pausing to catch her breath. "Not opponents of climate change action trying to disrupt, but more militant advocates pushing for strident action."

"And doing it rather aggressively," Tony added as he gazed toward demonstrators clashing at the edge of a temporary grandstand with event organizers conducting a Townhall-like meeting.

"I must return to take notes for my next editorial. I'll take the kids for a few minutes if you could sneak closer and snap a few photos. Then I'll join the fray."

Tony hesitated, worried about exposing their kids to a dangerous situation. "Really? You sure?"

"These are climate activists, not deniers, and we're bystanders. We'll be safe, and I may learn something important."

She turned, grabbed Hannah's stroller, and strode to the grandstand before Tony could comment. Michael scampered after her. Tony pulled out his cell phone and edged closer to the melee. He wondered what she hoped to learn as he photographed the angry participants. After recording a minute-long video of a particularly vehement shouting match, he retreated to the chairs where Beth waited.

Later, on the bus back to their West Point Grey home, Beth voiced her concerns. "Odd, don't you think? Environmental activists who should be supporters, disrupting a Green Party event. I mean, it's like picking a fight with your friend. Why would they do it?"

Tony shook his head as he watched Hannah sleeping cradled in his arms. "Must be people frustrated with the slow pace of progress. They probably consider the Green Party as sympathetic to their cause but ineffective."

"Don't know. I haven't seen this before. And why aren't they attacking our traditional governing parties? Fighting with the Greens can't be helpful."

"Frustration," Tony repeated. "Frustration's a powerful motivator, and it won't always manifest itself in the most appropriate ways."

More than frustration, Tony thought as they strolled home from the bus stop. Something's changed, something he'd missed while he focused on his first months as a university professor. He'd detected no increase in proactive involvement from ClimateChange&U's faithful adherents. But citizen anger in the greater community had spiked. Was the public finally rebelling against the government's refusal to address climate change problems?

Chapter Twenty-Five

Wednesday, February 24, 2027

On a bleak late winter morning five months after Tony began working as an oceanography professor, Achara Zhu swept into his University of British Columbia office. Global temperatures may have been increasing for decades, but Vancouver winters were as foggy and drizzly as they'd ever been. Snow was rare, but the winter rains seldom stopped.

"I'm here," she announced before Tony lifted his gaze from his computer screen. "When do we start?"

He stared at the young woman's bright smile and black hair in a pageboy cut like so many of the university's oriental students. Her command of English and take-charge attitude didn't fit the stereotype.

Ms. Zhu had submitted a late application for admission to the Earth, Ocean, and Atmospheric Sciences graduate student program, and expressed an interest in Tony's acid ocean work. She said the American government's refusal to extend her family's US residency permit destroyed her opportunity to study at the Scripps Institute of Oceanography. UBC was her top non-American choice.

Tony hired her as a research assistant until classes began in September. Until now, their communication had been by email. He was expecting her arrival on March first and unprepared for the whirlwind that invaded his office five days early.

He stepped from behind his desk. "When you have the department office's paperwork completed."

"Done."

"Then, we should start. I'll show you the lab and your office. I've left two texts with relevant chapters marked and an outline of the project I'd like you to tackle. We can discuss it once you're settled."

On the way back to his office after getting Achara settled, Tony visited the department office to confirm she'd completed the formalities. She would be the first person working in his laboratory, and in September, his first graduate student. Messed-up paperwork would generate a bad impression.

Her arrival brought the good and the bad of Tony's time at the University of Victoria into focus. Positive features were easily identified. Three papers from one year's work strengthened his CV and helped secure his tenure track position at UBC. He'd also established collaborations with colleagues in ocean circulation and biochemical modelling. An old colleague, Marc Lavoie, provided new insights into plankton dynamics in a low pH environment.

Negative features were harder to quantify. The demise of Algal Energy, a company he'd devoted considerable time to during his years in Halifax, was a major disappointment. The sale of their start-up company to an energy conglomerate interested in biofuels netted Tony a substantial financial windfall. But it removed one driver of his interest in ocean acidification.

He'd also failed to integrate his interest in oceanic acidity with the work he did at the University of Victoria. Reinvigorating that interest would become job one as he launched his career as a university professor. His renewed collaboration with Marc on nutrient resupply to low pH phytoplankton blooms, and the experiments he had planned for Achara should help light a fire under that effort.

Achara waited outside his office when Tony returned after lunch. She strode in and set her laptop on the edge of his desk.

She fidgeted while he removed his raincoat and settled into his office chair. "During my four years as an undergraduate at Berkley, I learned a lot about US society and their attitude toward climate change."

He suspected something personal precipitated her hasty departure from the United States. *Perhaps, I underestimated her.* "First-hand knowledge is always valuable, but everyone's aware of their repudiation of the Paris Accord and other international efforts to reduce CO_2 emissions."

"Yes, yes, I knew about the Paris Accord and Canada's efforts to expand exports of heavy oil to Asia before my family moved from Thailand to the US. It took living there to realize the extent to which the American public, their governments, and industrial leaders cherish the idea the climate change fight is not their fight. They resigned the accord, but never joined the battle."

"But you're convinced we need to multiply our efforts in the battle against climate change."

She jumped from her chair and pointed at a graph Tony had tacked to his corkboard. "And my battleground will be the ecological response to increasing acidity."

He was pleased to hear it but wanted to test her resolve. "Not the ecological impacts of major changes in the thermohaline circulation. We know those changes will occur decades before pH is reduced to critical thresholds."

"Deep-water formation may shrink to inadequate levels to maintain the current circulation patterns by when, 2050?"

"Our best estimates are sooner, closer to 2045."

"Okay. And burgeoning growth from a low pH ocean may begin as early as 2080."

"I'd say closer to 2100, but for the sake of argument, let's say 2080."

Achara returned to her chair. "The cessation of deep-water formation won't dampen American interest in the expansion of coal and oil. The thermohaline circulation will slow, but unless we see a rapid change in circulation patterns, the Americans will continue burning coal. China and India will do the same."

"And before we get to a critical point for pH-related effects, it will be important to understand them better than we do now."

She turned her laptop and showed Tony her graph of atmospheric carbon dioxide concentrations versus date. "The blue line is the projection most experts use. It shows a gradual reduction in the rate of increase as conservation measures expand. But the US, China, and India, by far the three largest emitters, are increasing their emissions, not decreasing them. Projections accounting for their increased emissions produce the red line on my graph. We now hit the critical pH level in 2060, maybe even 2055."

Tony studied her graph for a few minutes. "I've also seen projections that assume the emissions for the big three will continue at present rates or even accelerating rates. The uncertainty in these predictions is huge, but let's go with your estimate."

"2055?"

Tony nodded. He was far from convinced they'd see impacts by 2055, but, if an early onset inspired her... "Our question becomes what oceanic conditions favour the generation of massive plankton blooms as acidity approaches the value we may see by 2055."

"Tropical waters with high nutrient inputs?"

Tony recalled his discussions with Marc Lavoie. "Or upwelling waters that also bring in nutrients."

After an hour discussing experiments to investigate the relationship between plankton growth and pH under various environmental conditions, Achara left to organize her accommodations for the coming months. Tony began assembling the laboratory equipment they would need.

At five, he smiled as he stepped into the incessant drizzle of a Vancouver winter and headed home. He was back in the game.

Four-year-old Michael greeted Tony inside their front door. "New school is fun. I played with two kids named Michael." He paused, a puzzled look on his face. "One's a girl."

Beth appeared in the kitchen doorway. Nineteen-month-old Hannah toddled out from behind her. "No, Michael, her name's Michela, not Michael."

Tony reached down to pick up Hannah. He hadn't seen her for ten hours, so he couldn't resist a little pampering.

He turned to Beth, pleased to see she remained as upbeat as she was the day they arrived. "And your day? Good as Mike's?"

She sighed as she turned with her arms outstretched. "Had our house for six months, and I still can't believe it. It's a dream come true, and it never ends."

"Like the Energizer Bunny."

She passed a thoroughly loved pink bunny to Hannah. "You generate the craziest outdated analogies, but yeah, like the Energizer Bunny, the good times keep going and going."

"Starting with our house."

She nodded before heading back to the kitchen. "Still can't believe how lucky we were to have money for a substantial down payment in this crazy real estate market."

He followed as Hannah banged her pink bunny on his head. "And your role in online journalism?"

"Too cutthroat. Planning to dump it once my slot conducting interviews on the national news network's environmental program gets established. Higher profile. It's already paying better, and I've had two opportunities to produce a larger segment."

"All's reasonably good."

Beth picked up the wine glass she'd left on the kitchen table. "I'd be happier if ClimateChange&U made more progress with the fence-sitters."

Tony hesitated. He was more concerned with environmental advocates who were getting more aggressive. "With the people who know in their hearts we must try harder to address the climate change issue, but won't commit?"

"They're important. Experts argue about why they don't buy in, but that hardly matters. The bottom line is we need them on board before we can convince governments to act."

"And the federal government's attitude?"

"Don't get me going. It's hopeless. Liberals and Conservatives are stuck in a climate change rut. The Liberals talk a more progressive line, but neither tries to bridge the widening gap between climate change goals and national accomplishments."

He glanced at his watch, keen to avoid a problem they'd beaten their heads against many times. "It's getting late. Better get dinner started."

Tony placed Hannah in her highchair. "What's on for tonight?"

"S'ghetti," Michael replied without hesitation. He thought every dinner should feature noodles, and spaghetti was his favourite.

"Ghetti," Hannah echoed, banging her spoon on her table.

Tony looked at his watch, frowning, before he opened the freezer door. "Okay, guys, you're in luck. We have left-over sauce."

He put the sauce in the microwave and started boiling the noodle water before adding soft bits of fruit to a bowl for Hannah.

"What about me?" Michael asked.

"What would you like?"

"Crackers and cheese."

"I'll slice some cheese. You know where to find the crackers. Six, okay?"

"Six?"

"Yeah, six. You can count to six, can't you?"

"I can count to a million."

"Well, stop at six. And one for Hannah."

After dinner, the rain stopped, and they walked to a lighted play area at the nearby community centre. Tony gazed at the McMonster houses and thought about the much smaller one they'd purchased.

Their two floors had three bedrooms, two baths, kitchen, dining room, living room, and a tiny alcove Tony planned to commandeer as a study.

Its location was ideal, close to Michael's school and shops for all their everyday needs. It sat on top of the Point Grey embankment, providing Tony with a short and relatively flat bicycle ride to the university.

They hadn't owned a car since shortly after Michael was born, and Tony couldn't foresee needing one soon. One of Vancouver's three car-share services would suffice for their occasional needs.

At the playground, Michael rushed to the monkey bars and other big kids' stuff while Beth strapped Hannah into a toddler swing.

"House is great," Tony said as he began pushing Hannah. "I'm super happy with having a house, but I'm struggling with the rest of our transition to suburban life."

"Like what's wrong."

"I'm disappointed with my time at U Vic, no breakthrough that makes my mark in the GCM world."

"Three papers, and you said they're solid."

"Solid, but pedestrian. I hoped for something earth-shattering, but it was too big an ambition. Lack of life from Algal Energy is another negative."

Beth retreated to a bench, a puzzled expression on her face. "But it's not your company anymore, or Clive's."

"Hoped I'd see something that showed they were building on the work we did."

"Less than six months. Isn't that a short time for a big announcement?"

"No papers at conferences by Yusuf or anyone else. I have this awful feeling the company's dead and buried, and no one's lamenting its passing."

"Jesus, you are getting negative."

"Blame it on the deteriorating climate. Every year we see more wildfires, more flooding, more God knows what else. Humanity is incapable of dealing with their root cause."

Beth shook her head as she took over pushing Hannah. "Story we've struggled with for years. You must have some good news, some reason for optimism?"

Tony smiled. She was right. He must escape from his tendency to slip into negative thoughts about the fight for climate change. The whirlwind that descended on his office that morning would have brought a smile to the most curmudgeonly countenance. She banished thoughts of Terrence Goddard and other climate change deniers, the Cuban project and its misuse of Algal Energy's technology, Algal Energy's demise, and his limited success at U Vic. Only the perfidy of governments withstood the force of Achara's enthusiasm. "You'll like this. Achara Zhu, my first student, appeared today."

"Thought you expected her next week?"

"Looking for an apartment. She dropped by to say hello, and she's so enthusiastic I have high hopes for a successful new focus on the old plankton productivity at low pH problem."

Beth laughed as she lowered Hannah to the ground. "Well, that's something. One piece of positive news to brighten Eeyore's gloomy outlook."

Chapter Twenty-Six

Thursday, March 25, 2027

Tony sat in his office clearing up loose ends before the Easter Weekend. A comment Achara made a month earlier popped into his head. On her first day at UBC, she'd said, "cessation of deep-water formation won't dampen American commitment to the expansion of coal and oil consumption."

He'd discounted her comment as the jaundiced view of someone mistreated by the US administration. The absence of deep-water formation would reduce the transport of water and heat from tropical to polar regions. A diminished Gulf Stream would be its most noticeable impact. Reductions in other surface currents were also important. How could the US government ignore environmental changes of that magnitude?

Discussions with Marc highlighted another impact. A more sluggish surface circulation would alter the dynamic at shelf edges around the globe. Surface currents often generated strong, along-shore flows. In a stagnant ocean, a more wind-driven circulation could generate more cross-shelf flows. They would produce upwelling of offshore water and a dynamic that trapped more carbon on the continental shelves.

In the current ocean, upwelling areas weren't very extensive, but shifting wind patterns could generate more. Add the broad shallow shelves Achara focuses on, and they'll form a massive area with enhanced production. Would these changes impact future trends?

He whipped off an email to Marc and strode to Achara's office. His latest thoughts originated from a comment she'd made. He couldn't ignore her input.

"You have a gargantuan problem," Achara said after Tony finished his explanation.

"What? A logic problem with my explanation?"

"A major political problem. The cowboys running the United States will use your ideas to justify their do-nothing approach to global warming. They'll see natural stabilization of temperatures and exclaim, 'all's well, full speed ahead'."

Tony stared with furrowed brows as he tried to decipher her thinking. She was reiterating the idea she expressed several months earlier. But was she succumbing to her emotions? "I'm not proposing temperature stabilization. Decreasing temperatures, possibly rapidly decreasing ones, will be inevitable."

Achara shook her head. "They'll say, 'Yankee ingenuity and the profit potential will inspire America's technological prowess.' They'll boast about solutions that stabilize carbon dioxide levels."

"What evidence do you have?"

She smiled. "None. Based entirely on conjecture—"

"Fueled by the way they treated your family?"

"And observations of my housemates, two American expatriates fleeing mistreatment." She thumped her fist on her desk, a comical gesture for such a tiny person. "I haven't misrepresented the situation."

"But a technical fix won't be possible."

"That won't stop them. They'll continue on their present course, confident they'll develop the cure when they need it."

They spent several minutes discussing where Tony's new ideas fit into Achara's thoughts about her graduate student project. They resolved nothing, but Tony returned to his office with a less confident stride. She'd pointed out some political implications he hadn't considered. Her concerns were important, and he couldn't ignore them.

In his office, Tony began turning his conceptual ideas into computer code. He wouldn't be ready to publish anything for months—months when he'd develop the models and collect the data he needed to constrain them. For now, he could focus on the science. He'd worry about how his results may be misused by politicians when he had something to report.

Tony saw the notice taped to the oceanography department's main door when he stepped outside on his way home. It wasn't there at 1 p.m., and its presence would annoy their department head. Their autocratic British dean with a military air wouldn't tolerate such an infringement of his mania for neatness. He always demanded everything remains in its proper place.

The makeshift notice described a question-and-answer session hosted by campus groups advocating for quicker action on climate change. It reminded Tony of the rabble-rousers' infiltration of a Green Party rally in Stanley Park five months earlier. He couldn't resist stopping to hear their pitch.

Tony locked his bike to a rack outside the Student Union Building and hustled inside. He recognized three of four students sitting at a table in the centre of the SUB conversation pit. The first led the Green Party's campus organization, and the others were active in Vancouver's two largest environmental groups.

The stranger in their midst appeared to be in charge. She focused on ClimateChange&U's advocacy for individual action. "Their idea of leading by example, hoping to convince governments to take up the challenge is not working."

"They've done good work," she insisted, something that encouraged Tony to stand a little straighter. "But it's time for more forceful action. Not violence," she added, nodding to her colleagues, "but a stronger voice that refuses to let governments ignore us."

The Green Party's campus leader stood waving a sheet that could have been a petition. "That's why we're here today organizing a recruitment drive. Our so-called civic leaders, a bunch of old fogeys, muddle along, gambling on our future." He spread his arms, encompassing the crowd. "Our future! We'll be stuck living in a degraded environment after they're long gone. If that's not the future you imagine, join us in our nonviolent effort to grab the climate change beast by the throat and throttle it."

He invited questions from the floor. When the conversation dragged on with little sign of new ideas, Tony slid out. He resumed his homeward journey. The leaders of this afternoon's recruitment drive appeared to have willing adherents. Tony doubted they'd form a formidable army in the battle to stop global warming. And how could they grab the climate change beast by the throat and throttle it in a nonviolent way?

*****

As Tony entered the Student Union, Beth stepped from her television network's Vancouver studios. A technical problem delayed their taping session, but she was pleased with her third feature segment in the weekly environment program on national TV. She hailed a cab, something she wouldn't normally contemplate, and hurried home to relieve Mrs. Findlay of responsibility for her two children.

They arrived home at the same moment—Tony by bicycle from the university and Beth pushing Hannah in her stroller while Michael skipped alongside. Michael's demeanor showed how much he enjoyed the time he spent at Mrs. Finlay's.

"Taping took longer than expected?" Tony said as he rolled his bike into its storage place under their front steps.

"Yeah, we had to redo an interview. Annoying, but everything's okay now. And I realized something while they patched up communication with our Saskatoon studio."

While he prepared their evening meal, Tony mentioned the thought Beth left hanging. "And your eureka moment?"

"I've compiled comments to my various posts on ClimateChange&U. You'll say nothing rigorous, but I'm like seeing changes."

"What sort of changes?"

"Less bitching from climate-change deniers. When I started posting opinion pieces, they dominated the responses. Now, they're a trivial annoyance. That's good. Probably not important, but it makes reading my mail more enjoyable. The fence-sitters are more interesting."

Tony shook his head. "You've been too focused on people who seem receptive to our cause but unwilling to join us for ages."

"Give me a break. They're important. The demographic we must reach, and something's working. Hits and comments are up. Many are from my fence-sitters saying they're ready to commit."

"Interesting. The numbers for our major focus, people who document their energy usage and report on changes, are flat. We're losing about as many correspondents as we gain. If overall numbers are up, it must be your editorials."

Beth fetched Hannah from the living room where she was annoying Michael and carried her into the kitchen. "I don't think it's changes we're making. The change is in the public's attitudes. They're finally turning on the deniers and losing patience with government inaction."

"Fits with something I observed this afternoon. I happened upon a meeting on climate change organized by the Green Party's campus rep and several activists from environmental groups. They advocated a more aggressive approach to generating government action."

"Move on from our lead by example approach on ClimateChange&U to direct political advocacy? Or are they talking about violent confrontations?"

"More strident political advocacy. I could get you the names of the leaders for a future editorial."

"Yeah, please. Should we move things up a notch on our site?"

Tony turned his attention back to dinner preparation, but his thoughts lingered over the violence question. The meeting organizers claimed they favoured a peaceful approach, but they were advocating confrontation. Peaceful confrontations could easily turn violent.

Two and a half months later, Beth arrived home from the television studio at three. She unlocked the front door after collecting Michael and Hannah from Mrs. Findlay's. Inside, Michael skipped to his scattered Legos. Hannah plopped onto the floor by a stacking toy. Beth turned on the kettle and sat back, trying to fathom the meaning of the impromptu strategy meeting.

Environmental leaders had announced weekend rallies in Ottawa and all ten provincial capitals. They claimed the gatherings would jump start a major push toward achieving Canada's Paris Accord commitments.

Everyone understood the problem. In 2015, Canada committed to reducing carbon emission by thirty percent. The 2030 deadline was less than four years away, and the country was falling far short. The organizers vowed to shake up the government. They promised exciting solutions that would grab the public's attention.

Everyone expected the networks to deploy news reporters, but why did Beth's producer insist she join the effort? She wasn't an accredited reporter and had no training for field interviews. She'd be a fish out of water and likely to get them into trouble.

Chapter Twenty-Seven

Friday, June 11, 2027

The vanload of reporters and camera operators arrived in Victoria at noon. At 1 p.m., Beth interviewed Karen Fairweather, Member of the British Columbia Legislative Assembly and the new leader of the provincial Green Party in a local television studio.

"Unless we have a drastic policy change, Canada will fall twenty-five to fifty percent short of achieving her Paris Climate Accord commitments," Ms. Fairweather said after Beth asked for her take on the situation. "We're seeing environmentalists' final effort to force the government to buckle down and achieve the goals they committed to."

"And your party supports this effort."

Ms. Fairweather sighed. "We have many common goals. We will agitate for change from within the legislature. They will push from the outside."

"The provincial government will presumably respond by saying British Columbians have done their part. The premier will point to projections showing BC's on target to meet our thirty percent reduction."

"Unwise to put words in the Premier's mouth, but he should make that point. We'll question his numbers showing BC remains five to ten percent short of achieving our targets. BC and British Columbians have done better than others across the country. But bragging about our success accomplishes nothing. The country has work to do. We must pull together and get the job done."

"If the Greens were in charge, what would you change?"

"Federally or Provincially?"

"Provincially."

"We'd make minor policy and regulatory changes to ensure we exceeded our Provincial targets by five to ten percent, rather than falling short by a similar amount. And we'd push the Federal Government and the other provinces to make a stronger effort. Our government shouldn't sit back and rest on its laurels."

After the interview, Beth sighed as she turned to her cameraman. "Accomplished what we needed. Now comes the hard part. Soliciting comments from busy field operatives with too many responsibilities."

By seven, she was exhausted. She'd learned a few tricks about grabbing a quick comment from rally organizers as they rushed past. She'd recorded a few quotes she hoped they could use. A meagre return for an afternoon's hard work.

After a quick meal, Beth returned to the fray. She found herself outside a police cordon with no access to the protesters' Beacon Hill Park campsites. As she watched the regular reporters struggle to get comments from the RCMP field commanders, she realized they may be observing a pivotal development in the weekend's activities. And she had a distinct advantage. She recognized the officer in charge, and he owed her a favour.

He'd led the Nova Scotia detachment thirty months earlier when Reverend Terrence Goddard broke through police security during a press conference at the Halifax Court House. Goddard attacked her with a paintball gun. It may have been a minor assault, but the high-profile nature of the event turned it into a public relations disaster for the police.

She fell into step beside Superintendent Berkshire as he strode away from a meeting with his field officers.

"I remember you, Ms. Manville, from that ridiculous incident in Halifax, and I thank you for your generosity. You could have caused the Force a lot of embarrassment." He paused, glancing at her television network ID. "Now, I suppose, you're looking for payback."

"I'm not reporting for the nightly news. I'm a correspondent on a weekly environmental affairs program looking for background information." Beth paused for a breath. Berkshire was walking so quickly she had to run to keep up. "Barricading rally participants inside the park seems like an unnecessarily aggressive move."

He stopped and gesticulated with his index finger raised. "We're not trying to barricade anyone inside the park. We're trying to keep bystanders like you outside while illegal campers inside the park disperse."

"Why not wait until tomorrow afternoon when they'd disperse without intervention? Looks like you're trying to generate a confrontation."

"A confrontation is your suggestion, not mine. Now, I have work to do. Good evening."

He turned and strode away at a pace Beth couldn't maintain. She wondered if she could have handled the conversation better but felt he'd answered her implied question. Someone higher in the chain of command ordered Superintendent Berkshire to evict the campers, something he was reluctant to do. And her cameraman had captured his rather aggressive response to her questions.

She bought a coffee in a nearby diner and typed her notes. At eleven, when Superintendent Berkshire's stormtroopers moved in, Beth was working on her third coffee. While her cameraman filmed the action, she solicited reactions from bystanders. At midnight, she retreated to her hotel room.

She was pleased with her evening's work. She'd assessed the situation correctly and collected the input her bosses demanded. She also had fodder for an editorial she could post on ClimateChange&U.

*****

Saturday morning, Tony got the kids up early. After breakfast, he left them in Mrs. Findlay's capable hands and hopped a cab to the Vancouver airport. At eleven, he found Beth in the restaurant next to her Victoria hotel, enjoying the last of a late-morning breakfast. He joined her for coffee, and she described her understanding of the previous night's events.

"The RCMP arrived before nine and set up roadblocks around Beacon Hill Park. I couldn't see clearly from my vantage point, but they seemed to be preventing entry. Around eleven, they moved in *en masse* and evicted everyone—men, women, kids— tore down their tents and ushered them out."

Tony stared across the street as he tried to conjure up the appropriate images. "Around midnight? Where did they go?"

"No idea. The cops escorted the campers to the park boundary but didn't seem intent on arresting people, and witnesses said physical force was minimal. The park's large, and many snuck back in. It became a farce."

"Sounds pointless and from what I read online, similar to responses in Ottawa and other provincial capitals. I wonder who made this strange decision."

Beth shook her head. "A senior boss at national headquarters? It wasn't the local onsite commander. And I have a theory for why."

Tony glanced up from his coffee, pleased to see Beth engaged in her problem and not paranoid about the possibility of confrontations. "Okay, let's have it."

"The police and presumably, their political masters wanted a confrontation to divert attention from the real reason for today's rally."

"And the protesters anticipated this and took a Gandhian nonviolent approach."

Beth nodded. "And that means something else. The police officers on the scene weren't pushing escalation. If they'd been intent on violence, they could have generated it."

Tony swallowed the last of his coffee and returned his mug to the table. "What's our agenda for this afternoon?"

"No active role. Watch and listen. I want to assess the crowd's mood and watch their reaction to unfolding events. Last night's experience suggests neither side wants a confrontation, but you never know."

"The Legislative Assembly?"

Beth nodded. "The lawn facing the parliament building. The speakers will occupy the steps leading to the portico, and they expect a spokesperson, hopefully, the Premier, will appear to address their concerns."

"Then we should find ourselves a vantage point and prepare to take notes."

The rally began on schedule at 2 p.m. They had microphones on a concrete pathway at the top of six broad stairs that separated the lawn from the Legislative Assembly's facade. Loudspeakers were mounted on pickups parked on the path.

The first three speakers approached the microphones, identified themselves, and launched into their spiels. They decried the police action to dislodge protesters camping in Beacon Hill Park. They called it an unnecessary attack designed to provoke retaliation from the campers. Resistance, they each gleefully announced, that didn't happen. Their words varied, but the message remained consistent.

They went on to describe the country's woeful efforts to meet its Paris Climate Accord commitments. They all ended by demanding concrete action to reach those goals by 2030.

The organizer controlling the flow of speakers paused between speakers three and four. He glanced at the Assembly portico where they'd positioned another microphone.

"See what they're doing," Beth said to Tony. "They're repeating the message the Green Party leader provided when I interviewed her yesterday. Waiting for the government to send a spokesperson to address this crowd."

"Ms. Fairweather predicted last night's fiasco?"

"Not in so many words, but the rest is straight from her script. They're waiting for the Premier or the Environment Minister to address the crowd, and if no one comes forward, they'll insist on a response before the crowd disperses."

Six more speakers addressed the crowd. The words changed as each attempted to engage the audience, but the message was unaltered. Finally, after the tenth speaker, the Legislative Assembly's main door opened. The environment minister, accompanied by an assistant and two security guards, emerged.

The rally organizer welcomed him, and the minister approached the portico mike. He began with platitudes, as politicians always do, before delivering his message.

"British Columbians and the British Columbia government deserve praise, not condemnation. We have reduced carbon emissions over the past decades and are on target to achieve the thirty percent reduction the federal government pledged us to by 2030. We welcome you here today and applaud the message you're transmitting. Take your message to the federal government and the provinces that are lagging. We've heard your message. We're there, we've done our part. Let's see that the rest of the country steps forward—"

He stopped in mid-sentence and stared to his right as commandos in camouflage gear stormed onto the portico. They prevented the minister from retreating inside, and one grabbed the microphone.

"We've heard useless bullshit from ministers and limp-wristed environmentalists afraid to back up their talk with actions. Their time is over. Help us put teeth in the talk and force the government to finally bite the bullet." He paused for a breath, and when he resumed his rant, the mike was dead. Someone inside the legislature had shut it off.

Seconds later, security forces with drawn weapons surrounded the militants and commandeered the rally organizers' microphones. They appealed for calm, but their efforts to quiet the crowd were pointless. Spectators were scattering in all directions.

Beth refused to abandon her post. She retreated a few metres and sheltered behind the Knowledge Totem, where she started dictating notes into her phone. Tony realized she was recording her impressions of the unfolding events and ventured forth to capture whatever he could with his cell phone camera. He recorded anything that caught his attention, hoping for something useful.

When Tony returned, Beth was leaning against the totem pole's concrete base, staring at the empty lawn. "Makes no sense," she said. "Unarmed vigilantes stormed the portico and intimidated the environment minister. Armed security forces appeared *en masse*, displaced the rally organizers, and hustled everyone away. What was their intent?"

"Whose?" Tony asked. "The vigilantes in camouflage gear, or the security forces?"

"Either, I guess. The commandos were unarmed, and they must have known the microphone they commandeered would be silenced. The security forces appeared more interested in controlling the organizers' microphones than in rescuing the environment minister."

"Like they knew he wasn't in danger."

"So, answer my question. Who's like pulling the strings, and what's their purpose?"

162

Tony couldn't answer Beth's rhetorical questions. They related to politics and the psychology of groups, not science. But one thing was clear. Interest in climate change was increasing. Time to put his nose to the grindstone and build on efforts to reinvigorate his long-time interest in ocean acidification. Recent developments convinced him it was the critical science question. One huge question remained. How could they convince society to take it seriously? The shenanigans they'd just witnessed suggested the time for that effort had arrived.

Chapter Twenty-Eight

Tuesday, July 20, 2027

Six weeks after the fiasco in Victoria, Beth tapped on Tony's open office door. "Should we invite Achara somewhere for afternoon coffee?"

He snorted without taking his eyes off his computer screen. In the five months since Achara arrived, he'd learned how determined she could be. "Dragging her away when something's working well is tougher than Chinese calculus. If you want coffee, I'm afraid it's you and me, babe."

"Tony, you must be more politically sensitive."

"What? Oh, Chinese calculus. Something I learned from Achara. She says it all the time."

"Does that mean she's finding your project difficult?"

Tony shook his head as he rose from his desk. "She uses it sarcastically or for trivial things, like getting a stuck reagent lid to open."

"Aren't you worried you'll be called before a university tribunal investigating inappropriate behaviour?"

"Nope, and, you know, I'm sure she'd laugh at your suggestion. She's been making solid progress for several months, and last Thursday, she unearthed something interesting. Our latest experiments suggested certain shallow tropical waters are candidates for early occurrences of high productivity."

"Unusually low pH, like now?"

"Under certain circumstances. Last week, she got a lead on field data that could confirm our prediction. She's chasing it down."

Beth turned after stepping into the bright summer sunshine. "Where to?"

"Starbucks at the bookstore or quieter places on University Boulevard."

"One of the quieter ones. Something weird's happening, and we must discuss it."

During their ten-minute walk to the café, Tony's mind wandered to Achara's latest reports of plankton activity in the Gulf of Thailand. Beth brought him back to her current reality.

"Like Cuppa Java," Beth said when he placed two coffee mugs on the window table she chose.

It wasn't. Cuppa Java was in an old wooden house in South End Halifax with painted-wood panelling and small double-hung windows. It was rather dark. The Boulevard Café was chrome and white plastic with large windows. The activity, not the venue, must have reminded her of their early days when they often met for coffee.

Beth took one sip of her coffee and launched into her story. "We've had one of those shellfish poisoning incidents in Australia."

"They happen."

Her cup wobbled, almost toppling when she set it on the table. "It's a big one, but that's not the weird part. The weird part is the overreaction in the blogosphere. Bloggers describe interference by alien invaders, pods of whales manipulating the ecosystem structure, and even terrorists sinking fishing boats. Their reports attribute the activity to someone or something disgusted with governments' failure to act on climate change."

Pods of whales reminded Tony of their dolphin escort during their field work in Cuba. He used his phone to access a sensationalist news site. He scratched his chin as he scanned the headlines. "That's crazy. Why link a wintertime outbreak to climate change? And invoking aliens or super-intelligent whales must be a joke."

"May be crazy, but it didn't go viral with nothing to it."

"You say they're blaming government inaction? How are governments reacting?"

"Denial. Like your reaction, calling it a joke. Forget them. What should we do?"

"By we, you mean ClimateChange&U?"

Beth snorted, then looked at Tony. Her staring eyes expressed her disbelief. "Yeah, how should we react on the website? Is this like last month's rally in Victoria, another example of someone trying to wake everyone up? Should we target governments, reminding them what we've been telling them for years? Tell them they can't continue to ignore the issue. They must make meaningful positive progress before it's too late, but how do we convince them?"

Tony held up his hand as he scanned more of the web chatter. He couldn't see how these latest revelations related to unarmed commandos storming a climate change rally. They'd interrupted a peaceful rally, prevented a provincial cabinet minister from escaping the scene, and then meekly surrendered to police after the crowd fled. "Have you considered the motivation of the activists who stormed the Legislative Assembly?"

"I have, but I'm like guessing you've something in mind."

"On the surface, it seemed like a useless suicide mission, disrupting a valid protest rally and accomplishing nothing. Reminded me of Reverend Goddard's attack on you five years ago in Halifax. This time, in the days after they were whisked away, colleagues of the arrested commandos distributed their manifesto. It's a very detailed and quite insightful assessment of the situation. It includes options for the government and the consequences of various choices. They released it in five detailed segments that got them maximum press coverage and ended with a very credible threat saying the next time they would mean business."

"We know this. What's your point?"

"Goddard's attack was the action of an irrational zealot. This latest was the carefully planned work of a well-informed army of environmental vigilantes."

"You're suggesting a link between the fiasco in Victoria and what's currently happening around the world." She shook her head. "I don't buy it."

"It does seem farfetched. Hold your fire on the website for a few hours. I'll catch up on the current situation and factor in the manifesto from our Victoria vigilantes. Then we'll craft a killer message."

She stood and collected the carrier bags that accompanied anyone responsible for toddlers. "I'm expected at Mrs. Findlay's to pick up Hannah. You do your homework, and we'll revisit it after you get home."

Tony finished his coffee and returned to his office. Along the way, he wondered how public outrage would impact his renewed interest in ocean pH. Achara had been working in his lab for five months. Her energy and unbridled passion boosted his enthusiasm for his collaboration with Marc Lavoie. Would this latest spike in public interest spark something more broad-based?

Achara leaned against the wall outside Tony's university office, staring at the screen of her tablet. "What's going on? What does it mean for our work?"

He stood back as she scurried inside.

Tony followed, sat behind his desk, and activated his computer. He manipulated the screen for several minutes.

"We've been fighting to convince governments here and abroad to take real action on climate change for thirty-five years," he said after he finally looked up. "The public involvement has waxed and waned. One campaign led by a Swedish school girl starting a decade ago had massive public support. But it didn't stop the relentless march to higher temperatures and CO_2 concentrations."

Achara had her phone in her hand and was whipping through websites at a pace Tony could never maintain. "You suggesting it's hopeless?"

"Not hopeless. We're not seeing the beginning of the end of global warming. Even if we're at a significant watershed in the climate change battle, the results we've seen this summer show we need more research. We've much to learn about the biological system we're currently observing plus the ones we expect in future decades."

"What about this?" Achara said as she slapped a paper on his desk. "It's by Olivia Grange and suggests predation by salps are a key factor in controlling phytoplankton production in highly productive coastal waters. Sounds like the future conditions we're predicting."

"Salps," Tony replied. "I remember those little buggers. They destroyed one of our large aquarium experiments when I was at Dalhousie. After that occurrence, I made numerous attempts to integrate predation into my models and settled on a generalized approach. I didn't distinguish between salps, Calanus, and other zooplankton predators. Marc Lavoie and I collaborated on some experiments when he was working in Bermuda a year ago, but we didn't get very far." He paused with brows furrowed. "You should consider that work as you develop your research proposal."

"Should I pursue it now?

"You could, for the next month while I'm paying your salary. Then you'll be focused on courses during your first terms as a grad student. In nine months, we'll know if there's a substantive change in emissions, and you can finalize your research project."

"If it's a continuation of the current work, I could start immediately."

He smiled, reminded of his impatience to get a jump start on his PhD project six years earlier. "That wouldn't be accepted. But you could propose a study that recognizes developments and generates a new project building on this summer's efforts."

After Achara left, Tony tackled the articles and commentary on the Australian outbreak. He couldn't accept aliens or another animal species as the responsible agents. Was a disgruntled individual, a rogue state, or an unidentified environmental advocacy group turned ecoterrorists behind the threats? *Something about the story, something I can't pinpoint, says wake up everyone, this is serious. It must have a logical answer. We need to find it.*

The investigation brought his oceanographic career into focus. It began with a significant contribution to a fascinating discovery. He pursued it until he became jaded by the extended time until their discovery would have an impact. He hoped his postdoc and a fresh approach to climate change research would generate studies with a more immediate impact. Then, more recently, Marc Lavoie and then Achara brought him back to his original focus. *Would this become the catalyst that brings my refocused research, our long-standing efforts to promote scientific awareness with ClimateChange&U, and Beth's newer, more political endeavours into alignment?*

Chapter Twenty-Nine

Thursday, July 22, 2027

The first thing Tony heard on Thursday morning was the official announcement on his clock radio. The newscaster claimed the G20 countries had agreed on a plan to curb emissions. It would keep global temperatures below the two-degree threshold mandated by the Paris Accord.

He shut off the radio, hopped out of bed, and joined Beth, Michael, and Hannah in the kitchen. He had a busy day in front of him and no time to worry about the latest, probably meaningless, federal government pronouncements. And they were only promising to achieve the original two degree target, not the more aggressive one and a half degree target they usually boasted about.

After wheeling his bike into his office, Tony stopped by Achara's office to see what progress she was making on her salp question. Numbered pins with green tops protruded from a world map on her corkboard. She pushed number twenty-three into the waters off northern South America and turned toward Tony.

"I'll get to your salps, but this is more interesting. Twenty-three reports of field studies in tropical areas. They show conditions like the ones that generated elevated productivity in our experiments."

"All year round?"

She shook her head before approaching her desk. "I'll investigate the well-studied sites to see how persistent they are."

Tony sat on the corner and scratched his chin. "Experiments I conducted at Dalhousie suggested massive increases in primary productivity when pH reaches a critical value. Our experiments found more modest increases at the higher pHs we'll see sooner."

Achara spun around and pointed at her map. "And this shows extensive areas are currently experiencing those conditions. It's happening now!"

"Whoa, slow down. You have a suitable starting point for what should be a stellar PhD project. This fall, you must focus on your courses, but you could compile results that establish their extent in time and space—"

Achara hammered her forefinger onto her map like a woodpecker chasing grubs. "This shows how extensive."

"In space, I agree, but you have no indication for time."

"I can do that. I already said I would."

Tony grabbed a blank sheet from Achara's desk and drew a crude graph with productivity enhancement on Y and pH on X.

"We have three points. Current productivity at pH 8.15, very elevated productivity at pH 7.5 from my Dal experiments, and somewhat elevated productivity at 7.7 from our current experiments. You'll need to fill this in."

"Is it linear, a step function, or something else?"

"Those could become the core experiments for your thesis project."

In his office, Tony sat back with a fresh cup of coffee and considered the difficulty he faced trying to keep her from the lab. She wouldn't find her courses overly challenging or literature research sufficiently time-consuming. She'd find a way, with or without approval or funding, to begin collecting data.

He'd have his course to teach and experimental work from his renewed collaboration with Marc Lavoie to conduct. He imagined Achara worming her way into his experiments and using them as cover for the measurements she wanted to make. She'd be distorting departmental regulations, but he wasn't inclined to object. They'd deal with infringement of departmental policies if they materialized.

At four thirty, Achara appeared in Tony's office doorway with reports of three more studies showing low pH and enhanced productivity. She also had a rough calculation of the potential for enhanced growth.

"Slow down," he said. "We must understand how low pH blooms persist before we estimate the net removal of carbon." He described the biogeochemical mechanisms for transport of organic material to the sediment. They were well-known. Those for returning silicate and other nutrients to the water column while sequestering carbon were less obvious.

"And the role of predators," Achara added. "We can't forget Olivia Grange's work."

"True. But we should start with the recycling of silicate."

"Why"

"Imagine separate mechanisms for returning silicate and carbon to the water column. Silica dissolution is a chemical process, but release of carbon dioxide from decomposition of organic matter is biological. Fundamentally different processes. We need a mechanism that returns nutrients to the water but retains carbon in the sediments. Silicate could be the key."

"But the textbooks always focus on nitrogen when talking about nutrient limitation. We're talking about the burial of organic matter, not exoskeletons. Why would we focus on silicate?"

Tony shook his head. "We should focus on silica because diatoms dominate many low pH blooms *and* ammonia because phytoplankton always need nitrogen. And don't forget something Marc Lavoie impressed on me months ago. Oxygen is necessary for many of these processes, and its supply may become limited."

"Got it," she said as she raised her right fist. "Cleaving phosphate and ammonia from organic matter are not oxidative processes. Releasing nitrate, nitrite, and carbon dioxide are."

That evening, Tony and Beth sat in their living room trying to digest the fallout from the formal announcements from the G20 countries. They highlighted coordinated plans to limit global temperature increases to the two degree worst-case target identified by the Paris Accord. Electrical production from coal and heavy oil would be eliminated within tight timelines. The complete elimination of electrical power generated by burning fossil fuels would follow.

The targets for transportation and the heating of homes and other buildings were similar. Coal and heavy oil would be eliminated, and other fossil fuel uses restricted.

Reporters labelled it Global Climate Action Day. They stressed the impacts on everyday life.

Beth was nursing Hannah when the details were announced. Michael was building his latest tower. He'd become quite a proficient Lego engineer, adding more intricate superstructures with the smaller Legos to Duplo bases. While Tony kept an eye on Michael's construction project, he pondered the meaning of the GCAD announcements for climate change research and environmental activism.

"What are you thinking?" Beth asked.

"The sensationalist claims of alien influences and whales manipulating the environment haven't generated this unprecedented international collaboration."

"I agree. We can't accept those explanations, but how do we explain it?"

"Is it a ruse, a scheme to make everyone think they have climate change under control? A lot of talk about regulation but upward pressure on carbon emissions continues."

"You mean smoke and mirrors. A scheme to kill growing public interest in finally taking climate change seriously. But nothing changes, and our push for climate action's set back years."

"Exactly! Does the rosy picture give the big emitters free rein to burn their way to fame and fortune? We'll find ourselves charging down the road to environmental Armageddon more rapidly than ever."

Beth rose from her chair and waltzed around the room, lulling Hannah to sleep. She placed the sleeping tyke in her cradle and knelt to help Michael with his construction project. Minutes later, she looked up, catching Tony's attention. "That doesn't work. If the new policies aren't implemented, carbon dioxide emissions and temperature will increase. Protests like last month's fiasco in Victoria show us people aren't buying the politicians' assurances everything will be okay. The citizens will realize they've been had, and they'll revolt." She shook her head. "There must be something else."

"I can't accept protests like the one in Victoria finally got through the politicians' thick skulls and caused this change. Even if they had, they couldn't bring it together so quickly." He paused, his head tipped to one side. "You're right. We're missing something important. Something about the timing."

An hour later, Michael was in bed and Hannah sleeping in her playpen. Beth returned to their Global Climate Action Day discussion. "You making sense of this?"

"Some. Can we start with the politics?"

Beth's brow furrowed. "If you wish. But isn't this a science story? And we already talked about the standoff in Victoria."

"We must understand the context. Twenty countries coming together on a common front means a plan in the works for some time. We're not witnessing a hasty response to recent threats."

"The opposition to government inertia has been building for some time."

He shook his head. "We didn't see it on ClimateChange&U. It reminded me of something Achara said in our first conversation."

"When she explained why she wanted to work with you?"

"That conversation. She said the US government wouldn't reduce carbon emissions to avoid changes in the global circulation patterns."

"Stopping the Gulf Stream wouldn't worry them?"

"That was her response. A manageable problem. They'd deal with it, but another ice age—that's a different matter."

"Explains why she wanted to work with you, but I don't see where it's taking us."

Tony paused again, recalling the image of Sir Gareth in his London Gentlemen's club sipping single malt scotches. "To my crazy conversation with Sir Gareth of Penarth. He claimed a mysterious consortium of industrialists would control global temperatures without curbing carbon emissions. That was a year ago. Are we seeing the impact of that initiative?"

"It would be Machiavellian. A cure that accepts humanity's inability to address carbon emissions and replaces it with a focus on temperature."

"They could make pronouncements like today's plans to shift away from coal and heavy oil. Then point to success controlling temperature and ignore the fact they've done nothing to reduce emissions."

"It provides a crazy logic that explains this week's observations. It sends us on a collision course with the low pH ocean you've been studying for five years. But can it be happening? Can a bunch of charlatans sell snake oil and manipulate world governments?"

Tony shook his head. "They may not be snake-oil salesmen. If they have a mechanism for controlling temperature without stopping carbon emissions..."

"But how can they do that?"

"No idea, but if they can..."

Could this be where Global Climate Action Day was taking everyone? Was it his eureka moment? Were global warming, carbon dioxide emissions, and climate cooling ocean acidification coalescing into a unified threat that would focus humanity's attention on ocean acidification? The work of Achara, Marc, and others was already showing evidence of enhanced sequestering of carbon in some circumstances. His recent modelling efforts suggested they could become important in the next few decades. Were they already witnessing the first benign-looking flurries in a snowstorm of monumental proportions?

The good news—these changes may indicate a significant turning point for his research. The bad news—the political and economic ramifications were mindboggling. What would they mean for ClimateChange&U and Beth's evolving interest in politics and environmental advocacy? How could he contribute to her efforts to influence the bulls of change rampaging through the china shop?

Postlude

Spring, 2050

Shortly after dawn on my first anniversary in Pemberton Meadows, I placed my morning pick-me-up on the front porch railing outside Michael's farmhouse. We hadn't had coffee for months, and the concoctions we called tea were getting further from traditional orange pekoe. It was hot, and I had no right to complain. We'd survived a year in our refuge tucked between huge snow-capped mountains. We were among a minuscule lucky few.

Life was hard for everyone in Pemberton. We struggled with the lack of things we once considered necessities, and for most, the loss of loved ones. Medical doctors were among the most frustrated. They had the knowledge to cure various ailments but lacked the medicines and medical infrastructure for all but the simplest procedures. That frustration extended to almost everyone. We had knowledge we longed to apply, but lacked the technology we needed to apply it.

The sun had recently risen on a beautiful spring day. The fields and gardens were planted. Everyone anticipated a day of celebration after weeks of hard work. Michael, Hannah, and I would have a muted celebration because we'd learned nothing about Beth's fate. The chances of hearing anything positive were fading into nothingness.

Michael joined me. "You set for today's celebration of the official completion of spring planting. First time it's been in May."

I picked up my cup. "I was imagining you put the date forward to make it coincide with our arrival one year ago today." I shook my head, smiling. "Silly idea. Anyone can see it's another effect, this time a positive one, of global warming."

"You're keeping track of the trends?"

"Numbers aren't as solid as I'd like, but we collect enough data to make estimates. Last year, global warming reached five degrees above preindustrial levels."

"You have confidence in the results?" Michael asked.

I looked up, surprised by his understanding of the importance of the increased uncertainty. It was trivial compared to everyone's survival problems but important for someone trying to understand what happened. "Everything comes with more caveats. It limits our real understanding, but we'll manage."

When Michael went inside, I returned to my meditations.

My first issue was the nature of the explosions that destroyed cities and ignited wildfires. Early reports suggested they were nuclear, but this had not been confirmed. Our coastal monitoring stations had radiation detectors. They were very sensitive, but only measured counts, not the radiation energy. Bill Robertson detected increased radioactivity at his Haida Gwaii station. It was far less than we expected for the numbers of powerful nuclear explosions some observers suggested, but the excess radiation had to come from somewhere.

My second concern was the rapid increases in global temperatures, carbon dioxide concentrations, and sea level. Concentrations that had been increasing smoothly leapt higher. The explosions and subsequent fires must be the cause, but we hadn't included step functions in our models. Our capacity to generate new models was limited, so we couldn't test our ideas about these new trends. Could we avoid stooping to unsubstantiated speculation?

My third problem was the lack of radio transmissions from elsewhere in North America. We'd only heard anecdotal reports of stragglers crossing the American's northern boundary into western Canada. They presumably joined the remnant populations on the Canadian prairies and eastern British Columbia, but we had no communication from most of North America.

We'd established radio communication with less than two hundred thousand people. What happened to the other five hundred million North Americans? How many were struggling to survive without any means of communication? Or worse still, were they living in a post-Apocalyptic dystopia that prevented communication?

The influx into the Pemberton Valley of refugees like Alice, Hannah, and me increased the population to approximately ten thousand. Many were transients, intent on finding unoccupied land they could homestead. Others hoped to expand the cultivated area of our valley.

Most were refugees from Vancouver. Ones arriving from Alberta and points east brought news of conditions on the prairies. None of it was good. Wildfires spreading north from the US, burned everything, including towns and cities.

Most of Pemberton and much of the nearby Mount Currie survived the fires. No fires reached Pemberton Meadows or other farmed areas. But the airport, the nearby golf courses and numerous homes and businesses south of town were lost.

Power supplied by the electrical grid failed, and fuel shipped in from elsewhere was no longer available. Local electricians diverted power from two wind turbines into the valley's electrical wires. They added power from self-sufficient homesteads with excess wind or photoelectric capacity to the grid. Their overall generating capacity was five megawatts, not a lot for a town of ten thousand, but better than nothing.

They'd also been to the Rutherford Creek Power plant, a nearby run-of-the-river hydropower facility operated by the now-defunct Provincial power authority. It was non-functional but appeared relatively undamaged. If they got it operating, they'd have approximately sixty megawatts of electrical capacity. That would be enough to supply Pemberton's basic needs with plenty to spare.

Over the next few months, we saw more interesting developments, ones that suggested our corner of the world was settling into a slow recovery. Zeke Barlow's arrival on Michael's doorstep illustrated this positive trend. He'd joined the first group escorted along the new trail from Toba Inlet to the Pemberton Valley.

After the firefighters attempting to save Vancouver gave up the fight, Zeke and a friend sailed along the BC coast. They rescued people trapped by the ever-expanding fires and, in one case, survivors from an overloaded boat that sank. His description of the destruction augmented reports I received from Bill Robertson on Haida Gwaii. The entire BC coast from Vancouver to the Alaska border was a wasteland. Gibsons, Sechelt, Powell River, Prince Rupert, and dozens of small, mostly indigenous, settlements were destroyed. Vancouver Island was no better. Nothing survived along its entire eastern side.

"Bella Coola?" I asked when Zeke finished his description. "It's at the head of an inlet protected by the mountains that saved us. We thought it might be okay."

"So did we. We sailed the entire length of the Burke Channel. When we saw trees in the North Bentinck Arm, we were hopeful, but it wasn't to be. Fires from the interior engulfed Bella Coola. Same thing happened farther north. Fires spread from the interior toward Prince Rupert."

Zeke brought us information that helped me understand why we were so alone in our little world. Places like Bella Coola and Prince Rupert had been attacked from all sides. If the fires spreading north along the coast didn't get them, those spreading west from the continent's interior did.

In Pemberton, new industries were popping up everywhere. One example was the business of escorting visitors along the trail from Toba Inlet. Another was the machine shop Michael and his housebuilding partner established. Previously they'd purchased brackets and other metallic fittings they needed. Those mass market items were no longer available. Their shop and the village blacksmith would produce the metal parts they needed. Pemberton had a saw mill and several specialty woodworking shops that would supply their lumber. The sophistication and variety of their raw materials may be limited, but they'd manage.

The lack of products supplied from larger centres was a widespread problem. Michael's machine shop filled one need. Other resurrected cottage industries filled others.

The caravan that brought Zeke to Pemberton brought me an important package. Michael called it the first piece of international mail delivered in post-Apocalyptic Pemberton. It was sent to me by Dan Delacour, a student who started working in Dr. K's Dalhousie University lab about the time I graduated. In the fall of 2027, we began a collaboration that lasted until everything collapsed. He collected environmental data from the Northeast Atlantic through the twenty thirties. His efforts became part of the UN sanctioned climate monitoring program in 2045 and continued into 2049. Our sampling at Tofino and Haida Gwaii was part of that effort. Dan was also more knowledgeable than I on many aspects of our problem. When I added his data to our climate monitoring data for the west coast of Canada and melded our insights, I'd have material for a comprehensive picture of the evolving climate change saga.

Those observations and my description of events Beth and I experienced from 2022 to 2027 would become my gift to posterity. Dan promised to write a companion narrative for the period between 2027 and 2032. It was in the package I'd just received.

The End

Here is a preview of the first three chapters of *Houses of Cards*, the second novel in my Road to Environmental Armageddon trilogy. It takes up the story starting in the summer of 2027. Daniel Delacour joins the struggle to understand the impacts of climate change on the marine environment. He and Elena Llewellyn strive to make the world take human-induced climate change seriously.

The Road to Environmental Armageddon

Book Two

Houses of Cards

Alan Kemister

In July 2027, the announcement of a coordinated global commitment to stabilize global temperatures catches everyone by surprise. Dan Delacour and two fellow graduate students at Nova Scotia's Dalhousie University struggle to understand the meaning of the promises and the regulations imposed by national governments. Dan's romantic involvement with a mysterious woman masquerading as a fellow student complicates their efforts. She leads him into a world of intrigue where influential leaders of the world's largest enterprises manipulate the climate crisis for their benefit. Are they, as some participants insist, also devoted to saving the world from environmental Armageddon?

Prelude

Summer, 2051

Greetings, everyone. *I'm Professor Tony Atherton, a climate change scientist. I'm here to help you understand how humanity made such a mess of the simple task of controlling global warming. By 2000, we knew we must reduce our carbon dioxide emissions. The 2015 Paris Climate Accord recognized this need. It mandated large reductions for the major industrial nations. Those reductions would keep global temperatures in the year 2030 to well below two degrees above preindustrial levels.*

When this story begins in 2027, we'd made almost no progress. We faced a future with temperatures far more than two degrees above background. They would generate sea-level rise, droughts, floods, wildfires, and increasingly erratic weather. We were headed toward the chaos we would experience in 2049, and humanity seemed unable to do anything about it.

You shall see, if you choose to read on, that a solution for global warming was imposed on the world in the summer of 2027. It provided a pause in the march to Environmental Armageddon. By 2041, the supposed cure was spinning out of control.

Our civilized life finally came crashing to a halt in May 2049. We became subsistence farmers in a preindustrial world that relied on barter. By the summer of 2051, my daughter, Hannah, my granddaughter Alice, and I were refugees living in the Pemberton Valley. We arrived from Vancouver in 2049. Alice's father, Zeke Barlow, joined us in 2050.

My son Michael and his family had lived in Pemberton for several years. During our second summer, He and I built a house and a large garden devoted to fruits and vegetables for Hannah, Alice, and me.

Pemberton became a strange amalgam of modern town and pioneering village. We had modern benefits like electricity and late-twentieth-century landline telephones.

Communication was improving as other communities established themselves in enclaves that could support human life. But oil was in short supply. We relied on animal power for most transport and labour. We stayed home most evenings, too exhausted for anything else after hard days with much manual labour.

Trade with outsiders was very limited. We depended on the resources of our small community. In that respect, we resembled a preindustrial town with cottage industries and complete reliance on the food we could grow in our valley. Growing larger amounts of more varied foods was a constant battle.

The Pemberton valley's pioneering folk were optimistic about their future. They welcomed the newcomers and developed inventive solutions to their problems. Most of the influx were happy to be alive and ready to pitch in.

I worked as hard as any but wasn't optimistic about our future. Three problems weighed on my mind.

The first was the lack of communication. We'd survived for two years after a mind-boggling catastrophe struck the globe. We had shortwave radio communication with other small enclaves of survivors. The ham radio messages documented massive explosions and fires. Survivors who struggled in from the Prairies confirmed these stories. But we knew little about eastern North America and nothing about Africa, Asia, or South America. If those areas survived the unexplained onslaught, shouldn't we have seen some evidence?

Messages from Europe suggested hundreds of nuclear explosions triggered the catastrophe, but atmospheric radiation levels were much less than calculations predicted. Did that mean something else caused the initial destruction and rampaging fires? Or did the explosions release less than the expected levels of radioactivity? I suppose I should have been happy. If radiation levels were as high as we expected, we wouldn't have survived the exposure.

My colleague Bill Robertson managed an ocean monitoring station from his home on Haida Gwaii. Radiation levels he measured were higher than we expected. That raised an interesting question. Why were atmospheric levels too low and oceanic levels too high? It also raised a practical problem. High radiation in the ocean could make seafood unsafe to eat. It also meant people living near the coast were subject to contamination by aerosols stirred up by wind and waves. Could we rely on natural processes stripping the radioactivity from ocean waters? Or would humans be stuck with dangerous levels of oceanic radiation for centuries?

The marine radioactivity problem changed our ideas on where we should live. Landlocked Pemberton was good. Masset, by the ocean on Haida Gwaii, was not.

My other problem was the increasing concentrations of carbon dioxide. Bill's measurements showed much higher carbon dioxide levels and a more acidic ocean. Temperatures were also noticeably warmer.

Before I was forced to abandon Vancouver, I'd studied the effect of a more acidic ocean on phytoplankton productivity. Bill's latest numbers described conditions that would generate the massive plankton blooms I'd been predicting for years. Would they extract so much *carbon dioxide from the ocean-atmosphere system that we'd experience serious global cooling? Could we survive a prolonged shift to colder temperatures?*

During the previous winter, I spent many hours pouring over data my British colleague Dan Delacour sent me from the Shetland Islands. It arrived on a yacht that transited the Northwest Passage during the fall of 2049. Merlin's Childe with her skipper, Claire Fitzwilliam, and crewmembers Tomas Matthews, Luna Grange, and Carys Delacour overwintered somewhere in Alaska. Claire left Dan's package with Bill Robertson on Haida Gwaii in the spring of 2050. I didn't get it until the fall. By that time, Merlin's Childe had left for places unknown.

Dan collected climate monitoring data from the northeast Atlantic from 2045 until the cataclysm in May 2049. Bill and I collected similar data for the BC coast from stations off Vancouver Island and Haida Gwaii. I merged Dan's observations with the ones we made. Dan and I then used tedious shortwave radio transmissions to add newer results. Assessing the data with our now limited computing capacity would take some time. Undeterred, we tackled the job with enthusiasm. We now had results that should help us understand what happened in May 2049 and maybe even generate solid predictions of future trends.

The package Claire delivered from Shetland contained a manuscript Dan wrote. It summarized events between 2027 and 2032 and complemented my description of our experiences earlier in the 2020s. Between 2022 and 2027, I stood at the forefront of climate change research. Between 2027 and 2032, Dan carried the torch.

Claire and her crew, several of them actors in Dan's story, got so close without me getting a chance to meet them and discuss their roles in the events leading up to 2049. I was unlikely to get another opportunity to talk to them, but I could read Dan's depiction of a critical five-year period. This is Dan and his wife Elena Llewellyn's story, told in third person as we'd agreed to several years earlier. It includes input from several others.

Part One

An industrial Solution

Chapter One

Friday, July 16, 2027

Dan Delacour thumped his desk, rattling mugs and pencils, and toppling a book onto the floor. "Yes!"

The Dalhousie University graduate student was on a role. Three major improvements to his mathematical model for deep-water formation in the Labrador Sea worked flawlessly. One more adjustment and he'd have the tool he needed to address the impact of climate change on a key process in ocean circulation.

He glanced at his watch. Four forty-five, too early for dinner but too late to start that final tweak. *And I've been working like a dog. I deserve a little diversion.*

He turned to the online news feeds. The headline, ALIEN INTERFERENCE IN SHELLFISH POISONING, grabbed his attention. A reporter invoking manipulation by extraterrestrials amplified his interest in an already hot topic. After pondering the significance of inconsistencies in several stories about Australia's latest harmful algal bloom, Dan checked the time. *Shit! Now I'm late, and I have a stupid commitment.*

He hurried to the Muse, the Dalhousie University Association of Graduate Student's pub on the university campus in south end Halifax. He refused to let his sister's carpenter disrupt his Friday evening get together with fellow oceanography students for fish and chips with pitchers of beer and lively conversation.

Elena Llewellyn, the non-scientist in their group, made room by shifting her chair. The free-spirited young woman was a tiny animated Welsh pixie; a throwback to sixty years earlier when flower power and free love prevailed. Her tie-dyed top and long flowing cotton skirt didn't mesh with the increasing regimentation and conservative Christian orthodoxy of North America in 2027.

She placed her hand on Dan's thigh and teased him with her pinkie. He gently lifted her hand off his thigh. When she smiled and slid closer, the light dawned. She was sending him signals he'd totally missed, ones he'd be a fool to ignore. The realization distracted him from the pub-table speculation about the Australian algal bloom's cause and accusations of sabotage in the sinking of a fishing boat.

His recent experiences proved he was a failure at balancing his interest in climate change and his thesis with interest in girlfriends. Climate controversies were heating up. Did he want to ruin another relationship when he couldn't balance his conflicting interests?

"They've gone overboard as usual," the hulking John Jeffries said. "A red tide with shellfish poisoning on the Great Barrier Reef is trivial. It will soon be forgotten."

Dan glanced at the others, trying to read their reaction to John's regressive perspective, before responding. "Outbreaks may be commonplace, but no shellfish were involved. Direct transmission of algal toxins to humans is unusual."

"But not unprecedented," John replied, scowling while shaking his head. "Every time someone farts, your lot cries climate change crisis."

Dan rolled his eyes. "Jesus, John, don't turn everything into a confrontation. If phycotoxin poisoning without ingesting contaminated seafood is happening, someone must inform the health authorities. It may have nothing to do with climate change."

Madison Jeffries jumped in, defending her husband. "But Dan, the story went viral because reporters suggested aliens orchestrated the outbreak to highlight the climate change problem."

Dan snorted. "Gutter press. When challenged, they couldn't identify their sources."

"Or wouldn't," John added. "No reporter willingly reveals confidential sources. But it's the environmentalists' fault. They're always stirring the pot."

Two servers arrived with plates of fish and chips. Elena leaned toward Dan as the others tucked in. "I knew you'd make it and what you'd order, so I did the honours."

He smiled, another indication of Elena's overtly solicitous and, frankly, rather possessive behaviour. *I'm not complaining, but what caused it, and why now, when something strange is happening to our world?*

After an interlude when everyone focused on their fish, Anna Pawlak brandished her fork like a conductor's baton. "Aliens threatening Earth's citizens if they don't curb carbon dioxide emissions is absurd."

"That story grabbed everyone's attention and caused panic because it sparked people's imaginations," Elena interjected with her carefully modulated English accent. "Aliens arrive and notice global warming is out of control. They threaten the world with dire consequences unless we curb emissions. Governments downplay the significance of the reports and question the aliens' existence. That's a story with legs."

Dan chugged the last of his beer, slammed his glass on the table, and stood. "I agree with Anna, the story doesn't hold water. I hate to miss the discussion of its limitations, but I'm late. Gotta run."

Startled by his sudden movement, Elena spilled ketchup on her shirt. She struggled to clean the red smear as Dan grabbed his pack and charged toward the exit.

"Dan! Bloody hell, Dan!" Elena yelled minutes later as he strode toward his new digs.

He turned. She stood five metres away, bent over with her hands on her knees as she gasped for air. Several cloth bags lay beside her.

He rushed back. "You okay?"

"Crikey! Where's the disaster?"

"Sorry. You've been trying to catch my attention?"

The gasps became guffaws as she sank to the sidewalk, choking on her laughter. "Yeah! It's hot as Hades, and I've been yelling for ages. What's the bleeding hurry?"

"Late heading home to talk to a carpenter." He paused, eyeing the assortment of bags she always carried. "Give me some of your stuff. I'll deal with my problem, and then I'm all yours."

She pointed back toward the university. "But your flat's that way."

Dan hesitated. His recent move was serendipitous. He'd broken up with his latest girlfriend, an all-too-frequent occurrence, and needed new accommodation when his sister contacted him about house sitting. *How did Elena know?* "My sister's new house. Being renovated and I'm looking after it."

"Lead on, Macduff," she said while holding out several bags. "I need your help. Then you can impersonate the big bad wolf and have your way with me."

The sexually charged invitation, a clear amplification of the signals she'd been sending at the pub, surprised him. They'd been platonic friends for months and seldom alone. He may have been preoccupied with his work and unreceptive to her hints, but her interest was now perfectly clear. He shrugged his shoulders before grabbing her bags and hurrying home. She was older and more interested in climate than the undergraduates he'd previously dated. Would that make the difference?

The carpenter was gathering his tools when they arrived. He kept glancing at Elena as he instructed Dan on the next morning's engineered flooring delivery.

Did her rapt attention and coy smiles suggest she was interested in his instructions, or was it flirtation? And what were they laughing about as she escorted the young stud to the door?

When she returned, Dan cocked his head and raised an eyebrow. "Well?"

"Would you explain a paper?"

"Explain a paper? Not what I expected."

"A serious science paper from the *Journal of Deep-Sea Research.* I'm not sure I understand it."

He sighed. The situation was getting crazier by the minute. "Where is it?"

She pulled a stack of documents from a bag. "A study of underground vents in ocean sediments. Here's the paper and several others it referenced."

"Sounds geochemical. You should ask John. He's into that sort of research."

Elena hesitated before handing Dan the papers. Her olive skin tone didn't hide her flushed appearance. "I, um, well, I'd rather you looked at it. John confuses me when he explains anything."

That couldn't be true. John provided clear explanations. Was the paper an excuse, a Trojan horse designed to breach his defences? *She's effing gorgeous, and I've no intention of rebuffing her advances, but what's her motivation?*

"Coffee?" he asked.

"If it's no trouble, but I would appreciate your ideas. Perhaps you can read whilst I make coffee."

He showed her the construction zone that was the kitchen and assembled the laboratory funnel in a ring stand he used to make drip coffee.

Dan retreated to the minimally furnished living room, placed a Led Zeppelin LP on the platter of his outdated stereo, and positioned the tonearm. He attacked the first paper as the opening riff to 'Whole Lotta Love' filled the room. He smiled as he disappeared into the world of scientific research. *My kind of background music.*

Elena brought him coffee and bustled about the house and garden. As he neared the end of her stack of documents, she joined him on the sofa. She'd played both sides of *Led Zeppelin II* and replaced Led Zep with the Doors.

She poked him as Jim Morrison screamed the refrain from 'Light My Fire'. When he looked up, the Welsh beauty was snuggled next to him, stark naked, with a big grin on her face.

Dan took a deep breath and tried to relax his voice. "Lost your clothes, did you?"

"Had to deal with the ketchup you spilled on my top, and I wanted clean knickers for tomorrow." She snuggled closer and slid her hand under his T-shirt. "I washed them in your awesome bathroom and pegged everything to the drying rack on the deck."

"That means you're staying?"

"Well, yeah. You wouldn't kick out a naked girl, would you?"

He smiled, no longer in doubt about where their evening was heading. "Probably not. Gets cold out there at night." He leaned over and kissed her.

She returned the kiss as she pulled him into an embrace that propelled them toward horizontal on his loveseat.

Seconds later, she squirmed away and sat with her hands folded in her lap. "Tell me about my paper."

"What, now?"

She pointed at two bulging joints on an end table. "Patience, Romeo. I want your assessment before we get to my other entertainments."

Dan wilted in multiple ways as he turned to retrieve the article. "What can I tell you?"

"What it says, so I can determine if I understand it correctly. Then I have some nutty ideas for you."

The paper described the transport of biologically important gases from sediments near the base of a mid-ocean ridge. The critical observation was oxygen escaping from tube-like structures.

"Is that normal?" Elena asked when he finished his description.

He shook his head. "Organic matter decomposition consumes oxygen and produces carbon dioxide and ammonia, so you shouldn't see oxygen escaping from the sediments."

"What about photosynthesis? It generates oxygen when it produces organic matter."

"Photosynthesis needs sunlight. It can't occur at the ocean floor."

She grabbed the paper and pointed at a paragraph on the fourth page. "But Dan, they saw oxygen."

"They suggest an unknown biological process releases oxygen through those tubes. They admit they don't understand it."

"Good. That's what I hoped. Now, what about this one?" She stood and turned, bending forward stiff-legged as she fished another paper from her bags.

Dan stared wide-eyed at her blatant sexual display.

The second paper was short, a one-page letter to *Nature*. It described a pod of deep-diving whales detected by sonar as investigators approached the same study site.

After a quick read, he handed it back. "Biology. No idea what it means."

"But should whales be that deep?"

"Don't know how deep an individual whale might dive, but I doubt you'd see a whole pod at depth."

"What does it mean? The oxygen, the tubes, and the whales scarpering when the oceanographers approached?"

Dan scowled. *Why's she teasing me mercilessly with unanswerable questions?* "No idea."

"Here's my theory. Whales are the super-intelligent species on Earth. They congregate at places like the one your fellow oceanographers found and communicate by telepathy. The whales instruct less intelligent animals to build the tubes in the sediment and produce oxygen they breathe. They also plant thoughts in humans' brains that influence our activities."

"Good grief! What produced these crazy ideas?"

"Term assignment for my summer school course. The professor challenged us to imagine how different the world would be if we discredit a basic life premise." She looked up, her smile and twinkling eyes, bewitching.

He nodded his encouragement. "I get it. You postulated whales are the most intelligent animals."

"Makes sense. They have the biggest brains."

Dan shook his head. Everyone knew brain size wasn't proportional to intelligence. "They don't manufacture tools, store knowledge, or have a sophisticated language."

"That's why I've hypothesized non-verbal communication, and it needn't be a technological society. It could have an intellectual focus, like eastern philosophies. Anyway, it's not meant to be real. It's an exercise in logical thinking. But it would explain the Australian business we were discussing."

His brow furrowed as he tried to link this discussion with the earlier one at the pub. "How do super-intelligent whales come into that story?"

"Suppose whales are convinced humans allowed global warming to go too far and made the shellfish generate the toxins."

She was technically wrong. Phytoplankton, not shellfish, generated the toxins.

"Then," she continued, "they instilled the idea aliens generated the toxicity and threatened humanity if we did nothing about global warming. That would explain our current worldwide drama. And I can explain other inexplicable events using intervention by whales."

His eyes widened as he considered her idea's screwy logic. "Okay, I'll give you one thing. If whales communicate in this way, it gives credibility to world leaders receiving strange messages no one can trace. But, if I played your game and imagined a basic premise is wrong, I'd imagine aliens with superior technology sent the messages."

"You could tackle that premise if you were taking the course, but I'm sticking to whales as the pre-eminent intelligence on Earth. I need your help searching for errors in my exposition."

Dan sighed, remembering her inaccurate reference to shellfish. "You want to start now?"

She grabbed a joint and skipped toward the stairs. "No, silly, not now. Time for a little diversion."

At the top, she leaned against a doorframe, impatiently twirling her index finger. Dan picked her up, carried her into the bedroom, and lowered her onto his rickety bed.

Chapter Two

Saturday, July 17, 2027

Elena lay in Dan's bed feigning sleep while she enjoyed the warmth of early morning sun streaming in the east-facing window. He rose, collected fresh clothes, disappeared into the *en-suite* bathroom, and turned on the shower.

Her newfound lover was open-minded and considerate, accepting without sarcastic comment her mostly over-the-top behaviour. When she stood at the top of the stairs enticing him into bed, he took charge in the most masterful and delicious way. Complete opposite of public-school educated Brits she'd encountered—erudite, forceful, and demanding in public, then meek, mild losers in bed.

Brown eyes, short brown hair, slightly above average height and no bulging muscles. Her nondescript Canadian lover might blend into a crowd, but he was attentive, a great lover, and whip smart. *What more could I want?*

Someone pounding on Dan's front door interrupted her reverie. The sound of running water stopped, and seconds later, he rushed from the bathroom and down the stairs. Elena crawled out of bed, found a Loverboy T-shirt at the top of the stack in his bureau drawer, and pulled it over her head. She checked its length before descending the stairs. *What if he rushed down so quickly because he expected an irate girlfriend on the stoop?*

Before she reached the bottom step, he'd pulled open the door. He stood soaking wet with dishevelled spiked-up hair, wearing only blue jeans. He looked so damned buff as he confronted two fit, clean-shaven men with close-cropped hair, dark suits, and aviator sunglasses. Their loutish demeanours reminded her of a dictator's body guards in a third-rate movie.

The older man pushed onto the threshold and presented his official-looking identification. "Mr. Delacour, were from the Canadian Security Intelligence Service. The Prime Minister requests your immediate presence in Ottawa at a hearing on global warming."

Dan stared, a puzzled expression on his face. "What if I'm busy?"

"Yesterday's declaration gives the PM wide-ranging authority to address the alien demands. It includes co-opting the efforts of individual citizens."

"What?" Dan exclaimed.

Elena stopped, her mouth hanging open. Rumours suggesting aliens created the phycotoxin outbreak and threatened governments had gone viral, first in the blogosphere and then in the mainline media. Governments reacted, insisting alien control of the phycotoxin outbreak was a hoax. Was the Canadian government now responding to the hoax?

"Pack an overnight bag," agent number one said as he passed Dan a single sheet with an official-looking letterhead.

He scanned it quickly and passed it to Elena. She glared at the agents after reading the prime ministerial letter *requesting* Dan's attendance.

"I can handle today's flooring delivery," she said as she returned Dan's letter. She was cheesed off with how these plods had ruined her meticulously planned weekend but wouldn't admit it.

The second officer nodded toward Elena. "Listen to the little lady. The sooner we leave, the sooner you return."

Dan shrugged and headed upstairs. The older agent stared at her T-shirt. "Loverboy, eh? You weren't even alive when they were popular."

She smiled, trying to ignore their sexist behaviour. First one called her 'little lady' then the second stared lasciviously. She didn't want them sniffing around and finding the second joint and the rest of her stash. Better to keep them here in the front hall, distracted by her appearance. "Dan's really into these old rock bands. Isn't this one Canadian?"

"Yeah, Calgary. Wicked old band. Attended a Loverboy concert when I was a teenager."

Dan returned properly dressed and carrying his overnight bag. He diverted into the living room for his laptop. At the front door, he passed her his house key and followed the agents to their black SUV.

Elena watched until they turned the corner, then repaired to the living room to search for a Loverboy LP in Dan's extensive collection. She found *Keep it Up*, placed it on his turntable, and cranked the volume. She collected the joint still sitting on the end table and retrieved the clothes she'd hung outside. The flooring delivery could arrive at any moment, and she didn't want to encourage another misogynistic performance like the one she'd just endured.

*****

In their vehicle, the first agent passed Dan a manila envelope. He stared at the bulky package, wondering what was really going on. Why had they appeared on his doorstep without notice, why him rather than someone more senior, and how the hell could he contribute to an ill-defined process without an opportunity to prepare?

When he calmed down, he opened the envelope and perused the top sheet. It described emergency hearings in the national parliament on the scientific basis for climate change. The second page outlined the subject Dan would address during an afternoon presentation. When he looked up, he realized they were on the road to the Shearwater military airport.

Once they were airborne, he wasted several minutes staring out the window of the executive jet considering two questions. Why was the government invoking interference by aliens? Why invite him to this high-level meeting?

The first was political. Aliens as the meeting's driving force was not credible. Were they introduced to divert a gullible public's attention from the government's real motive?

He had a potential answer to his second question. Dr. Heinrich Keizer, his thesis supervisor, was a member of the national climate change task force mentioned in the PM's letter. The invitation must be his doing.

His other concern was personal. An opportunity to present his results to senior politicians should have been exciting. But his initial reaction had been annoyance at anyone interrupting his weekend with Elena. *How did she so thoroughly upend my priorities?*

After turning away from the window, Dan focused on his one chance to influence government action. It demanded a flawless description for a non-specialist audience, but he lacked time to generate a fresh presentation. He located his PowerPoint file for a recent talk he gave to high school students and tweaked it to suit the current situation.

In Ottawa, the parliamentary hearing dragged on. After half an hour of political posturing and ten scientific presentations that mostly described local or regional impacts, Dan got his opportunity to extend the scope to the global scale.

He described the impact of global warming on Atlantic-wide circulation patterns. Warming temperatures meant less cold water sank into the abyss and flowed towards the tropics. A direct consequence was weaker warm currents like the Gulf Stream that returned surface water to the north.

"Our analysis suggests the vertical transport will cease in 2045. That means a massive reduction in northward flowing warm water and an absence of the Gulf

Stream as we know it. We'll see colder winters in Europe and more ice in the Barents Sea. Berlin is north of Saskatoon. Without the Gulf Stream it's winters will be as cold."

He concluded with a plea for oceanographic research into deep-water formation and ongoing monitoring of environmental conditions in the Labrador Sea. The graph with the drop-dead date prominently displayed remained visible on the screen behind him.

The chairman gazed at the government side of the committee table. "Questions?"

"Could we treat the formation region like a heat pump and withdraw valuable heat from these waters while keeping the present circulation pattern intact?"

Dan stared at the member. *Did he understand the scale?* "The amount of heat removal would be massive and the distances vast. It wouldn't be practical."

The chairman shifted his gaze to the opposition's side. A New Democratic Party member raised his hand. "Your graph shows a range of dates for the doomsday you're projecting. Are you suggesting it could occur as early as 2035? That's only eight years away."

Dan smiled. *This guy understands the implications of my results.* "My date represents the central tendency from the analysis, the most probable value. It has some uncertainty. Twenty thirty-five would be the earliest possible date."

The chairman glanced at the clock and dismissed Dan before calling the next witness.

Dan muttered about the partisan nature of the questions as he hurried away. He almost collided with a clerk outside the hearing room. The modern-day Bob Cratchit handed Dan a sealed envelope.

"Plane ticket for your trip home and cash for your expenses. You're booked on an evening flight, but if you'd prefer to stay over, the airline will rebook you."

"Anything you need from me?"

The clerk consulted his tablet. "We have a copy of your slides, and your comments were recorded. You're good to go. Thank you for your contribution."

Dr. Krueger stepped past the clerk and accompanied Dan to the exit. "Don't be despondent. You gave us the input we need—a solid description of what you're doing and why it's important, without speculation or political diatribes."

Dan snorted. He'd contemplated a pitch for environmental action but deleted the extra slides as he listened to the talks. "But aren't we here to push for action?"

"We are, but we must accept the politicians' plodding, methodical ways. Your job was presenting a clear picture. The task force scientists will synthesize everything and make our case. You've made it easier, better than the less focused presentations."

"I hope you're right. I only heard politicians trying to score points off each other."

"Trust me. It was worthwhile. And you're set to make an important contribution. Once you've finished your thesis, you'll have many opportunities."

"You think so?"

"The world's major carbon emitters will commit to reaching their Paris Accord targets by 2030. Your results will be critical for predicting how the improvements alter current projections."

Dan shook his head. "I don't believe it. The changes are too great. They'll have too big an impact on people and the economy. The current panic will blow over, and government leaders will return to fancy talk and no action."

"Trust me," Dr. K repeated. "Governments are committed to major reductions in fossil fuel use. We'll see economic repercussions because the time frame's restricted. Environmental changes may be large and rapid. You must gather the data and perfect your models. Get home and get to it."

A different Elena Llewellyn greeted Dan when he arrived home. A ponytail, plain yellow top, and walking shorts had replaced the long flowing hair, tie-dyed T-shirts, and wraparound cotton skirts. The simpler, more modern getup exuded sophistication.

She pointed into the dining room. "The flooring's stacked and ready for installation Monday. And I've been everywhere, clearing the debris and making it more liveable."

"You *have* been busy," he replied as he pulled her into a hug.

"I also fetched some clothes," she added, "and when I realized you were coming home tonight, I visited the market."

He pushed her away and cocked his head, eyebrows raised. *She's playing the hausfrau role, but what's her real agenda?* "You're planning an extended stay?"

"It's quiet here. My place is pandemonium because one flatmate has two friends staying." She tilted her head, mimicking his posture. "I can leave if you want me to."

Dan shook his head before heading to the kitchen. "I'm not kicking you out, but what's the deal?"

This wasn't the Welsh nymph who lured him into wild marijuana-fuelled sexual adventures. More like the practical friend he'd known since she arrived in Halifax to begin graduate studies in political philosophy. *Either version was preferable to being alone, but why had she reverted?*

She snuggled against him as he grabbed a beer. "Tell me what happened after those scary secret agents hauled you away."

He twisted the cap off his beer, tore open a bag of nachos, retreated to his living room sofa, and related the gory details of his trip to Ottawa. "Boring and anticlimactic," he concluded.

"Crikey. From the way they talked, I imagined the Prime Minister and half the cabinet soaking up your pearls of wisdom."

"Complete absence of VIPs except for the Environment Minister, and she only stayed for fifteen minutes," he said with a chuckle as he recalled the platitudes she spouted.

"So only committee and task force members like Dr. Krueger."

"And no discussion or debate," he replied, wondering how she knew Dr. K was there. "After we made our presentations, they whisked us away."

She snuggled closer. "Strange, isn't it? They go to the effort of getting you together—"

"At great cost."

"Yeah, really. Why couldn't you email your talk and participate by videoconference? Sending an executive jet for one participant is absurd. Talk about reducing carbon emissions. And after all that, no discussion. Absolutely crazy."

"Dr. K suggested it's the way Ottawa committees work. We were part of a public data-gathering exercise that's mostly for show. They want the discussion later, behind closed doors. And they never give a damn about squandering the taxpayer's money."

"But governments have been subject to more disruptions and protests in recent months, and they now seem ready to act. I hope their data gathering works. Wouldn't want them to make nonsense of it."

Dan bit his lower lip as he pushed her to arms-length. *She's too damned well informed.*

"That's what Dr. K said. They'll act, and it's our job to make sure they do it from the best knowledge base. But I don't believe it."

"Writing's on the wall. Things will change."

He scratched the stubble on his jaw. "The United States has increased its carbon emissions since the implementation of the Paris climate accords. And economic expansion in countries like China and India has overwhelmed their efforts to control carbon emissions. How can these countries reverse course and reduce emissions in forty-one months?"

"Believe me, big changes are coming, and they'll happen in a matter of days and weeks, not months and years."

"But do governments have the will?"

Elena nodded. "They've gone to the precipice and realize they can't go further without falling. We should be prepared."

"Prepared, how?"

"Oh Dan, don't be naïve. We need fuel for cooking and basic foodstuffs that won't perish."

"You're kidding. They needn't reduce greenhouse gases by that much."

"Think about it. We're facing restricted air transport, rationing or expensive fuel for vehicles, massive shifts from coal and heavy oil to lighter oil and natural gas. The supply system's precarious and disruptions will occur."

Dan shook his head. *Was she was making a mountain from a molehill, or did she have inside information she was keeping from me?*

Chapter Three

Sunday, July 18, 2027

Dan woke to the sound of someone tapping on a computer keyboard. He opened one eye.

Elena sat by the window wearing his Loverboy T-shirt. A mug rested on the windowsill.

Her delicate elfin features and flawless complexion looked paler in the early morning light. Sunlight streaming through her unkempt hair picked out the red highlights in the dominant brown.

He stretched. "You're up early."

She pointed at the clock on his bedside table. "It's gone seven. I was reading news from the old country. You want a report, or should I return to bed?"

She abandoned her computer without waiting for an answer, tugged the shirt over her head, and dropped it on the floor. He pulled aside the sheet. The news could wait.

Later, Dan had eggs sizzling on the stove. Elena appeared outside the deck door, naked and dripping from a morning swim.

"Forget your swimsuit?"

"Do I need one?"

"What happens if we invite friends over?"

She rubbed her wet hair with a towel. "Steve and Anna." She paused when Dan raised his eyebrows. "They're your most serious friends, and we'll need serious allies as we march forward.

"Allies? March forward? What are you talking about?"

"Countries will respond, but everything won't go smoothly. When opponents raise questions about the science, you'll need serious allies like Steve and Anna to help answer them."

Steve Matthews was thirty and older than most of his graduate student colleagues. He was a sometimes austere, physical oceanography student, studying fluid dynamics. The bookish Anna Pawlak was another pure scientist, fascinated by the elegance of mathematical descriptions of sub-atomic particles.

"Should we invite them?"

"Yeah, today. The weather's beautiful, and we can discuss your trip to Ottawa. No time to buy a bathing suit, but I will organize dinner."

"I thought you wanted emergency supplies?"

"We'll be free in the afternoon. You agree?"

He shrugged. He should focus on his research project, and the updated scenarios Dr. K mentioned in Ottawa, but he couldn't simply push Elena into the background. "I've nothing pressing."

She raced away and returned with her phone. She described the pool to Steve, but not to Anna.

After breakfast, they visited the home centre to buy disposable propane cylinders for Dan's camp stove. Others were buying propane and gasoline-powered electrical generators, but store shelves weren't stripped bare.

After a quick lunch at a trendy café, Elena visited the grocery store, and Dan returned home to devote a few hours to his project.

Anna and Steve arrived at four o'clock and wheeled their bicycles onto the porch.

Dan nodded toward the door. "You could take them inside."

"They'll be safe locked to the railing, and it's probably easier."

While Steve locked their bikes, Anna pulled her swimsuit from her backpack and turned to Elena with a gigantic smile on her face. "Steve told me about the pool. Must I assume you simply forgot to mention it?"

Elena headed inside. "I planned to go in without one. I thought you might join me."

"But you wouldn't give me a choice. And what about the guys? You expect them to join your skinny-dipping party?"

Steve followed with two bottles of wine from his bike bags. "I'm not interested in frolicking naked in anyone's backyard."

Dan took the bottles, putting the white in the fridge and the red on the counter. "The pool's secluded enough. You needn't worry about the neighbours."

Steve reddened. "That's not the problem."

Anna looked at Steve before responding to Elena's suggestion. "I think not. Where can I change?"

Elena sighed before leading Anna to the bedroom. They returned a few minutes later with Anna in a one-piece Speedo suit and Elena in the tiniest bikini Dan had ever seen. She'd only been a few square centimetres less than honest when she implied she had no swimsuit.

After their swim, Anna glanced at the house. "So, Elena, what's the deal? You now living here."

Elena's response skipped important details. "I came over Friday to ask Dan about a paper and stayed because he needed someone to manage things whilst he was in Ottawa."

Anna scoffed. "More complicated than that."

"Stayed for the weekend. Now it's up to Dan."

Dan scowled, wondering why Elena suggested he was in charge. "No point. In a few weeks, I'll be apartment hunting."

Steve gazed at the house and yard. "What's the story?"

"My sister's house. Her family's moving from Winnipeg next month. I've been holding the fort while they get renovations done."

"Then, you'll move out?" Anna asked.

"Three kids and a bloody great dog. And no suggestion I stay."

Steve turned toward Dan, with his head tilted to the side. "Winnipeg. Business transfers?"

"Yeah."

"I wonder if they'll be moving that quickly."

"Why not?" Anna asked.

"The web suggests governments plan to make reductions in carbon emissions from carbon pricing and regulations that reduce travel," Steve responded.

Dan's eyes narrowed. Steve always remained aloof from political talk. His sudden interest was as surprising as Elena's. "Why would that affect anything? If you're transferred, you go. If fuel goes up, you shrug your shoulders and pay."

"That's not what I'm seeing. Their employers may delay their transfers."

Dan turned to Elena. "You've been surfing the web. What are you seeing?"

He expected her to engage, but she remained silent, her eyes brimming with tears. *Something he said... or something else?*

Shortly after nine, Steve and Anna wobbled home on their bicycles. Dan and Elena turned to the kitchen.

"I'm amazed you pulled together such a fantastic dinner," he said as he surveyed the mess. "Hamburgers never tasted so good."

She organized everything into neat piles and loaded the dishwasher. "Three trips to the local greengrocer. You can discover my other secrets if we make this living arrangement permanent."

"But I'll soon be apartment hunting."

"I can't tolerate my place and Kim's scatty friends. I'm better here, and we can search for another flat together."

He stepped back, his heart racing. *Where is she going? We started with a steamy night together. Now, after two days, she's pushing a long-term commitment.* "You sure you're ready for that?"

"You don't listen," she replied as she filled the sink with soapy water. "Big things are happening, and I plan to share them with you." She turned from the sink, beaming as she flicked suds in his direction. "And we know damn well it's what you want."

When they woke Monday morning, the trickle of rumours had become a flood. Inflammatory tweets and blog postings by various rabblerousers warned of drastic reaction from governments everywhere. Better-known commentators discussed the need for worldwide initiatives to reduce carbon emissions. They insisted concrete action was imminent.

Government spokesmen from the G20 countries denied every rumour. The similarity of the insipid replies smacked of conspiracy. They downplayed the need for urgency using almost identical words and ignored questions about local concerns.

Dan's immediate priorities hadn't changed. He trekked to the university and began reformulating his models. His new scenario anticipated carbon dioxide increases from the G20 countries would end abruptly.

He was busy writing computer code when Steve strolled into his office. "We wanted to thank you for yesterday. Jolted us from ruts we'd been living in."

"Thank Elena. It was her show."

"You can pass the message."

Dan nodded as Steve commandeered a chair. "I need to finish my thesis, and this crisis lets me add something practical."

"To a thesis focused on theoretical arguments based on physical principles? You want something from me?"

"Your latest models to illustrate the impact of my work in your real-world situation."

"Okay. The code's available. You can make your changes, rerun the models, and compare the results."

Steve held up his hand. "Your revised model that accommodates our new reality, the one we'll soon be experiencing."

"That's a new problem. It may take months to develop an understanding I can model."

"Come on, Dan, we know you've been thinking of little else since Saturday. You'll get it sorted."

Dan laughed, thinking of the distractions Elena provided. "Hope so, but I only started this morning, and life's getting complicated. I'll send you the code for the current model today, and you can help me develop the new scenario."

"You're on," Steve said as he strode to the door. "The paper we produce will make our marks in the field."

Dan shook his head. Steve was the third person in two days who'd said the new political machinations would make his career, but he was far from convinced.

He returned to his programming with greater enthusiasm. He looked up when Elena jangled a ring with a key and small plastic figurine in his face. The six-centimetre-high figure looked like something from a sex toy store. "Oops, sorry, didn't realize you'd come in. Been here long?"

Elena laughed. "About ten minutes. You mutter to yourself when you're working."

"People have mentioned it. Only happens when I'm into something."

"You were definitely into something, and it wasn't pornography. I peeked."

Half an hour later, Dan transferred the results of his day's efforts to an off-site memory bank and gathered his stuff. He found a sticky note on his desk near where Elena had been sitting.

<See you at six. If you're late, you'll regret it.> No signature, just a tiny drawing of an elf or fairy.

He arrived home at ten minutes before six. Elena's knee-length black dress and elaborate gold earrings didn't reflect the playfulness her note promised.

She accosted him before he kicked off his shoes. "Your sister phoned. Their arrival's been delayed by six weeks. There's also important new info on the web."

Dan's shoulders sagged. *Had life's grubby details steamrolled another romantic opportunity?*

"Does Gabby want me to call back?"

"After nine. We should have dinner, and you must see what's happening elsewhere."

"Can't you tell me while I prepare something?"

"I'd rather go out. It might be our last chance."

"Things aren't getting that crazy..." Her pained expression suggested she thought it was a real possibility. "Okay, I shouldn't doubt your judgement when I haven't seen the evidence. Where should we go?"

"The Five Fishermen."

It was one of Halifax's most expensive restaurants, and they'd need a taxi to get there. "I can't afford that."

"It's on me. My flatmates returned next month's rent. Plenty for one big fling before austerity destroys our options."

Dan smiled, kissed her, and ascended the stairs to find more formal clothes. It didn't take an Einstein to realize she'd already made the reservation.

End of Book Two preview

About the author:

Alan Kemister is the pen name of a Halifax Nova Scotia based scientist experimenting with creative writing. He has a keen interest in environmental science and dabbled in yachting and golf before turning to fiction after retirement. He's written more than thirty published short stories and one poem. Several of these stories appeared in anthologies produced by Halifax's Evergreen Writers Group: *Out of the Mist: 22 Atlantic Canadian Ghost Stories* released in 2014, and *Off Highway: Journeys of Nova Scotia Writers*, in 2017. A third Evergreen Writers group anthology, *Water's Edge* was published in the spring of 2020 at the height of the COVID-19 pandemic.

Alan has self-published *A Body in the Sacristy* and *Tilting at Windmills*, his first two Barrettsport Mysteries featuring Detective Goodyear and the fictional South Shore town of Barrettsport Nova Scotia. *The Souring Seas* is a change of pace, the first in a series of novels about the hazards of ignoring human-induced climate change.

Tilting at Windmills, A Body in the Sacristy, Out of the Mist: 22 Atlantic Canadian Ghost Stories, Off Highway: Journeys of Nova Scotia Writers, and *Water's Edge* are available on Amazon in paperback and e-book formats.

Links:

E-mail: alkemi47@gmail.com
Facebook: https://www.facebook.com/Phil.Yeats47
Website: https://alankemisterauthor.wordpress.com